THE KEY
TO CHINTAK

THE ZAMORIAN CHRONICLES

JOHN
HOWARD

Published by Antony Rowe Publishing Services in 2005
2 Whittle Drive
Highfield Industrial Estate
Eastbourne
East Sussex
BN23 6QT
England

ISBN 1-905200-13-7 (children's edition)

Cover Designed by Jurgen Ziewe
www.lightandmagic.co.uk

Printed and bound by Antony Rowe Ltd, Eastbourne

Thanks to soooo many people for helping me along the way – far too many to list, but you know who you are. Special thanks to my wife Julie and beautiful baby daughter, Neve.

Wow, I'm a dad!

Mustn't forget my mum and dad. Sleep well.

Only Millie can read what's written on the rest of this page

The Key to Chintak - The Zamorian Chronicles, will be a massive hit worldwide. Of that I have no doubt.

Foreword by G.P. Taylor

When I first started down the road of self publishing I had to sell my cherished motorbike to fund my dream – I never imagined it would lead me to where I am now. A 9 book - 3 film deal has quickly followed with Shadowmancer - Wormwood and Tersias all becoming best sellers.

In one month, Shadowmancer was picked up by a mainstream publisher and turned into worldwide success. The book was a New York Times #1 best-seller and is published in 43 languages. Since that time I have been asked to endorse many books. This is the first self published book that I wanted to put my name to. *The Key to Chintak* has something for everyone and is an amazing read. It has a blend of excitement and mystery that will keep the young reader enthralled throughout. You will fall in love with Millie - she makes Harry Potter look like a wimp! The action goes on from page to page and takes you around the world combining history with mystery. Well written, exciting, entertaining, it is truly dynamic and a must read...There are a lot of fantasy books out there - but this is one of the best I have seen. The Author, John Howard, deserves all the success I know he has coming to him. Anyone who walks away from a highly paid job to visit 4000 kids across 40 schools, to promote his book, deserves to make it! If you are going to read one book this year then make it this one.

READ IT NOW!
You will not be disappointed.

Secrets are hidden in some copies of this edition.
If you find them, you could be in for an amazing surprise.

Check out www.zamorian.com for details.

CHAPTER ONE

THE INVISIBLE TRUTH

'Hmm … most peculiar, most peculiar indeed,' muttered Arthur to himself. His job as a museum curator often turned up puzzling artefacts. However, none had caught his imagination quite as much as the ancient black book that now lay before him in his study. It had been subjected to all manner of tests by some of the world's leading archaeologists and scientists, all of whom had reached the same conclusion. It had never been written in or on and thus provided no clues to its ownership or intended use.

This particular afternoon Arthur's granddaughter Millie, who'd been living with him since she was six, was flicking through a magazine. 'Grandad,' she said in her most inquisitive voice.

'Yessss,' answered Arthur in a manner that implied he was busy.

'This article is wrong.'

'OK … tell me why it's wrong?'

'Well it talks about the world's continents …'

'OK,' he replied, as if waiting for the punch line.

'… But doesn't mention the hidden one. There *is* a hidden one, right?'

'Not as far as I know.'

'Well, the book must be wrong then,' she said impatiently.

'Yes … what book would that be?'

'The black one in your study. The one called *The Key to Chintak.*'

'I haven't got a book by that name. Besides there *really*

isn't a hidden continent. I mean where would you hide it?' he said chuckling to himself rather loudly.

Millie dragged herself off the sofa and stomped into her grandad's study. 'THAT BOOK!' she exclaimed, pointing to the one that intrigued him so. 'Look,' she leaned forward and flipped the book shut, pulling her best stubborn face in the process, 'the writing on the front – *The Key to Chintak.*'

Arthur peered at her forlornly over the top of his half-rimmed glasses.

'What?' said Millie, crossing her arms.

'Millie my love, there's *no* writing on the cover or inside. That's why this book is such a mystery.'

'Grandad, your eyes must be bad because I can clearly read what's written on the cover *and* some of what's inside. Personally I think it sounds like quite an adventure.'

Arthur stared back at her, unable to speak.

*

Twelve-year-old Millie Jarman had been born on the outskirts of Midhurst, a small English town, on a particularly splendid summer's day. Her proud parents, Sally and David, wished for no more than a healthy child and on 17th August their wish was granted. The six years that followed Millie's birth were relatively stress-free, although she developed quite a stubborn streak and much preferred the word 'no' to all else.

Millie had wavy brown hair, skin that tanned at the merest appearance of the sun, and the most impelling bright blue eyes. Her snub nose was the only hint of her father's side, but even though she looked more like her mum, a daddy's girl she was. She was often at his side and always saw him as her great protector. Some of this was no doubt linked to the fact that her father was Arthur's son.

Apart from being a rather ungainly man Arthur's features were mostly in keeping with those of a sixty-four-year-old grandad. His head, normally covered with one of the many hats from his vast and unusual collection, showed signs of hair only around the edges. The hair that sprouted from the rest of his head seemed to have made its way down to his ears and nose but, strangely, he seemed incapable of growing a beard or moustache!

His nose was mostly accompanied by a pair of gravity defying half-rimmed glasses that always remained glued to his face. A face that was finished off with a pointy chin – a great target for any stray gravy that accompanied his favourite Sunday roast – and unusually small lips.

*

Millie never met her other grandparents as they died some time before she was born. This made her appreciate the one she did have even more. The time spent with Arthur after school, until her parents finished work, was always good fun. He was an avid story-teller and Millie loved to listen to him recount how he won wars single-handedly or how he discovered some great treasure while on an expedition somewhere or other. She sensed he was being slightly economical with the truth, but it didn't matter to her one bit.

Sally and David had their collective futures pretty well mapped out, but it all went horribly wrong one cold January morning when they were on their way to drop Millie off at school.

The ice on the windscreen was particularly harsh, and it took longer than normal to heat up the inside of the car. They set off on their usual route, but were twice diverted by weather-enforced road closures.

They rounded a bend as an oncoming van lost control

and slid across the road in front of them. David had no time to react before ploughing into it.

Sally and David were dead before their car came to rest at the bottom of an embankment. Millie, who remembers nothing of the accident, was cut out at the scene. Amazingly she suffered only minor scratches, and was able to leave hospital in no time at all. It took her a while to come to terms with the fact that her parents had 'gone to sleep forever in the clouds'. This was the best way her grandad could think of telling his – now adopted – six-year-old granddaughter that she would never see her mum and dad again.

The first few months after the accident were especially fraught for Millie, but as time wore on she started to come out of the shell into which she'd retreated, and slowly became her old self again.

Living with her grandad made Millie grow up fast. She certainly knew more about the world, and the wonders and tragedies it held, than all of her school friends. She sometimes failed to grasp why they didn't want to talk about ancient times and fabled ruins as much as about make-up and clothes. That's probably why she had more friends who were boys. They seemed more interested in adventure stories and they didn't cry so much when she kicked and slapped them for making fun of her 'old parent'.

It wasn't until six years after the accident that the two remaining members of the Jarman family made a discovery that dramatically changed the direction of their lives.

*

'Grandad, shut your mouth before the flies get in!' said Millie, still unsure why he was so shocked about her reading the book. She knew he didn't really like her poking around his things, but surely he was going a little over the top. After all, she'd only flicked through the first few pages.

'Millie, this book has no writing in it.'

'Grandad, can you *really* not see any writing in it? I'm telling you the truth. It's called *The Key to Chintak* and tells of a hidden continent and a lost key – or a lost something or other. Can't quite remember, but it does sound like fun.'

'OK, I'm game,' said Arthur as he flicked over the cover. 'What does it say on this page then?'

Millie looked at the page, at her grandad, and then back at the page again. 'Nothing,' she said faintly.

'Aha!' said Arthur triumphantly. 'I thought so. You were having me on all along.'

Millie screwed up her face. 'When I say nothing, I mean nothing except the same words as the cover – *The Key to Chintak*. The story starts on the *next* page.' Millie leaned forward, turned over the page and started to read.

I, Fitar, along with all other Zamorians, am a descendant of the planet Zamora, which is in a galaxy far outside your own.

We – the children of Zamora – need help to escape our prison of eternal life. The power invested in this book will choose the person best skilled to aid us in this task. If you are reading this then you are that person. You are the Chosen One.

Only you can decide if you wish to take on the deadly forces that will be put in your way if you try to help us. If you choose to, then you will first have to reassemble the key to the gateway that leads to the hidden continent – the Key to Chintak.

You should understand that whatever dangers you experience prior to assembling the key and opening the gateway will not compare to what lies ahead of you after that point.

Please help us.

'Do you want me to continue?'

'Grandad, I said do you want me to continue?'

Millie could tell the full extent of her reading had started to work itself through her grandad's head as the colour, which had vanished from his face, suddenly made a welcome reappearance.

She began to realise just what might be in store for her if the book *was* to be believed. Could she really be the only one to read it and if so could she really be the Chosen One – whatever that meant? Up until a few minutes ago she had considered herself to be a fairly ordinary twelve-year-old girl, whose main worries were anything but adventures involving a missing key, mysterious people, and a whole new continent. Not to mention the 'deadly forces' and what might lie ahead if she *actually* opened the gateway.

Sure, Millie had looked at the book before – she was somehow drawn to it – when her grandad was in another room, but she never really took a great deal of interest in what was written inside. She actually believed it to be an adventure story penned by someone with a vivid imagination. Most probably her grandad himself.

'So my twelve-year-old granddaughter can read a book that no one else can see writing in, telling her to save a lost race in a continent that no one knows exists!' Arthur scratched his head, sat up straight and gazed into Millie's eyes.

'Er ... well ... basically ... yes.'

Arthur's inbuilt curiosity, which had led him into archaeology in the first place, was for once overridden by another urge. The urge to protect his granddaughter. 'Millie, the book talks of deadly forces and although I can't believe I'm saying this, it obviously carries some mystical powers, as you seem to be able to read from its blank pages!'

'I know what the book said, Grandad, but I have to read on. I know it talks of great danger, but maybe I have already put us in danger by having read this far. Maybe only by reading on will we be safe.'

Arthur stared curiously at Millie, churning her words over in his mind. 'Better sit yourself down then,' he said slowly.

Millie plonked herself down in a leather-clad beast of a chair. It had a huge back and deep chunky arms that made it difficult to tell from behind if anyone was in it. The chair had often provided Millie with cover when she wanted to nose through whatever took her interest on the desk. It also paid testament to the lack of cleaning that took place, because whenever someone fell back into its cavernous grip, billows of dust would be exhaled from its clutches.

There were three other chairs scattered around the room. Millie found this to be most amusing, because guests never usually strayed past the forbidding oak door to the study. *She* was allowed in, but only when her grandad was there. Wishful thinking on his side of course!

*

Millie always loved to go into her grandad's study. The distinctive smell of all things ancient forever took her back to the days when she first used to visit with her parents, and creep off with her grandad to explore its wonders.

The room was fairly large but felt cramped, as it was

strewn with the weird and wonderful. The desk that took up most of one wall was a very grand affair. Its dark brown wooden top was adorned with deep green leather that had clearly seen better days, although its frayed edges and random studs seemed to blend in well with the surroundings. A new desk somehow just wouldn't have been right.

In the centre was a very eerie-looking lamp. The base was made up of a blackish lump of something which might have been an animal of some sort. Only a good clean and sunlight would have revealed its true identity. The shade was equally sinister-looking and made of dark stained glass. Millie couldn't remember the thing ever working.

As the only window always had its curtains drawn, the light was provided by a set of three spotlights. Actually only one was working. One seemed to be enough though.

Apart from the lamp, and piles of paperwork, there were various artefacts dotted around the desk that had no use but to provide their owner with something to prod every now and then when bored. Great stories, often more than one per item, were attached to each of them.

Posters of animals and faraway places haphazardly covered the walls. One of them, of a kangaroo, was even upside down.

Conspicuous by its absence was a computer. Arthur couldn't abide them, and were it not for Millie's studies, one would never have made it into the house. He did know how to use them, though, as they controlled the lives of everyone at the museum.

A huge pile of atlases of all shapes, sizes and colours occupied what little space there was between the desk and the wall. They were stacked haphazardly in no apparent order and were it not for the desk legs and the wall itself they would have long since succumbed to gravity.

*

Millie flipped the book open half-way just out of curiosity, but looked slightly taken aback by what she saw. She quickly turned to the next page and then the next at an ever-increasing pace. On each turn her expression became more and more drawn.

'What is it, Millie? What does it say?'

She kept flicking ahead until her grandad leaned over and stopped her.

'Millie, what can you see?'

'Nothing!'

'It's *something,* as it seems to be troubling you. Tell me what it is. Right now I don't think you could say anything that would surprise me.'

Millie looked up at her grandad. 'No, Grandad, I really do mean *nothing*. All the pages are blank.'

Arthur looked puzzled at first, but then flipped the book shut. 'What does it say on the front?'

'*The Key to Chintak*,' Millie replied, before it suddenly dawned on her that whatever made her special before was still there and relief painted its way across her face.

With that Arthur turned over the first page. 'Same as the cover?' he enquired.

Millie nodded. Both of them drew deep breaths as he slowly turned over the next page.

Millie's face lit up. 'Yes, Grandad, it looks the same as before, but I don't understand. How come I can't see anything on those other pages?'

'Hopefully, my dear, that will be explained in what you *can* read.'

As he couldn't see any writing, all of this was slightly surreal to Arthur. Even though he was more than a little apprehensive about what might be ahead, he was eager to find out. 'Read on,' he said hurriedly.

Millie dispensed a disapproving glance at his tone, turned back to the book and read aloud.

For you to understand our plight I must first tell you about the Zamorian balance of life, called Juju. On Zamora everyone lived until they were two hundred as long as there were two children for every adult. The more children there were the longer the adults would live and vice versa.

The only real threat to our existence came from meteors that often passed close to Zamora. We needed an escape plan in case one looked set to strike our planet. Because of this Zamorian scientists created a device called Molto that allowed us to travel anywhere in any universe and in great numbers if necessary.

'Stop!' said Arthur, who was now rummaging around on his desk before eventually conjuring up a tape recorder. He placed it in front of Millie and sat back in his chair, clutching a notepad and pencil. 'Carry on,' he said eagerly.

You believe the core of your planet to be molten, but it is nothing of the kind. In fact it is a hidden continent. It is a weightless sphere, bigger in mass than all the other continents put together, and more than capable of supporting our race. We named this continent Chintak and set up a Zamorian research base there. The base of course always maintained the Juju balance.

I must stress that even if we did have to leave Zamora for Earth we never intended to conquer any other part of your planet, or seek to integrate our races. If all had gone to plan your people would never have known we existed.

Arthur's frantic scribbling did little to distract Millie who barely took a breath before reading on.

All Zamorians are born with a special power that can only be used when they reach adulthood. However, that all changed when Zardrot became an adult. He was the first to have multiple powers and he used them to kill anyone who opposed him in his quest to rule our planet. He was eventually caught and tried for the murders of three high-ranking officials, but two days before his execution he escaped and went into hiding on Earth.

Once our leaders found out where he was, the research base in Chintak was abandoned, thus upsetting the Juju balance and in turn sentencing Zardrot to death within days. However, a year later a probe picked up traces of Zamorian DNA on Earth. Further analysis proved that Zardrot must have spawned a child which carried his genetic make-up, but was immune to the Juju balance. We were unable to trace accurately the location of the child, but as the centuries passed none of our fears were realised and probes reported back ever-diminishing signs of Zamorian DNA activity. Hopefully – for us – some of that activity still remains as only someone of Zamorian descent can read this book.

Millie's words tailed off and silence filled the study. It seemed like days, not minutes, before either she or Arthur chose to speak.

'It would seem we now know why you're somewhat special to these people,' said Arthur, who was more than a little bemused.

Millie raised her head and met her grandad's eyes. 'I'm confused! Alien relatives – are they my cousins?'

Now it was Arthur's turn to stare blankly.

'I always wanted some distant relatives, but I'd rather

hoped they would be from this planet!' Although Millie said this with a grin on her face, trying her hardest to look casual, Arthur knew she was far from calm. Shock was beginning to set in, but it didn't stop her from rambling on. 'I wonder if I have a special power? I wonder if I'll get it soon or if I have to wait until I'm eighteen? I hope I can vanish and reappear, as it would be a good way of getting out when I'm grounded ...'

'Millie!'

'Grandad, which one of my parents had Zamorian powers?'

'MILLIE, STOP! Neither of them did and nor do you. The book must be wrong. You are an ordinary human child, with an ordinary life.'

Millie repositioned herself in her chair. 'How many ordinary children,' she paused for effect and leaned closer to her grandad, 'human children that is ... do you know who can read blank pages from a book written by an unknown race from an unknown planet?'

Arthur opened and closed his mouth without uttering a word. Millie just raised her eyebrows.

As Arthur turned these thoughts over in his mind, he watched Millie trawl back through the text she'd just read aloud. This time she stayed silent, except for the odd incoherent mumble, as her finger trailed across the pages from side to side.

Eventually she looked up. 'Grandad, I'm going to read on. I have to know what happened to the children and where exactly I fit into all this.'

CHAPTER TWO

THE KEY

Zamorians never visited Earth again until the fateful day the Belendrian Six condemned our adult population to death. Belendrian was the name given to a Zamorian – like Zardrot – who possessed multiple powers.

Before any law abiding Zamorian adult could do anything about it the six had used Molto to transfer themselves and every single Zamorian child to the hidden continent of Chintak.

They sabotaged the Molto controls, stopping anyone else leaving Zamora and thus condemning them to death. Without their children it was only a matter of time before life ceased to exist.

The death of millions caused by so few.

The Belendrian Six then became the only remaining Zamorian adults. As they were outnumbered almost a million to one by Zamorian children this meant they would effectively live for ever.

Their reason for committing such an atrocity was simple. Greed. Greed for eternal life, and greed for the riches of this planet. They also believed that they would suffer the same fate as Zardrot had they been found out as Belendrians.

Unlike us children the Belendrians set up home on the Earth's surface. All Belendrians have the ability to change their appearance so they had no problem assuming human form and fitting into your society.

To stop any of us escaping they cursed the gateway to Chintak. The curse was simple. Any Zamorian or human

19

passing either way between the Earth's surface and Chintak would fall foul of the headless curse.

Millie, who'd just reached into a drawer to retrieve a jelly baby, wrinkled her nose at the thought of what she'd just read. She didn't want to look at her grandad for fear of what he might say, although his intermittent tutting noises were a good indication. Millie dropped the jelly baby back into the bag – suddenly the appeal of biting its head off had diminished – and continued.

As time wore on Aurora, who'd placed the curse, became more and more remorseful for what he'd done to his fellow Zamorians. Kiptiziz, the leader of the six, and the most powerful, recognised this and grew increasingly worried about his state of mind. For this reason he forced Aurora to curse himself. This took away his ability to curse, and made it impossible for him to reverse the one he had placed on Chintak.

This drove Aurora to even greater depths of despair. A year after casting his last curse he made this book and passed it through the gateway to Chintak with instructions to script what you are now reading. It was then that I started writing and with Aurora's guidance continued to do so right up to this year – 1729 – the year I pass the book back.

Most importantly, he made a key, in secret, to the Chintak gateway. We named it the Key to Chintak. It is this key that you have to find.

A knock at the front door diverted both Millie's and Arthur's attention from the book. 'Ignore it,' said Millie, with just a cursory look in her grandad's direction.

There was another, much louder, knock.

Millie reluctantly hauled herself out of the chair. 'Maybe a little break will do us good,' she said, as she left the room.

'Try one,' said the eager face that greeted Millie at the door. The face belonged to Ted and his offer centred on a crumpled piece of kitchen towel clutched in his hand.

Ted was Millie's best friend. He went to her school and tended to be at her side most of the time, although, since the start of the school summer holidays, she hadn't seen him for a few days.

'Try one,' he insisted.

'I heard you the first time and the answer is no. I have to rush – sorry!'

This comment resulted in the most dispirited of looks on Ted's face.

His face was a mixture of hope and despair at the best of times. He had a small mouth that seemed to contradict his big, startled looking eyes. Why his nose pointed to one side wasn't clear, although it wasn't to do with a rugby accident, as he would have you believe. He was shorter and stockier than Millie and had particularly big feet.

They had similar hobbies and pastimes and he shared her mischievous and adventurous view on life. What made him different from Millie was his obsession with creating the weirdest sweets imaginable.

'Ted, now isn't a good time. I've something really important to do.'

His response to her statement was more quizzical than she desired. 'Oh really. What would that be, then? Anything I can help with?'

'No.'

'Millie, who is it?' hollered Arthur from the study, his voice laced with more than a little impatience.

'It's OK, Grandad. It's Ted. I'm just coming.' Millie

pulled the door to, exposing just her face to the outside world.

'Hmm, sounds interesting. What are you two up to?' he probed, trying vainly to peek over her shoulder while perched on tiptoes.

'Nothing really … OK … what have you made this time? I'll try one and then I must get on,' she said as she motioned towards the tiny bundle clutched in his hand. She'd hoped her change of direction would stop him asking what was really occupying her. She didn't think he would believe her and she had no inclination to try and make him do so. All she wanted was to return to the book as quickly as possible, and if that meant she had to try another of his odd creations then so be it.

Ted wasn't convinced and her sudden change of mind only roused his curiosity further. 'Exactly *what* have you got in there?'

'An alien from another planet.' She said the first thing that popped into her mind and delivered it with a straight face and a sarcastic tone.

Again Ted's face looked dispirited. 'If you must know I'm discussing "women's things" with my grandad.' Millie was never quite sure what 'woman's things' really meant, but she'd often seen on television that the phrase was a sure-fire way to clear a room of the opposite sex. Besides it sounded grown up.

'Er … right, OK,' was Ted's mumbled reply. Either he knew more than she about its meaning or they'd both been watching the same programmes! Whichever it was, it did the trick. He started to edge away from the door.

'Before you go – what's in the kitchen towel?'

'Ted's Bears,' he said, looking eager again.

Millie peered into the paper and poked a finger amongst

the contents before plucking out the smallest one available.

'I melted a few things together in a pan and came up with them. They don't look like bears yet, of course, and I'm not so sure they're fully set,' he looked at Millie hopefully, 'but they sure taste good.'

She slipped it into her mouth and Ted continued. 'The main ingredient is jelly babies, but—'

The thought of the Headless Curse and her resultant lack of appetite with real jelly babies caused her to spit Ted's creation straight back out again.

'Maybe a touch more sugar,' she said, apologetically. Ted turned and made his way towards the gate, muttering loudly to himself. Normally Millie would chase after him to try and make things better, but today wasn't a normal day. Instead she chose to shout ''Bye then,' in his general direction before pushing the door to. She knew Ted would be fine tomorrow because this wasn't the first time one of his creations had met with such a response. Although in this case – unlike with his Fondant Snot Gobblers – Ted's Bears actually tasted quite good!

Millie returned to the study to find her grandad puzzling over a couple of atlases he'd rescued from the pile stacked against the wall. In pulling them out he'd actually straightened the rest up rather too neatly. This just didn't seem to fit in with the surroundings and she found herself having to suppress the urge to mess them up again.

'What are you searching for?'

'Just waiting for you,' he mumbled, trailing a finger over a page.

Millie peered inquisitively over his shoulder, 'I don't think you'll find Chintak in there! What say we read about the key?'

Arthur shut both books simultaneously with great aplomb,

scattering dust across the room in the process. 'Who was at the door?'

'You already asked me that.'

Millie put her grandad's wandering mind down to the shock of what was unfolding before him. That and a quick nip from his hip flask sneakily taken when she was standing at the front door talking to Ted.

He dropped the atlases back on top of the others causing all of them to defy gravity in a lurch towards the floor. Millie smiled inwardly. Once again the study had resumed its role as the untidiest room in the house.

Arthur could see she wanted to plough on with the book, as with her abrupt reply she'd also flipped over to the next page. 'Carry on then,' he said, and Millie did just that.

Aurora's plan was to find a direct descendant of Zardrot who could help us. That person became known as the Chosen One. Obviously we hope that the Chosen One, being partly human, will not carry Zardrot's twisted hatred of the Zamorian race.

The Key to Chintak is made up of five separate parts. It could not be constructed in one piece, as Aurora believed the other Belendrians would have detected its presence. It is imperative that the key is not assembled until you stand before the place where this book was discovered. As you put the last piece with the others you must say the word CHINTAK and the gateway will appear. Do not take this warning lightly. If you do not do as instructed then we believe that you will be sucked into a bottomless void, never to be seen again.

Another deep breath and a series of tuts from her grandad told Millie that his concern for her was deepening with every page. She chose not to look up, but to read on and deal with the fallout later.

Just before losing his cursing power, Aurora cursed each part of the key. He wanted to take as many precautions as possible in case any of his fellow Belendrians happened to find them. If a Zamorian nears a key piece then evil forces will work against them – resulting in death. The curses became active one day after he hid each key piece.

We hope that as a Zamorian descendant with human genes none of the curses placed by Aurora will affect you, as you are neither wholly one nor the other. In case they do, Aurora inscribed a counter-curse on each part of the key that will only appear when you hold it in your hand. All effects of the curse will be reversed once you read the inscription aloud.

This was the last thing Aurora did for us before Kiptiziz killed him.

'Nice man, this Kiptiziz,' said Arthur, almost trance-like.

Millie was feeling more concerned with every passing moment but felt compelled to read on.

This brings me to today. The day I pass this book into the unknown. I will sign off with my name. When you get to that point you have a choice to make. If you choose to help us then turn the book upside down and back to front, place your hands on the cover and declare so. If you truly are of Zamorian descent and mean what you say then the whereabouts of the first piece of the Key to Chintak will be revealed to you. Aurora has made sure that only the person to whom the book reveals its secrets can open the gateway.

You must carry this book with you at all times on your journey to act as your guide. Aurora also invested some powers in it to help you on your way.

Each of the five parts of the key is in a different continent. When you discover one, place it on the cover of this book and the location of the next will be revealed to you. You must find all five. Assemble them as instructed and open the gateway to Chintak. Once you have done this we will be able to communicate with you.

I hope, for the sake of all Zamorian children trapped in Chintak, that Zamora's historical records were correct and there is indeed still a Zamorian descendant on Earth who will be able to help us.

Fitar.

For the umpteenth time the book had referred directly to a Zamorian descendant and both Millie and Arthur knew who that person was. Millie looked rather drawn. Her face was a picture of worry, as if reading the book had finally taken its toll her normally resilient mind.

Could she really help the Zamorian children? She was obviously the one they considered to be their saviour, but could she really do it? 'Grandad, I have to help them,' she said, choosing to ignore her own self-doubts.

Arthur pulled himself upright in his chair as the enormity of what Millie had just read began to sink in. 'No, Millie, I can't let you! It's far too dangerous. I think your adventurous spirit has got the better of you and I simply will not allow you to put your life in so much danger. The children of Zamora have coped without you until now and they'll just have to continue that way.'

'I have to, Grandad. I just have to … besides I'll not be alone in trying to help them.'

'And what makes you say that?'

'Because you'll be with me. Apart from anything else, I'm the only one that can read the book.'

'True, but I have my notes and tape.' Arthur held his notepad aloft, flapping the pages in Millie's face. However when he opened it his triumphant look soon disappeared.

'Grandad, what is it?'

He continued to flick back through the pages, having seemingly not heard the question.

'Grandad?'

Arthur slowly raised his head. 'Everything I wrote has vanished.' He handed the notepad to Millie, who looked puzzled.

'Well?' he said.

'Er, Grandad, *I* can read your notes. They're a little jumbled and you really do need to learn to spell better, but I can still read them.'

She then started to recount some of what she saw and as she did so Arthur picked up his tape recorder and proceeded to rewind it. When he pressed *play* the tape leaped into life, but he heard nothing apart from the background hissing that filled the air.

'I hate hearing myself on tape. I sound like a mouse,' squeaked Millie.

'I can't hear anything, Millie. Not a thing, apart from some background noise.'

Millie shrugged.

Arthur just sat there drumming his fingers on the desk. He could have muttered anything at that point; he certainly had lots of material to pick from, but chose to say, 'The Belendrians knew that Zamorian DNA most likely still existed on Earth. That's not good news Millie.'

As quick as a flash she came back with a response. 'They would have known that for centuries, Grandad, and still one of us is here. Providing I am one, of course. But I'll need to turn the book over to find out.' Both of them looked towards the book and then back at each other.

'Well, I could try to find the five pieces that make up the key on my own, and speak to you back here as I go,' said Arthur in his best leadership-like voice.

'Except you can't read the book, you may fall foul of any curses that are aimed at just humans, and let's not forget the book says that only *I* can assemble the key.'

'Fair points.'

'Oh, and there's also the small matter of me being only twelve years old, so you couldn't leave me on my own anyway!' Millie looked like an expectant puppy waiting to be thrown its favourite ball.

'Well, it would seem Zamorian words are for your eyes only,' said Arthur resignedly, turning his attention back to the book.

The tension in the room increased to an even greater level as Millie picked it up and turned it upside down and back to front. She flipped open the cover and riffled through the pages. 'Nothing new there,' she said quietly.

'Well, you first have to put your hand on the cover and say what Fitar instructed, I guess,' said Arthur, now, with his granddaughter, totally hooked on what the book might turn up next.

Millie placed one hand on the cover. 'What do I have to say again?'

'Er, that you are of Zamorian descent and want to help, or something like that.' His muddled look and vague response did nothing to calm her nerves.

Millie could feel the sweat building on her palm that was now pressed hard against the cover. She took a deep breath and said, 'I, Millie Jarman, a descendant of Zardrot, truly wish to help the Children of Zamora.'

Neither of them was quite sure exactly what would

happen next. A flashing light or some deep meaningful words booming out from the inner reaches of the book, perhaps? Instead they were greeted with silence. The study was still dimly lit and no noise could be heard from the black book that lay pressed beneath Millie's sweating palm. Nothing had happened at all.

Arthur glanced across at his granddaughter. 'Open it. I guess there will be some more writing inside now.'

Millie peeled her hand clear of the cover and slowly opened the book. As Arthur wasn't able to read from it anyway he had to rely on her expression and it didn't look promising. She flipped over a few pages, paused, and then slowly closed it again.

'Well?'

Millie chose not to respond.

'I guess you can't see anything then?'

'You guessed right.' She wanted to say more, but seemed exhausted by the prospect.

'Maybe you shouldn't have mentioned Zardrot. Maybe because he was a Belendrian the book doesn't take kindly to his name?'

This seemed to be just the thing she wanted to hear. No sooner had Arthur finished the sentence then Millie had again pressed the palm of one hand onto the cover. 'I, Millie Jarman, a … Zamorian descendant, truly wish to help the Children of Zamora.'

Again nothing happened and again no text greeted the ever-eager eyes of the young girl now positively slumped in her chair. 'I don't understand, Grandad. How could I have got so far? How could I have been able to read what I did before if I wasn't the Chosen One – if I wasn't a Zamorian descendant?' she said despondently.

'I have to admit it doesn't make sense.'

Suddenly Millie sat bolt upright, looked at her grandad and then pulled herself forward on her chair and closer to the book. She flipped it over and the right way up and proceeded to leaf through the pages silently until she reached the one she was obviously searching for. Her finger slid down the page until it stopped and made its way across. 'Aha! Got ya.'

'What?'

'I think I know what I did wrong.'

'Which was?'

'The book says place BOTH hands on the cover. Don't know why, but it's worth a shot.' With that she turned it over and into position and placed both hands face down on the cover. Somehow this felt different. Somehow this felt right.

'I, Millie Jarman, a … Zamorian descendant, truly wish to help the Children of Zamora.'

As soon as her words tailed off she felt a surge of energy rocket through her and the book started to glow hot. So hot that even Arthur, who was a couple of feet away, could feel its warmth. Millie, however, did not feel the heat. Instead, all she could feel was an overwhelming surge of well-being, an almost indescribable feeling of elation, as if all her birthdays and Christmases had come at once.

As if someone had just told her she really, really, was of Zamorian descent and she really, really, could help the Children of Zamora.

The feeling subsided and she turned to face her grandad, who motioned back towards the book and said, 'Well, are you going to open it or not?'

CHAPTER THREE

ASIA

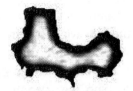

Instead of blank pages, this time Millie was greeted with instructions on where to find the first part of the key.

Make your way to the banks of the river Yamuna in Agra, the capital of the Mogul monarchs. There you will find the tomb of Queen Mumtaz, the Taj Mahal. The first piece of the key lies within the handle that adorns the door leading to the Gardens of Paradise.

Millie stopped and cast a somewhat confused gaze towards her grandad who took his time before saying, 'And?'

'And nothing. That's it.' Millie flicked through the next few pages, all of which stared blankly back at her. Neither of them was sure what they expected to be told, but even so they somehow felt a little short-changed by what was on offer.

'In the door handle … all sounds rather too simple to me,' said Arthur, while desperately trying to suppress his urge to smile about the fact that maybe saving another race wasn't going to be as hard as he first expected. 'Obviously we aren't going to be able to just waltz up and remove the handle, but I'm sure I can pull a few strings via the museum to carry out a little, how would you say, research.' Yes,

Arthur was *very* pleased with himself.

'Right,' was Millie's reply. Her feelings were slightly different as she rather hoped it might be a little harder than tinkering with a handle and then moving on.

She cleared her mind before firing off some more questions. 'I know the Taj Mahal is in India, Grandad, but what are the Mogul monarchs and who is Queen Mumtaz?'

'The Taj Mahal was built as a resting place for Queen Mumtaz by the king, who was deeply in love with her. It took decades to complete and legend has it the king never fully recovered from the loss of his wife.'

Millie knew she was staring at her grandad with a faint awestruck expression, but couldn't help herself. She just loved the fact that he seemed to know everything about everything and if he didn't he could sure sound convincing when he made up the answers! 'And what were the Mogul monarchs?'

'Not what, who. They were the rulers at the time before the British came to power.' A raised hand told Arthur that Millie had heard enough. She'd long since learned that however interesting a subject might be and however much she loved to listen, if she didn't stop him early he would go on for hours. She did feel a touch guilty however as Arthur looked a little disheartened at being cut off in full flow.

'How many times have I told you not to wave your hand like that? I'm not a dog!'

Suitably berated, Millie turned her attention back to the book that still lay open before her. 'Grandad, a picture of the key has just appeared. It wasn't there before.' She pointed to the place on the page where the image was.

Arthur shook his head, 'I can't see it, my love. Can you draw it for me?' He reached into a pile of what could best be described as desk rubble and, like a magician, theatrically plucked out a blank sheet of paper which he passed to Millie. She picked up a pencil and proceeded to sketch out what she could see.

'It's not that good, but it's pretty close. I've even included the jagged edge around the outside. It's sort of like a section of a cog. What do you make of it?' she said, handing it to Arthur.

Arthur couldn't comment, because all he saw was an empty page. He could see Millie putting pencil to paper and sketching away, but for him the page remained blank and Millie could tell by his expression that this was the case. 'Don't worry, Grandad, I know what it looks like and will recognise it when I see it.' With that she folded up the sketch and used it to mark the page.

She closed the book, tucked it under her arm and slid off her chair to face her grandad. 'Shall we?'

*

Time dragged by, even though there was a relatively short amount of it between the closing of the book and the airport check-in desk the intrepid travellers now stood before.

During the intervening period the pair had kept their discussions about what may lay ahead to a minimum, preferring instead to adopt the head-in-the-sand approach. While alone in her bedroom, though, Millie kept trying to conjure up powers she hoped would reveal themselves when summoned. She did this to no avail as everything she tried – even gargling while standing on one leg with her fingers in her ears – produced not a single response.

Their adventure was to start in the school summer holidays, but Arthur still took the precaution of agreeing some additional time off for Millie. He gained the school's approval after he told them he was taking her on a once-in-a-lifetime educational trip. However, he sincerely hoped their journey would take a lot less time than the five weeks she had left of the official holidays. Millie's inheritance from her parents at least meant the trip would be well funded.

*

At the airport Millie rambled on about a vast array of subjects. Questions about the length of the check-in queue, what happened when someone went through the 'beepy' gate and whether she could accompany her bag through the X-ray machine were beginning to make Arthur question his desire to board the flight to India. This was after all only the first leg of what looked set to be quite an arduous journey.

Fortunately for him Millie sat quietly on the plane happily watching the same movie twice over, even though there was a varied choice, eating far too much chocolate, and snoozing peacefully.

Even though she slept on the flight Millie was still glad to see the bed in their modest hotel in a downtown suburb of Delhi. It was only a matter of minutes after arriving that she climbed into its clutches and nestled down. Arthur too slept soundly, thanks to a fair old dose of jet lag and one too many 'complimentaries'. The next morning they journeyed to Agra aboard a train that, as with most new things, was a source of great amusement to Millie. In between listening to her views on the Indian railway system and their joint admiration of the spectacular scenery, Arthur went over his story many times with his young accomplice.

'Grandad, I've got it, I promise. You have a letter from the museum that states you're on a fact-finding tour of the great historical doors of the world and you want some private time to explore the one that leads to the Gardens of Paradise.'

Arthur settled back in his seat. 'And leave the talking to

me.'

'Trust me, I will.'

The train pulled into Agra and they got a taxi straight to the Taj Mahal. Millie leaped from the cab, scaring the driver in the process.

A quick wave of some rupees from Arthur reassured him that both of his passengers weren't about to make a run for it without paying.

As Arthur stepped from the taxi he couldn't help being overcome by the beauty that punctured the hazy skyline before him. The Taj Mahal was a magnificent sight and this was underlined by the fact that even Millie stood silently, mouth open wide, for all of two seconds.

'That, my girl, is truly a wonder of the world.' Arthur's own wonderment was soon forgotten when he looked down to discover Millie was gone. His heart sank, as he cursed himself for losing sight of her. Quickly he scanned behind him and towards the Taj Ganj, the area that still felt and smelt as if it held true to its former roots as a bustling and colourful bazaar. People spewed from every building and each street corner seemed alive with activity.

A couple of panic-stricken minutes passed before Arthur felt a tap on his shoulder. 'It's said that Mumtaz Mahal ran a stall in the Taj Ganj selling jewels.' Arthur turned to be met by a tall Indian man who was wearing a khaki uniform with the words *Official Guide* blazoned across the breast pocket.

'Not now, I'm—'

'Trying to find a little girl about this tall and wearing a blue baseball cap,' interrupted the guide, holding his hand to his waist to depict height.

'What have you done with her? Where is she? If you have—'

Again the guide interrupted, '*Now* I see from whom she

got her forthright manner.' He pointed over his shoulder towards the grand forecourt that formed the gateway to the Taj Mahal. 'She told me about your historical mission to visit this part of the world and research our magnificent entrance. Come, I'll take you to her.'

Arthur, now feeling somewhat ashamed at his outburst, followed the man towards the entrance. In an effort to break the silence he enquired, 'You were saying about Mumtaz Mahal?'

If the guide was flustered by the abrasive approach of the Jarman family then his reply didn't show it. 'Mumtaz Mahal must have stood out from the crowd, as history tells us that the young Shah Jahan first met her when she was working in the Taj Ganj, before he became king. A long and happy marriage and many children were the result of that meeting. Alas, as you are aware, her tragic death caused Shah great sorrow and led him to create the Taj Mahal in her memory.'

Arthur's impression of a nodding dog was cut short when, to his great relief, he caught sight of his granddaughter. Millie, however, seemed oblivious to the anguish she'd put him through.

'There isn't one,' she said, hands on hips.

'Millie, I told you not to leave my side *and* I told you to let me sort things out.'

'I know and I will. I mean … I will next time.' She smiled coyly and tilted her head to one side.

'There isn't one what?' Arthur's tone was short and abrupt.

'A handle.'

'Ah yes,' said the guard cutting in, 'that's one thing the young lady didn't properly explain.'

Millie opened her mouth to speak, but quick glances from both the guide and Arthur caused her for once to keep her opinion to herself.

'This door has never had a handle on it.' A tug on his arm by a rather flustered tourist caused the guide to divert his attention elsewhere. 'Sorry, would you excuse me a minute?'

'Grandad, I don't understand. How can there be no handle? The book said—'

'Has it ever occurred to you that the book may have been written by the Belendrians to draw you out into the open? Maybe, just maybe, this guy not three feet from us, this very helpful guide, is in fact one of them?' Arthur said in a hushed tone

Of course it had occurred to Millie, but she didn't want to say. That's one of the thoughts that she'd conveniently chosen to bury at the back of her mind, but the mere mention of the possibility made her shudder and edge just a little closer to her grandad.

Before she could reply, the guide, free from the distraction of the inquisitive tourist, returned to their side. 'As I was saying there has never been a handle on *this* door, but I understand the original door was adorned with quite a masterpiece.'

'The original door?' blurted Millie.

'Yes. The original door was studded with silver rupees and proved irresistible to local rebels, who stole it in 1764. Its whereabouts has been a mystery ever since although it's believed that the rupees were taken from it and divided amongst the looters. Legend has it that the handle itself never actually left the area, and if rumours are to be believed, then it still resides within the boundaries of the Taj Ganj. Where, exactly, nobody is certain.'

Arthur removed his sweat-drenched hat and scratched his head. 'Nobody is certain, you say, but what is the uncertain line of thought?'

'I don't understand,' replied the guard, who all of sudden seemed to lose his composure and was clearly uneasy at the direction of questioning. 'Oh, I think you misunderstand my English. What I mean is … nobody knows. Do you still wish to examine the current door?'

'No, but thank you very much for your time. It has been most informative.' With those words from Arthur the guard nodded graciously and disappeared back into the throng.

Millie and Arthur remained rooted to the spot and both were now almost certainly thinking the same thing. *How on earth were they going to find the piece to the key if nobody had any idea of the whereabouts of the handle it was inside of?* Suddenly India felt like a very big haystack.

'Grandad, I'm not convinced by what he said – that nobody knows its whereabouts. Did you notice the way he shifted suspiciously when you asked about the certainty of who might have it?' Being a fine one herself, Millie recognised a liar a mile off.

'I think you're right, but where do we start?'

'There looks like a good place,' Millie pointed over her grandad's shoulder and into the bustle of the Taj Ganj.

'I just don't know, Millie. What chance have we got?'

'Grandad, if we find the key we'll also find the handle and then we can return it to its rightful owners. Just imagine how that would make people here feel?'

Arthur looked down at his feisty little granddaughter and smiled.

*

After spending the best part of a week trudging around the streets of the Taj Ganj they were running short of ideas and humour. They'd tried everywhere: from museums to local dealers in all types of artefacts.

The temperature, day or night, always seemed to be nudging a hundred plus and the heat and humidity were making Arthur feel a similar age. Even Millie, sporting a sari, or 'big sheet' as she unlovingly called it, was feeling the energy draining from her with each passing hour.

Their inquiries were beginning to get them noticed and there were times when they were sure people actually closed up shop when they approached. Their greatest fear, that one of the Belendrians was nearby and they would happen across him, or worse still, that he would seek out the inquisitive pair of strangers, was never far from their minds.

'If only the key had been given some sort of homing device to lead us to it, then the task would have been much simpler,' said Millie, mopping her brow with her sari.

'Simple tasks are obviously not for the Chosen One,' said Arthur wryly. 'Which brings me to my next point. Are you SURE you really are the Chosen One?'

Patience and belief were obviously wearing thin.

'Well maybe I should choose to leave you at the hotel, not the one in Agra, but the one in …' Millie's words tailed off, and her grandad could see she was staring intently at someone in the crowd of people that always seemed to frequent the area of parkland bordering their hotel.

'What is it Millie?'

'That man – his left leg – look at the tattoo,' she said.

Not far from the pair a fair-skinned man was stretched out on the grass. Millie thought he must be English, as his glowing skin, peeling nose, and general attire pointed to the one race that always insist on frying themselves whenever the sun appears.

The pair of intrepid and somewhat sweaty adventurers, eased closer to the man, but they failed to do so unnoticed.

'Can I help you?' said the man, who was shielding his

eyes from the sun and trying to evaluate the unlikely duo.

As Millie drew closer she resisted the urge to smile at the man's dress sense. It seemed he was quite happy to burn every part of his body except his feet, which were nicely protected by a huge pair of grey socks and chunky sandals. He was in his thirties, with a smattering of grey woven through his rather unkempt ginger hair. His build suggested a liking for the local cuisine and his teeth, crooked and stained yellow, had definitely seen better days. On the face of it this man was quite unremarkable, except for the tattoo on his left leg. Unless Millie was mistaken, apart from having no jagged edge, his tattoo looked remarkably similar to the key piece they were hunting for. Millie pointed to the tattoo, 'What is that?' she quizzed the stranger.

He cast an uneasy glance at Arthur and then back to Millie. 'A tattoo,' he replied with raised eyebrows and a sly grin.

Millie flexed her own brows, crossed her arms and dropped onto one leg.

Arthur stepped forward and interjected before Millie had a chance to say what she was thinking. He wasn't entirely sure what that might be, but figured it was probably not polite.

'Sorry, let's try that again. My name is Arthur Jarman and this is my granddaughter Millie.'

'We come in peace ... blah, blah, blah. What's the tattoo of?' Millie cut in.

'Millie!' exclaimed Arthur. 'I do apologise. We've had a long day, and the sun seems to have affected my delightful granddaughter's manners.'

Millie puffed out her cheeks, switched feet, and bored her eyes into the ground.

'I'm a historian and was drawn to the most unusual tattoo

on your leg as it reminded me of something I'd seen in a book many moons ago. I – we – were just wondering if you know what it is?'

The man stared at the pair unsure if they were real or just manufactured by too much sun, drink and lack of sleep. 'OK. Well actually I have no idea what it is. I just asked the tattooist for something different and he did this.'

Sensing this wasn't what they wanted to hear, and seeing Millie's none-too-pleased expression, the man continued, 'You could always ask the guy in the tattoo parlour. I had it done in the Taj Ganj. Just follow the main street until you get to a shop called Mirage. Then go down the side of it and follow the smaller alley that splinters off to the right – at the end of which you will find the tattoo parlour. It doesn't look too inviting, but I had this done a few weeks back and I'm still alive!'

Millie and Arthur smiled thankfully. This seemed to be a great relief to the man as his desire to talk about body art was tempered with a great urge to run away from his inquisitors.

As they walked off Millie stopped in her tracks and turned to face her grandad. 'Grandad, you could see it. You could see the drawing on the man's leg. So I would say that wasn't the part of the key we're searching for, but as it resembled the shape it might just be—'

'The door handle that contains the key,' said Arthur, finishing the sentence for her.

For the first time since they'd been in India it seemed that they had finally got a lucky break and it was just the tonic required to lift the hearts of the weary travellers.

'Well, at least you have a rough idea what we're looking for now,' said Millie, disguising her feeling that she was no longer special in that respect.

CHAPTER FOUR

THE TATTOO PARLOUR

Arthur and Millie thought they'd covered almost every part of the sprawling mass that made up the Taj Ganj, but they were clearly mistaken because the route to the front door of the tattoo parlour was not one they'd taken before. Nor was it one they wished to take again. The alley-way leading to the parlour was littered with all sorts of debris, not to mention some very odd people skulking silently in every doorway, each one keen to conceal, rather than reveal, his face. Even in the doorway next to the parlour, where nobody appeared to be standing, Millie felt, almost sixth sense-like, the presence of someone watching her.

Although the shop didn't look inviting the alternative of hanging around outside in the dimly-lit alley, filled with smoke as if straight from a film set, was much less appealing. Even though it was the lesser of two evils they entered the shop with deep trepidation.

If at all possible there was more smoke inside the shop than outside. A ceiling fan with two missing blades made a vain attempt to move the stale, dank air that sat heavily in the waiting area, along with a few potential clients lined up against one wall. Grotesque pictures and bizarre symbols lined the opposite wall and a plant pot doubling as an ashtray dominated the centre of the room.

'Can I be of assistance?' said a voice from across the room.

Millie and Arthur made their way through the haze towards the voice, carefully avoiding the plant pot and the frothing dog lying just in front of the counter. The voice itself portrayed a crystal-clear English accent at odds with its surroundings. The accompanying face also didn't seem to belong in a place so obviously devoid of civilisation.

'Are you lost?'

'Er, no, my Grandad would like to see your tattoo book.'

The face peered over the counter, looked at Millie, and introduced itself. 'My name is Ranjit, and you are?'

'Millie, and this is my grandad Arthur.'

Ranjit came out from behind the counter and bent down to talk to Millie. He just didn't seem right. She had no real reason to form such an early opinion of the man, but she couldn't help herself. Sure, his accent and demeanour didn't fit in with the surroundings, although that in itself wasn't enough to distrust someone. There was something else about him. Something she couldn't quite put her finger on.

It wasn't his height, something Millie was never intimidated by. She had spent a good deal of time with adults and so she was used to being towered over. It wasn't his look, almost noble and charming. It was just something else. Something sinister.

'I'm not sure this is a place for little girls, and between you and me don't you think your grandad is a bit old for tattoos?'

'I'm NOT a little girl AND my grandad doesn't want a tattoo. He just wants to see the different ones you offer.'

Such a strong-willed response was clearly not expected, as Ranjit took a few seconds to reply. 'I see, and why would that be then?'

Millie looked to her grandad, for once stuck for an answer.

'Because I'm interested in regional art and am writing a paper about it for the museum I work for.' Millie was more than relieved with her grandad's response, as she wasn't sure how long she could stand peering up the nose of the creepy shopkeeper.

Ranjit rose to his feet and pointed to a mound of books on the dusty counter. 'Feel free.'

Arthur scooped up the pile and made his way, with Millie in tow, towards the nearest seats. He plonked the books down on his lap as he sunk into the dirty plastic that lined his chair. Millie took up residence on the seat beside him, but not before pulling out a large roll of toilet paper from her rucksack and tearing off a chunk to wipe the chair down. She then duly disposed of the paper in the plant pot, where it immediately exploded into life as it came into contact with a still smouldering cigarette butt. The smoke produced only added to the seedy ambience of the place and caused not a raised eyebrow amongst the people present.

'Let's see if we can find the picture and then maybe it will have a name attached that could lead us to it. Sure we could ask Ranjit, but I don't know what it is … I just don't trust him,' whispered Arthur.

Millie didn't feel the need to concur.

It took almost twenty minutes for them to work their way through the pile of books, but not once did they come across anything that resembled the tattoo on the stranger's leg.

'Are you after anything in particular?' said Ranjit, who was now standing before them. 'It's only that I need the books back for other people to look at. Other people who actually *want* a tattoo that is.'

Arthur had no choice, but to ask him straight out. 'We saw a man in the town who had a tattoo that greatly interested me. It was a piece of art like none other I've seen before and he said it was done here.'

Suddenly a thought flashed through Millie's mind. She reached into her rucksack, making sure the precious black book was out of sight, and pulled out the piece of paper she'd sketched the key on – the piece of paper her grandad saw as blank. '*That* is what we're looking for,' she said thrusting it in Ranjit's face.

He took the paper and unfolded it. Arthur was just about to say something when he realised what Millie was up to. If Ranjit could see the drawing then there would be no doubt. *He* must be a Belendrian.

'Ranjit, Ranjit,' called a voice from behind the counter.

Ranjit looked towards the voice and then back to cast another curious glance at the paper.

'Ranjit, your father is on the phone and he wants to know when you'll be home. He wants you there at seven and told me to remind you not to be late.'

'Tell him I'll be there. No! Tell him I'll *try* to be there. Oh and tell him in English. That should do the trick.'

He turned his attention back towards the paper and then to Millie and Arthur. 'Curious drawing this one.'

Millie tried desperately not to look at her grandad and she just knew he was doing the same. Now was not the time to look any guiltier than they already did.

'Was it done with invisible ink?' He looked up grinning, but was a little puzzled to see that Millie and Arthur weren't similarly amused.

Arthur was the first to shake the blank expression from his face. 'Er … yes … sorry. My granddaughter has a rather warped sense of humour. I'll sketch you the tattoo we saw.'

Ranjit handed Arthur the paper and a pen, but just as he was about to draw Millie said without thinking, 'Other side.'

This made Ranjit lean forward and re-examine the paper. 'Why the other side? Both are blank.' As he looked towards Millie, Arthur flipped it over.

Millie said the first thing that came into her head.

'Because there are, there are … fewer creases on that side.'

'If I may say so, you're just a little weird. The creases are the same on both sides!' Normally Millie wouldn't take such a comment thrown at her, especially from such an extremely weird and creepy man himself, but on this occasion she chose to bite her lip and stay silent. Even she realised that you can only put your foot in your mouth so many times in one day.

Arthur started to sketch out what he remembered of the tattoo, but before he'd completed half of it Ranjit grabbed his writing hand and said, 'You have to leave!' Suddenly his tone had changed altogether. Gone was the mild mannered and clear-cut approach of before to be replaced by a few sharp words and an unquestionable motion towards the door.

'LEAVE, I SAID!'

Arthur slowly rose to his feet. 'Young man, old age has blessed me with two things you clearly do not possess.' Arthur now stood face to face with Ranjit, who still had hold of his writing hand. The look on Arthur's face and the way his chest had suddenly puffed out wasn't something Millie had ever seen before. Like everyone else in the room, who'd now diverted their attention towards Ranjit and Arthur, Millie was curious as to what might happen next.

'And what two things would they be then?'

'Manners.'

'And?'

'A rare contagious skin disease!' Millie couldn't help herself. She'd no idea what her grandad was going to say next, but figured her comment would do the trick. Ranjit quickly released his grip and brushed his hand on his trousers. Arthur, suppressing his urge to smile, turned to leave.

'Ranjit, your father is still on the phone. He wants to speak with you personally.' The second voice from behind the misty counter belonged to a young girl, clearly frightened at having to deliver the message.

'Hello.' She nodded courteously towards Millie and Arthur, who was still clutching the paper.

'Don't talk to them Mia! AND I have told you before, tell my father I'll TRY to be home at seven. Need I remind you that without this job you would be on the streets and the way you're going, young lady, that's where you're heading? Now get back to the phone and do as you're told!'

'There's really no need to be so rude!' Millie blurted out.

'Leave now or …' Ranjit swivelled round to face Millie and lowered his face to hers.

'Or what?' Millie was on a roll and would have said more had it not been for Arthur's intervention.

'Let's go.' He led Millie across the smoke-filled assault course and out into the forbidding alley. No sooner did they leave than it seemed the whole shop followed suit. Everyone filed out, head down, and scuttled off into the darkness. Even the frothing dog looked too scared to stick around, as it too made a hasty retreat into the night.

Not that it was easy to tell, but nightfall had snuffed out the sun, making their surroundings even more menacing than before. Suddenly neither of them felt so courageous any more.

'You really don't want to be here when he comes out. Nasty piece of work, that one. Not as nasty as his father, but nasty none the less.' They both spun round to be greeted by one of the men who'd been patiently waiting in the tattoo parlour. He was very short. Millie stood almost nose to nose with him, and his general appearance was one of someone who'd obviously fallen on hard times. Before another word was said he too had vanished into the shadows.

Their courage was ebbing away by the second and Millie did something she hadn't done for some years. She slipped her hand into her grandad's and squeezed hard. He looked down and said, 'Let's get out of here now!'

However, before they could retreat back up the alley they were distracted by yet more activity from the tattoo parlour behind them. Although the shop's façade was partly obscured by mist, they could both distinguish the figure hurrying out of the shop. It was Ranjit, and had he not been backing out, barking orders to his frightened shop assistant, he would have spotted them both.

Millie and Arthur slipped silently into a pitch-black doorway as Ranjit shouted, 'You lock up. I have to go now. I'm sure even *you* can't mess that up.'

When he'd finished his dressing-down Ranjit turned to scan the apparently empty alley-way before him. He stood menacingly looking up and down into the darkness. To Arthur and Millie's horror he fixed his eyes on their doorway. 'I know you're there. I can see you.'

Their hearts raced and Millie's stomach actually felt as if it was trying to get out of her mouth and make a run for it all by itself. She squeezed her grandad's hand even tighter. The humidity and their situation were causing both of them to perspire heavily, but however annoying it felt to have sweat dribbling from their noses neither of them were tempted to brush it off. Each remained motionless, holding their breath.

Millie felt something brush her leg and was just about to scream when Arthur clasped his hand over her mouth. 'Don't move,' he whispered.

'Do I have to come over there and get you?'

Both of them stood rigid, hoping and praying the answer was no.

'If I do you'll not live to see another day.'

Millie slipped her hand inside her rucksack and felt for the black book. If the book had powers that could help her, now would be a good time to find out, but she couldn't get her bag open properly and her grandad nudged her to stop moving.

'OK!' snapped Ranjit, and started towards them.

Suddenly the dark, stinky doorway that was their only cover now seemed like a very unwise choice. Bins blocked their way to one side, leaving them with little choice but to contemplate trying to escape past their fast-approaching assailant. Each step towards them narrowed their options further, but they were gripped by fear and unable to move.

'Ranjit!' Not for the first time a voice diverted his attention. Mia had appeared at the shop door, a paper bag in one hand, and a torch in the other. 'Ranjit, you forgot your bag.'

Millie and Arthur couldn't have been more relieved to hear Mia's voice, but their delight was to be short-lived.

Mia held out the bag and pointed the torch at Ranjit, momentarily causing him to tilt his head forward and shield his eyes from the brightness. The beam of light cast in the direction of her boss also caught Millie and Arthur in its glare. Were it not for being temporarily blinded, Ranjit would have seen from Mia's expression that something wasn't right.

'We have to go. We have to go right now,' whispered Millie, tugging on her grandad's arm. Before they could move Mia lowered the torch and shouted 'Suna, here Suna,' and Millie felt something dash past her legs. It was the frothing dog who like everyone else connected with Ranjit, was clearly scared of him. Suna scampered towards Mia and came to rest behind her legs.

To their great relief Ranjit walked back towards his shop and turned his attention to the dog. 'I have told you before, you useless bag of bones. One day you're going to push me too far and then, my furry friend, I'll have you boiled down for glue.' Millie and Arthur were horrified, but both wisely remained silent.

Ranjit rose up, grabbed the bag, and without saying another word he disappeared into the night. Suna trotted alongside him, but not before first casting a backward glance directly towards the doorway.

Mia pointed the torch up and down the alley and into each hidden doorway. 'They're gone, you can come out now. Nobody else is here.' She shone the torch at their feet and for the first time in what seemed like days they felt safe enough to step out from the shadows.

'You're unwise to cross him. Many have done so before and have never been heard of again.'

The pair joined Mia's side and Arthur was the first to speak, 'Thank you.'

'Yes, thank you,' echoed Millie.

'What brings you here?'

Arthur reached into his pocket and pulled out the paper containing his sketch of the tattoo, 'This.'

Mia took one glance at it. 'Follow me.' She led them back into the shop and locked the door, choosing not to switch the light on. Even the torch was extinguished, leaving only the dimmest of street lights to cast an eerie glow on the proceedings.

'It's not safe for you here.'

'Why? I don't understand. I'm a historian and I'm just researching—' Arthur's speech was cut short by the sound of footsteps in the alley outside.

'Don't move.' Millie and Arthur were in no mood to

disagree with Mia's instructions.

The footsteps made their way to the door and the handle was flexed several times.

'Damn!' came the now all-too-familiar voice of Ranjit.

'He must have forgotten something,' said Mia in the most hushed of tones.

'What do we do?' whispered Millie.

'Nothing. He doesn't have his keys today.'

They reeled slightly back in their stance as they saw him press his face up against the window. They could see him because of the light behind, but he couldn't see them. At least they hoped he couldn't.

The door rattled loudly once more. 'MIA! MIA! Where are you? That damn girl, why isn't she here?'

As quick as he came back he disappeared again. All three stood silent straining their ears for any outside activity.

'I don't want to know your reason for seeking out the handle. Whatever it is, surely it's not worth your lives? Believe me, that's what's at stake here.'

Millie edged a little closer to Mia. 'Thank you for your concern, but we must find the key.'

Mia looked at her quizzically. 'What key?'

'She means handle,' said Arthur, frowning at Millie. 'She gets confused.'

'Yes, sorry, I mean handle. Can you help us? You must believe me. We have to find it. We just have to.'

Mia stood motionless trying to work the pair out. 'Ranjit doesn't get on with his father, Manik. There has been trouble between them for as long as I've known them. You see, Ranjit doesn't want to follow in his father's footsteps and take over the family import and export business. The feud between them can often get very strained and they seem to stop at nothing to aggravate each other. That's why he only speaks to his father in English. He has done so for almost a year now, because he knows it annoys him so much. That's also why he acquired this business. He wanted to get as far away from his father's empire as possible and this place proved the ideal way of realising that desire.

Manik, though, is not to be messed with. His fearsome reputation precedes him, and it's obvious that were Ranjit not his son he would have disappeared a long time ago. About the only thing the two seem to have in common is their ability to remove from their path anything that blocks it. Dead or alive.'

'Are you serious? I mean this is the twenty-first century. Not the dark ages. Surely they can't just make people disappear?' said Arthur, who'd also now edged a little closer to Mia.

'I am *deadly* serious.' Her mood changed and she seemed to somehow sink into her shoes. Tears streaked slowly down her grubby face, accompanying her sudden lack of stature. 'My parents owned this shop and did not want to sell up. It may not appear much to you, but it was their livelihood, and they paid for their stubbornness with their lives. When I went to the authorities I was just told to stop wasting their time. Oh yes, I am deadly serious.'

'Why don't you run away?' quizzed Millie, clearly shocked by what she was being told.

'Where could I run? I have no money. The house we had was taken by Ranjit for one of his friends. I only have the food he gives me daily, and I sleep in the shop.'

Arthur reached into his pocket, pulled out his wallet and from it a stash of rupees. 'Here, take these and go.'

The sight of that much money to a girl so poor was almost too much for her to take. 'Why would you do such a thing?'

'Please take it.' Mia didn't wait to be offered a third time, but snatched the money from his hand and clutched it tightly to her chest, clearly afraid that such an offer wouldn't stand for too long. Tears again welled in her eyes.

Millie felt drawn to join her but took a deep breath and regained her composure before saying, 'Could you help us, please?'

Mia held out her other hand, took the paper from Arthur, and examined his artwork. 'This is the handle from the original door that led to the gardens of the Taj Mahal. Manik has it.'

'Go on,' said Arthur, after briefly exchanging glances with Millie.

'It had always been rumoured that the handle never left this area and most people were sure who would have it if that were the case. Manik's reputation and connections in high places ensured that it remained just that – a rumour.'

'How do you know this?'

'Give her time, Millie.'

Mia drew a long deep breath. 'I know this because I overheard a conversation between Ranjit and his father. I was alone with Ranjit one evening in the shop when he sent me on an errand. As I made my way up the alley I realised I'd not locked the shop as instructed. Not wanting to upset him I returned, only to discover I'd left the keys on the counter. It was when I crept back in and retrieved them that I overheard him arguing with his father on the phone in the back room. It seemed he wanted to upset his father particularly deeply on this occasion.'

Arthur leaned ever closer. 'In what way?'

'A traveller happened upon our shop earlier that day and not liking anything in the books he enquired if there were any other unusual designs on offer. It wasn't until I overheard the telephone conversation later between Ranjit and Manik that I realised the significance of the artwork Ranjit decided to tattoo on the stranger's leg.'

'The handle?' whispered Millie.

Mia nodded.

'But why did he do that?' asked Arthur.

'Out of spite. Manik had stopped him seeing a girl who took his fancy and he got back at him in the most hurtful way possible. His father was furious and was screaming at him down the phone. I didn't stay to hear any more as I was frightened for myself. I took the keys, crept out, locked the door behind me and didn't return for a full half-hour. Nothing was ever mentioned and all unusual tattoo requests were met with a resounding "no" from then on.'

Mia handed back the sketch. 'And now you must leave. Heed my warning. It's not safe for you to stay in Agra.'

Arthur took the drawing and tucked it into his pocket.

'Thank you for the money. I'm truly grateful. I have friends afar and I'll travel to them.' She walked to the door, stared out into the darkness, and beckoned Millie and Arthur over.

Arthur clutched Millie's hand. 'Millie, it's time to go. Hold my hand and stay right by my side.'

Mia unlocked the door and edged out into the alley. 'Stay there,' she said, waving them back into the shop. 'I'm going to check it's clear.'

Millie peered out gingerly into the night. So much so Arthur felt the need to tug her back. 'Grandad, she's gone.'

'Let's just give her a minute.'

A minute passed – followed by another few – and still they stood alone and helpless in the doorway. 'Grandad, I don't like this. Let's go now. Something is wrong.'

'Shhh, Millie, listen.' Footsteps could be heard approaching from the opposite end of the alley to which Mia had disappeared. Arthur squeezed Millie's hand tighter and pulled her out of the shop door. He'd just broken into a run, almost sweeping Millie off her feet in the process, when the footsteps spoke.

'It's me, Mia. Don't go that way!'

Arthur stopped abruptly and spun round, pulling Millie with him.

Mia motioned towards her. 'Quick, follow me. I think there's someone hiding in the shadows that way.'

Millie pulled her grandad towards the beckoning Mia. 'Come on, come on. Let's go.'

They followed Mia to the end of the alley and back into the relative normality of the main part of the Taj Ganj. Suddenly the roar of the street traders and the bustle of the local children – clambering over each other to catch sight of a threadbare travelling snake charmer – seemed rather normal and most welcome indeed.

'Mia, it's not safe for you here either. Make good use of the money and start a fresh life for yourself. Thank you for helping us.' Arthur could tell she was paying little attention to his words and great attention to her surroundings. Her eyes darted from person to person and her hands twitched nervously.

Millie tapped Mia's hand. 'Where does Manik live?'

Mia crouched down and brushed Millie's hair from her face. 'If you want it that much then you will find it. You have been very kind to me and I'm not about to repay that kindness by sending you to a perilous place. I must go now. Thank you for the money.' With that she disappeared seamlessly into the crowd.

'Come on, Grandad; let's get back to the hotel. Let's get out of here.' For once Arthur was in total agreement with his granddaughter and they too blended into the masses as they made their way back to the relative sanctuary of their hotel.

CHAPTER FIVE

THE SECRET ROOM

Millie woke to see her grandad peering intently out of the hotel window at something below. Her attempt to roll over and catch some more shut-eye was interrupted by her incessant curiosity. 'What are you looking at?'

'Some sort of fuss outside. There are lots of people milling around in the gardens, but I can't make out what's happening.'

Millie wrestled with her pillow and shuffled her feet under the bedclothes. 'Is *your* bed uncomfortable, Grandad?'

'No.'

'Then why are you up so early?'

'It's not early. It's past ten.'

Millie sat bolt upright. She'd slept twelve hours straight through! Not unusual in normal circumstances, but decidedly so after the events of yesterday and the prospect of what the day might hold. 'I have to get up. We have to get going.' As she clambered out of bed she clapped her eyes on the suitcases waiting patiently by the door.

'I've left you some clothes out for the journey home. Everything else is packed except what you're wearing and your wash things. You can put them in a side—'

Millie, who was still waking up, took a few seconds to formulate the words in her mind, but when they came out Arthur was left in no doubt about her take on the proceedings. 'We can't stop now! We just can't. We are so close. All we have to do is find Manik and get the key piece.'

'Millie, listen to yourself. *All* we have to do! Do you not remember anything from yesterday? The danger we've been warned about, and that's before we've even got anywhere near the key piece. Don't pretend you weren't scared yesterday. I was, and I'm not afraid to admit it. Millie, my love, all the adventure and war stories I've told you about me … well—'

'Grandad, you were my adventure and war hero yesterday when you stood up to Ranjit in the shop.' Millie figured her grandad was about to confess to being slightly economical with the truth about his past, but she already knew that, and it didn't bother her in the slightest. She meant what she just said. She was bursting with pride and admiration when he rose to his feet yesterday and faced off with Ranjit in the shop. 'Not to mention how well you held your nerve when we were trapped in that doorway.'

Arthur could do no more than smile, as he perched himself on the side of Millie's bed. 'You were brave too, but we haven't even got near the *first* key piece yet. Do you think we're just going to waltz up to Manik and he will just hand it over? That's providing he really has it, of course.'

Millie leaned her head on her grandad's arm. 'Of course I realise the danger, but I realise more the pain and suffering of the Children of Zamora. We have to carry on for their sakes.'

Arthur sank his head into his hands and rubbed his nose, something he always did when in deep thought. 'OK, we'll try.'

Millie leaped up and slung her arms round his neck, hugging him harder than ever before. 'But if we don't find it today, we leave. I've already checked us out of here. It's not safe. We'll take our bags to the airport and leave them there.

'But!'

'No buts, Millie. That's the deal. If we don't get it today we go back home.'

'But!'

'*That's* the deal.' Arthur held his hand out. 'Well?'

Millie reluctantly placed her hand in his and shook. 'Deal.'

'Now go and get changed as I want to get out of here.' Millie released her grip, uncrossed the fingers on her other hand hidden behind her back, and skipped away to the bathroom.

*

While Arthur was in debate with the hotel receptionist Millie wandered outside to see what the fuss had been earlier. Just as she did so, an ambulance pulled away from where a mass of people were gathered, with two police cars following swiftly behind.

'What happened?' she asked in the crowd's general direction.

'Somebody's dead,' a fair skinned man replied. 'Gruesome, really,' he continued.

'Why?'

'His left leg was missing,' he said, before at last turning to face his inquisitor. 'Oh sorry, I didn't realise you were so young. Me telling you that has made you look rather ill.'

She was not looking ill because of the thought of a missing leg. It was the thought of the person to whom the leg belonged that was responsible for that. 'Was he wearing grey socks and sandals?'

'Excuse me?'

'On the remaining leg that is.'

'What a peculiar thing to ask. Yes I think he was, but—'

'And ginger hair? Did he have ginger hair?'

The man, clearly spooked by such odd questions from a

little girl, started to edge back towards the crowd. 'Yes!' he said, before beating a hasty retreat.

Millie ran back to the hotel and slid to a halt beside her grandad.

'What is it, Millie? You look flustered.'

She knew if she told him the truth they would be on their way home there and then. 'Just trying to flag down a taxi. I think I'm too small to catch their attention,' she said in a low voice, as she picked up her case. 'Are we all done now?'

Arthur nodded, grabbed his things and they both made their way outside, where a dozen taxis stood neatly in line. 'Blimey, where did all those come from? There weren't any a minute ago.' Before Arthur could reply she rushed over to the nearest one and offered up her case. Arthur followed and they both piled in and set off for the airport.

He was going to ask Millie what she was really up to, but was distracted by the crowd that was still gathered. 'I wonder what that was about.'

Millie gazed out of the opposite window and pretended not to hear.

*

Once more they found themselves standing nervously in the shadows outside the tattoo parlour. In the time it took them to drop their bags with Left Luggage at the airport and return to the alley they'd debated many ideas on how they were going to track down Manik. Asking around was risky, but Millie reasoned that the riskier the plan, the less likely they were to be caught. Well that was Millie's reasoning, and she'd somehow managed to convince her grandad it was his too.

'Remind me again, Millie, why is this the best plan?'

'Well, I doubt anyone would expect us actually to follow

Ranjit home and then try and snatch the key piece in broad daylight,' she said, almost convincingly.

'They don't expect us to do it because it would be so stupid,' was his whispered reply.

Millie patted her grandad's back. 'Exactly!'

They knew Ranjit was in the shop as they'd seen him turn the *Open* sign to *Closed* on the door earlier. What he was up to meanwhile was a mystery, but all they could do was just sit and wait. A fight further up the alley had distracted them both until Millie felt something dig into her leg. 'Don't kick me!' she exclaimed.

Arthur took his concentration off the fight and was just about to reply when he saw Ranjit making his way out of the shop with Suna trotting along beside. 'Look, Millie. He is leaving and we nearly missed him.' True enough they nearly had. Millie berated herself inwardly for not staying more focused.

They kept a safe distance behind Ranjit as he wove his way through the maze of side streets that made up the Taj Ganj. Every now and then Suna would cast a glance backwards, but her master never followed suit.

The dingy alley-ways of before were first replaced with smart suburbs and then by stately-looking homes dotted uniformly along tree-lined streets, but the grandest of all around was the house Ranjit and Suna came to a halt outside of. Ranjit punched in a code on the gate that obligingly and ever so gently swung open to let him and Suna in. It took so long to open fully and then to start its journey back that Millie and Arthur had time to slip in unnoticed, take refuge behind a tree and see the front door close behind Ranjit.

'Now what?' said Arthur, mopping his brow. The sun and the humidity were at their worst and the pair of them were soaked through.

'Shhh! What's that noise?' said Millie, raising her finger to her lips.

Arthur cupped a hand to his ear and whispered, 'Sounds like something … swishing. Whatever it is it's on the other side of this tree.'

Millie craned her neck ever so slowly around the tree to see Suna sitting there, tail merrily wagging, and obviously pleased to see them. The feeling was not mutual and Millie waved her hand to try and frighten her new playmate away, but this just seemed to excite Suna even more.

'Get rid of it. It's going to give us away!'

'Do you think I'm trying to play with it? I *am* trying to get rid of it, but the dumb dog won't budge.'

SLAM! The noise of the front door shutting and voices rapidly approaching did nothing to calm their anxiety. What it did do however was cause Suna to dart round and join Millie and Arthur behind the tree. Now all three of them sat nervously huddled together as the voices approached.

'Why are we going out here?' Ranjit's voice was by now instantly recognisable. Millie and Arthur huddled a little closer, trying desperately not to breathe as loud as their lungs demanded. Even Suna stopped panting.

'I have something to show you, my son.' The pair passed the tree and the sound of their footsteps dimmed as they made their way towards a distant part of the garden.

Millie turned to her grandad and said, 'Ranjit must be with Manik. Let's follow them.' Before Arthur could reply she was on her way, leaving him with no choice but to follow behind, with Suna cautiously bringing up the rear. They zigzagged their way across the expansive grounds, making full use of the vast array of trees as shelter.

Manik stopped in front of a huge iron gate, pulled a key out from behind a loose brick and stuck it in the lock. The gate creaked open. He stepped forward and beckoned his son inside. The trepidation on Ranjit's face and rustiness of the gate both indicated to the watching pair that this was a path not well trodden.

'I bet that's where the handle and the key are, Grandad. I just bet you.'

Millie as always was first to move off, but Arthur quickly made up the ground. Suna had decided enough was enough and unnoticed by the other two made off in the opposite direction back towards the house. Arthur held Millie back as she went to look through the open gate. 'Don't do anything stupid. I want you to stay by my side.'

'OK.'

They edged forward to see an open courtyard that was surrounded by high walls and contained nothing except the odd tree, a slightly raised platform area, and some candle holders on the walls. They watched engrossed as Manik left his son standing by the raised platform. He walked over to a particular candle holder, pulled it down, and then walked back to join Ranjit.

Millie and Arthur couldn't hear the discussion that ensued, but it concluded when Manik stepped onto the platform and stood patiently for a few moments.

The ground started to vibrate and a large section of the floor rose up in front of the raised platform. All who were watching stood mesmerised by the events unfolding before them. What was the floor had now become a building of some size and still it lumbered its way upwards.

'Grandad, check that out. Unreal.' Arthur was too dumbfounded to reply properly. Instead he just grunted.

When the building finally stopped rising and the dust had settled it was not as impressive as Millie first imagined it was going to be. It was a bland, box shaped structure, which stood about twenty foot square with no distinctive markings whatsoever.

A stone door, previously obscured by the dust, slowly opened and Manik stepped inside, swiftly followed by his son. Millie took this as her opportunity to get in closer and listen to what was being said and maybe, just maybe, sneak a peek at what was inside. She darted over to the side of the building and flung herself against it. Only then could she see her grandad still standing at the gate waving furiously at her. She waved back at him, motioning him to join her, which he duly did.

'I told you to stay by my side!'

'Actually you told me not to do anything stupid!'

'One of these days, Millie. One of these days ...'

The voices inside became raised. 'I don't understand, father. Why are you showing me this now when you have just spent the entire morning moaning about me knowing too much?'

'I have my reasons.'

'Do you actually trust me now? Well, that would be a first!'

'Ranjit, did you take care of the man with the tattoo?'

'Yes, I told you I did.'

'And the old man and the young girl?'

'They had checked out.'

Millie and Arthur had plenty to say at this point, but a sudden rush of fear seemed to have removed their ability to speak.

'*I* will deal with them then, my son, but first I have to tie up another loose end.'

'Which is?'

'You.'

BANG!

The first bang was followed by two more and the sound of a body thumping to the ground.

'Sleep well, my son. Sleep well.' Footsteps heading in their direction were all the encouragement they needed to make a quick dash for cover behind the nearest tree.

Manik emerged dusting himself down. Considering what he'd just done he looked remarkably at ease with himself. All that was left for him to do was to reset the candle holder and watch the room make its way back down into the ground. He stood, arms crossed, until the area became the quiet idyllic courtyard it was before and then promptly left, locking the gate behind him.

Millie and Arthur waited for several minutes before speaking.

'What does he mean, that he will deal with us?'

Millie shrugged. 'Grandad, let's just retrieve the key piece and scram.'

Arthur nodded. 'Wait here. I want to make sure we can get out of here as quick as we can when we have found the key piece,' he said. He headed off to tug on the candle holder before walking back past Millie and over to the courtyard entrance. 'Come with me,' he instructed, as he passed Millie on his way to the locked gate. Arthur checked the coast was clear, then slipped his hand through and felt for the loose brick with the key behind it, but despite all his efforts it was out of reach. Just as he was about to give up the gate opened and Millie appeared outside.

'Climbed over,' she said, as she came back into the courtyard and headed towards the raised platform. 'Shall we?'

Millie got to the platform first and stepped onto it, but nothing happened. She stepped off and on to no avail before Arthur arrived.

'You probably don't weigh enough. Here, let me try,' he said – quite happy that she at least needed him for something. Millie gave way to her grandad who climbed on, immediately bringing the ground to life and the room up, and as it did so she wandered over to the door that was slowly coming into view.

She could see the expression on her grandad's face and responded accordingly. 'Don't worry! I'm not going to go in without you.'

Whether she meant it or not Arthur wasn't going to find out because once the room had settled and the door had opened Millie was pulled in, as if a bungee rope were tied to her waist. She was pulled with such force that her feet left the ground and within a flash she was gone. Arthur's horror was further compounded when the door slid shut and the room started its descent back into the ground. His constant jumping on the platform and jiggling of the candle holder had no effect and within a very short space of time he was standing there alone helplessly staring at the floor.

The room was unimaginably dark inside. If there were really shades of black, then this was the darkest. Millie had yet to worry about the light or even that the room was no longer above ground. Her focus was purely on breathing. She'd been thrown into a corner by whatever force dragged her in. Her lungs were not responding as expected and she felt the most intense screaming pain in her head. Her energy was being sapped from her and she barely had strength to open her rucksack and pull out the book. 'Help me. Please help me,' she said as she cuddled it close to her chest. As soon as she did so she felt her lungs filling with air, but the head pain continued unabated.

The book must be protecting whichever part of my body I hold it against, she thought to herself. Breath restored, she reached back into her bag and pulled out a torch, battling all the time to think straight as the pain ripped through her head. The beam of light that sliced through the darkness allowed her, for the first time, to check the surroundings properly.

Ranjit's body lay directly ahead, about ten feet away, and just behind him stood a large stone with two items laid out on top.

The handle and the key piece.

Even through the pain she felt elated to have found what she was looking for, though she was clearly affected by the curse that accompanied it.

Millie knew what she had to do. The book had told her that to counter the curse she needed to hold the key piece and read the inscription. What she didn't need was for her torch to go out!

'NOOO. NOT NOW,' she hissed to herself, banging it several times, but when it came back on she jerked viciously back against the wall and hugged the book even tighter. Ranjit was now standing before her, eyes open and demonic, hands out and trailing blood.

She wanted to scream, but didn't have the energy, so lashed out instead as he leaned forward and tried to grab the book. Without that she would have no chance and she was in no mood to surrender it easily. Her right foot connected with him and he stumbled back a few paces, only to come at her again. It seemed the curse made full use of anything it could find because Ranjit's actions were clearly not those of a dead man.

Millie used what little energy she had to get to her feet and run at Ranjit and in the general direction of the key piece. This unbalanced him and he went tumbling back, knocking both artefacts off the centre stone. The handle landed on the sandy floor directly below the stone, but the key piece rolled off to the other side of the room. In all the commotion Millie dropped the torch and again the room was shrouded in darkness.

She quickly fell to her knees and felt around only to touch someone's hand, causing her to leap back across the room. The distance between her and the key piece had now doubled and the crippling head pain thankfully receded.

The thought flashed through her mind that not being able to see might just be an advantage. After all, *she* knew where the key piece was – wherever the pain was worst – but her attacker didn't know *her* whereabouts.

She stood up and waited silently for any noise in the room, all the time clutching the book firmly to her chest, but its protective action was wearing thin because the air in the room was starting to run out.

It was now deadly silent and for a moment she just froze to the spot, but she didn't remain there long, as she could hear Ranjit's sudden onrush. She quickly slid sideways and was mightily relieved to hear him bounce off the wall where she had been standing, and crumple to the floor.

This was her moment. She ran flat out towards the opposite corner of the room, each pace bringing her more and more pain, drawing more and more breath from her ever depleted lungs until she too crashed into the wall and fell to her knees.

Almost delirious with pain and lack of oxygen she felt around on the sandy floor – and then she found it. Merely touching it sent even more pain rocketing through her body. She felt as if she was about to explode, but the glow from the key piece provided just enough light for her to read the inscription. '*If you close your eyes then you can come too* ...' she read, just before she passed out.

*

'Millie! Millie! Wake up! Please wake up!' She came round to a most welcome sight. Arthur had crouched down, cradling her in his arms with anguish painted across his face. She looked around the room and tried to take it all in. She hadn't seen it in daylight before and somehow it seemed much bigger. The sight of Ranjit's dead body only a couple of feet away, with one arm outstretched before it, made her shudder at the thought that he was so close when she read out the counter-curse.

'The room just pulled you in and sank back into the ground. It all happened so fast, Millie, there was nothing I could do. I tried everything, then all of a sudden it just came back up again and I found you lying here.'

'Grandad, it wasn't your fault. It was the curse. At least now we know it *does* affect me and we can prepare ourselves. The book helped me though. Without it I would have been a goner.' She unclasped her right hand and the key piece fell to the floor.

'So this is what it looks like,' said Arthur, retrieving it and blowing off the sand, before examining it intently. 'There's no inscription.' he said in a low voice.

The blank key piece was unremarkable, except that it appeared to be glowing ever so slightly. A trait, no doubt, that would attract people to it, and the other pieces, were they to exhibit a similar glow. Maybe that was the reason Manik chose to hide it in such an elaborate place? Maybe he thought it was valuable, or possessed some hidden power that would one day reveal itself to him? Whatever the reason, he was about to lose his most prized possession.

Millie sat up and took it back off him. 'There was,' she murmured as she toyed with it in her hand.

They weren't given any more time to debate the

inscription because the room had now started to rumble, causing the pair of them to leap immediately to their feet. 'Run, Grandad, the door is closing!' Millie said as she grabbed his hand and hurtled towards the ever-decreasing shaft of daylight. They made it through just in time, falling to the ground outside. By the time they'd composed themselves again the room had completely vanished and the courtyard was restored to normality.

'It must be on a timer of some sort. I was in there with you for ages before you finally came round.'

'I'm just glad to be out!' Millie said, sweat cascading down her face. 'Are you ready to go?' A swift nod and they were both on their feet, out of the gate, and down the garden. As they drew level with the front of the house a car pulled up outside and they took refuge behind the tree they'd previously occupied with Suna.

They sat silently and listened as first the gate opened and then the front door. Manik appeared at the top of the steps and was soon joined by a distinguished-looking gentleman in some sort of official uniform. The uniform was worn with panache by a man with great presence, who seemed to be made entirely of muscle. His round face had an inappropriate handlebar moustache that looked most unbecoming for a man so well built. They were clearly good friends, both greeting each other with broad smiles and firm hearty handshakes.

Millie and Arthur overheard the two men talk about old times before moving on to the real point of the meeting – them. A few strained glances were exchanged behind the tree when they overheard Manik describing their appearance and his desire to 'be rid of the interfering pair'. A minute's silence prompted Millie to peek around the tree to see what was going on. She did so just in time to see Manik come back out of the house and hand over a large brown envelope to his visitor. More handshakes were exchanged before they parted.

As before, once the coast was clear, Millie and Arthur made a swift exit, thanks to the lumbering mechanics of the main gate. 'Grandad, if we go to the airport now he may be there waiting for us,' said Millie, as she hurried along.

'Who do you think he was?'

Millie shrugged, 'Not sure, but he looked official. He could be police, customs, anything.'

Thoughts on how to leave the country were batted between them as they retraced their steps to the Taj Ganj.

'I have an idea,' said Millie, as she stopped dead in her tracks.

'Which is?'

'TAXI!' She hailed a passing cab. It pulled up alongside and Millie flung open the door, hopped in, and gestured Arthur to join her.

He stepped inside, to be greeted by the driver enquiring their destination.

Arthur turned to Millie who instructed the driver to make his way to the hotel they'd checked out of earlier in the day. 'The hotel, Millie? Are you mad?'

'Think about it, Grandad. It's the only place they know we've left. They're not going to check it again. I would say the first place they'll check is the airport because they probably figured we have left our bags there.'

'OK, fair point, but what do you want at the hotel?'

'They have an Internet connection and I want to use it. It's all part of my plan. Don't worry; I'll explain when we get there.' Millie wasn't too keen to explain her plan before then because she wasn't actually sure she had one!

The taxi pulled up outside the hotel and Millie jumped out

and ran inside. By the time Arthur had caught up she was already sitting at the terminal. 'What are you planning to do, Millie?'

She raced her fingers across the keys. 'Aha! That should do it.'

'Do what?'

'I'm sending an email to the Indian High Commission in the UK and copying in some global news companies to make sure. I pulled their contact details off a search engine.'

Arthur, still none the wiser said, 'In English please.'

Millie's fingers came to rest and she glanced up. 'We don't know who that official was speaking to Manik, but we do know he wants rid of us. This means we don't know whom we can trust here, and if we head to the airport we're very likely to be picked up. I've just written a mail saying if they want to recover the handle that was on the stolen door that originally led to the Gardens of Paradise, then they should go to Manik's address. I've also given instructions on how to find the secret room there.'

Millie carried on typing while Arthur stood over her in wonder at how someone so young could have such a devious mind. 'Very good idea, young lady. When they find the room they'll also find Ranjit's body, which will incriminate Manik. So if they don't get him for the stolen door handle they'll get him for Ranjit's murder. One thing though. How is that going to help us get out via the airport?'

'That's why I'm informing the news people. They must all have teams on the ground here and will probably respond quicker than the High Commission. They'll put people on the story, which will ensure the authorities have to act properly. Simple really!'

'Very good, but it doesn't answer my question.'

Millie stopped typing and said, 'I've added in this mail

that there's a certain amount of corruption here and the news crews might want to station some people at the airport in case Manik gets wind of what's happening and tries to make a run for it.'

Arthur started to nod slowly. 'Ingenious. There won't be a corrupt official in sight with the news crews around. Especially one connected to Manik.'

'Exactly! Now, Grandad, shall I press send?' A simple nod of the head was all she needed and the mail was away.

Millie smiled. 'Grandad, there's one thing we need to know before we get to the airport and that's where we're going next.'

Arthur took Millie's hand and led her away down a quiet hallway where she placed the book on the ground and the key piece on top.

Once again she was filled with the most amazing feelings as light from the book flooded the hallway.

Once again she would find instructions inside about the location of the next piece.

Once again they set off into the unknown with a potent mixture of excitement and fear.

CHAPTER SIX

AUSTRALIA

Journey to the heart of the Aboriginal homeland and seek out the largest cavern within the greatest monolith so worshipped by the indigenous people of that land. Use your unique knowledge to retrace the footsteps of Ausvaldomic. The cave drawings will help in your quest.

Millie and Arthur's route through the airport and onto the plane was unhindered, thanks in no small part to a number of news teams already present when they arrived.

'Good plan, my girl. Very good plan,' said Arthur as he boarded the plane with Millie at his side. She just smiled and tried hard not to look too smug.

It wasn't long into the flight before she started going over the clue to the whereabouts of the next piece of the key. 'Grandad, the "Aboriginal homeland" is Australia, right?'

'Yep.'

'And the greatest monolith?'

Arthur smiled and said, 'Also in Australia!'

If Millie was amused by his comment then she didn't show it.

'I would say Millie that the greatest monolith has to be Ayres Rock, because it's the largest monolith in the world.'

'OK, Grandad, you know more about these things than I

do, but sometimes I wish the book was a bit more specific.'

'It certainly could be. It certainly could be,' mumbled Arthur into his in-flight magazine.

'Grandad, have you ever heard of Ausvaldomic?'

Arthur scratched his nose and stretched out his feet. A sure sign he didn't know the answer. 'Nope. Never heard of him, but once we get there I assume he will be common knowledge to the locals. At least I hope so anyway!'

Millie chuckled to herself. 'Well we could be there an awful long time if the locals don't know and it isn't Ayres Rock!'

*

Alas, the route to their ultimate destination was not a straightforward one. Stopovers were required in both Hong Kong and Perth, Australia.

Millie was looking forward to seeing the bright lights of Hong Kong and was very disappointed when told they wouldn't be leaving the airport due to a swift changeover of planes.

Perth didn't excite her as much as she thought Hong Kong would. However, her opinion changed once its easy-going nature and clean fresh air had been sampled. Far removed indeed from the hustle and bustle of India and the Taj Ganj in particular.

It wasn't long before jet lag got the better of them on arrival in downtown Perth and they were soon fully paid up members of the Land of Nod club – thanks to the sumptuous beds provided by the nearest hotel.

*

Her body clock and rousing dreams of India ensured Millie's sleep pattern was knocked out of kilter. Arthur didn't seem to be suffering at all; loud snoring and mumbling proved testament to that. Even when Millie turned the light on next to her bed and paced around the room Arthur did no more than jiggle a bit in his dreams.

Millie stood for ages staring out of the hotel window into the night wondering what might be in store for her. Thoughts about the danger she was going to face, and had already faced, were at the forefront of her mind. She knew she had to go on for the sake of the Zamorians, but her mind was clouded with contradiction. Could she really find all five parts to the key and hang on to her own life? Could both of them hang on to their lives for that matter? The more she thought about it the more she worried about her grandad's well-being and what she was putting him through.

Millie returned to her bedside, pulled her rucksack up onto the bed, unbuckled it and slid the book out. It was some time before she opened the cover and leafed through the pages, reading the visible text quietly to herself. This strengthened her resolve to carry on and made it easier for her to bury the worries deep in the back of her mind.

She turned her attention to thinking about how the book had saved her when she was trapped underground, gasping for breath in India. Or did it save her? Was it just her strong will, her own Zamorian powers maybe, that took over? She decided to see if the book could be called on to channel her powers there and then.

Back at the window, this time with the book clutched to her chest, she sought out something in the street below on which to focus her mind. Perth might be a nice place in the daytime, but at three in the morning when there's drizzle in the air, it's not such an inspiring sight.

A flickering street light would have to do. Millie hugged the book tighter and whispered that she wanted to extinguish the light.

Nothing.

Hugging it even tighter she wished for the opposite, that it would stay on permanently.

Again nothing.

None the wiser she moved away from the window and returned to her bed. She sat for a while and just stared at the book before finally slipping it back inside the rucksack and clambering under the covers. The feel of the quilt reminded her of how safe she used to feel as a kid – of course she was all grown up now – under its protective shield when faced by the prospect of having to fend off the 'bogeyman'. Could the book, she wondered, be a similar thing? Just there to make you feel better and strengthen your mind, but actually offering no real protection at all?

She hoped not. She really hoped not.

*

Millie awoke to the sound of rain beating against the window. 'Grandad, are you awake?'

'Yes.'

'I thought it was supposed to be sunny here?'

No response.

Millie checked the clock and closed her eyes. She only planned to rest for a few minutes more, but three hours later she was still sound asleep. 'Come on, young lady, we have another plane to catch,' said Arthur, stirring her back into life with his voice.

'I wasn't sleeping! I was just resting my eyes,' were her first words on stirring. Swiftly followed by, 'I just tried to wake YOU up a minute ago.'

'I see,' said Arthur. 'I think you must have nodded back off for longer than you imagined. I've been up almost two hours and out at the local library for most of it. It seems Ayres Rock *is* the place to go. Ausvaldomic was someone who, wait for it, entered one of the caves in the rock and vanished inside – only to reappear some time later and then vanish again into the desert. It's recorded as a myth and little more is written – at least in the books I found anyway. I sincerely hope once we actually get to Ayres Rock there will be more information on offer.'

Millie glanced at the clock, rubbed her eyes, and sleepily rose to her feet. 'Give me ten minutes.'

While she was in the bathroom Arthur stared out of the window at the rain beating down. A sole street lamp glaring away was the only thing out of the ordinary.

*

Another flight came and went before they found themselves sitting in a small café, killing time waiting for the next tour bus to Ayres Rock.

'So what will it be, Millie, 'roo or emu?'

Millie peered over her menu, 'What's 'roo?'

'Kangaroo. Tastes like chicken, apparently!'

'Yuck!' said Millie, slapping her menu down in disgust. 'I'm not eating that.'

Arthur, amused by her obvious dislike of the local cuisine, couldn't stop himself saying, 'Can't see "Yuck" on the menu. Is it one of the specials?'

'Grandad, you *really* aren't funny!'

Arthur persevered anyway. 'How about a burger?'

Millie sat up excitedly. '*Now* you are talking.'

'Croc' burgers I'm told are lovely,' said Arthur, as he chuckled away to himself. Millie slid back down in her chair, crossed her arms huffily, and said nothing.

'What will it be then?' said the robust waitress as she hovered over Millie, pad and pencil at the ready.

'Chips and one of your Orange Fizzy Slurps please.'

'Anything else?'

'No thanks.'

'And you sir?'

'Just a cup of coffee and the most fattening cake you can lay your hands on please,' he replied, as he gathered the menus together.

The waitress looked again at Millie who clearly had something on her mind. 'You have something to say dear?'

'Er, yes ... the chips are just potato, right?' she said sheepishly.

The waitress saw a smile spread across Arthur's face and said, 'Just potato my dear. Not a croc' or 'roo hidden in there anywhere.' She took the menus from Arthur's outstretched hand and started back towards the kitchen. 'The cakes however ...' she said, before disappearing into a steamy doorway. Millie grinned at her grandad, who now wasn't looking so pleased with himself.

The waitress returned with their order and stood over Arthur as he inspected his cake. 'Eat up. It won't bite you. Well, it probably won't.' A quick wink in Millie's direction and she was gone again.

The bus drew up shortly after the bill was paid and they were soon on board and on their way to Ayres Rock. The constant ramblings of the tour guide were beginning to bug Millie, and the guide in turn was losing patience with continually being asked the same question. 'I've told you, little girl, that I only tell credible stories of the past. Not fanciful, sunstroke-induced nonsense such as the story of Ausvaldomic.'

'Some tour guide you are,' she muttered, just loud enough for him to hear. Fortunately for her, Arthur was dozing. Had he heard her latest bout of bad manners he would have been none too happy.

Millie was sure the guide knew more, but his belief that this particular slice of history was rubbish, coupled with a fair old sprinkling of pig-headed stubbornness meant she'd got all she was going to get from him. She was most pleased to arrive at the small town that had grown up in the shadow of the rock, and even more pleased to part company with the bus and its annoying guide.

'Nice hat,' she said as she passed the guide, who was holding his cap out for tips, and stepped off the bus.

Arthur, still half asleep himself, missed the comment and left the bus completely oblivious to Millie's feelings about the trip down.

'Enjoyable that, wouldn't you say?'

'You were asleep for most of it!'

'Exactly! That's why I enjoyed it so.'

'While you were snoring away—'

Arthur raised his finger. 'I don't snore.'

Millie paused briefly, 'Like I was saying, while you were sleeping I asked the guide about Ausvaldomic, but he was reluctant to talk about him.'

'What *did* he say?'

'Nothing. Well, practically nothing. Basically he doesn't believe in the legend.'

'Stay there,' said Arthur. He turned back towards the bus and made a beeline for the guide. Millie stood watching as Arthur stuffed something in the guide's hand before exchanging words and gestures with him. The conversation concluded with the guide pointing in the general direction of the town, followed by the exchange of smiles, and within moments Arthur was back at Millie's side. 'Nice man he is.'

Millie looked over at the guide who was waving a five dollar bill in one hand, his face awash with grinning teeth. 'What did you tip him for? He was useless!'

'He told me the name of the best person to speak to about Ausvaldomic. Someone called Fre Kles – a local Aborigine who apparently knows everything there is to know about the subject.' Arthur led Millie off towards the town saying, 'Sometimes, my girl, you have to be a tad more diplomatic and charming than you are.'

Millie puffed out her shoulders, 'What do you mean? I'm diplomatic all the time. He was just an idiot, that's all!'

An ice cream and a seat out of the blazing sun soon restored the balance between the pair. The cool taste of her Strawberry Roo was all Millie needed to refocus her mind on the task ahead.

'G'day folks. Sure is a scorcher, wouldn't you agree?' Millie shielded her eyes from the sun and an Aboriginal man with deeply weathered skin came into view. His ragged black hair and general appearance showed he'd seen better days. 'My name is Felix. Pleased to meet you,' he said tipping an imaginary hat.

'G'day.' Millie winced at her grandad's attempt to sample the local dialect. 'My name is Arthur and this is my granddaughter Millie.'

'I see you folks sitting here and I'm guessing you're in need of a wholly knowledgeable and competent person to show you around.'

'Can you help us find one then?' Millie said while finishing the remnants of her ice cream.

Felix broke into a smile. 'Well yes, young miss, I do believe I can. I happen to know the best around.'

'And that would be you, I'm guessing?'

'Spot on my girl. Spot on.'

Millie couldn't help but smile and Felix used this as his invitation to join the pair – perching himself beside them on the wall they occupied outside the ice cream shop.

'Actually we're looking for someone in particular,' said Arthur, now that he'd polished off his Monster Chocolate

Boomerang Surprise.

'And who might that be?'

'Someone called Fre Kles.'

'You and a few other people too, mate,' replied Felix, as he ruffled his hair.

'Why?' said Arthur and Millie in stereo.

'Well nobody has seen Fre for some six months now. I was actually the last to see him when we shared a beer in that bar over there.' Felix pointed to a bar that looked as though it was straight out of an old cowboy movie.

'Do you remember what you spoke about with him?'

'As clear as if I said it myself, Arthur.'

'And?' Millie cut in, trying not to sound too eager.

'And … and … well let me see. Oh yes! Do you want a guide or not?'

Millie slipped her hand inside her rucksack and felt for the book. Fortunately it did *not* fulfil her wish for a power to shove her lolly stick up his nose without him noticing.

'We'll employ you as our guide. No problem,' said Arthur. 'Now please continue with your story.'

'Fre said to me that he'd finally worked out the writing on the cave walls. He said he found the answer written in the stars,' said Felix, scratching his chin. 'The next thing he said was pretty bizarre even by his standards. He said he'd already been in there – I think he meant the rock – and he was in awe of what he found.'

Millie leant a little closer and said, 'Then what?'

'His last words were that he was going to join them and become extinct himself.'

Arthur and Millie exchanged glances before she said, 'Who are them?'

Felix shrugged his shoulders. 'Beats me.'

Millie was sure her grandad drew the same conclusion as

her. 'Them' were the Children of Zamora.

'I've got to tell you guys that Fre was known round here as a bit of an eccentric to say the least. He was convinced that the legend of Ausvaldomic was true. He used to say that one of his distant forefathers saw Ausvaldomic sitting inside the caves writing something in the dust, but moments later he, Ausvaldomic that is, was gone. Apparently he was seen some time later wandering off into the desert and that was the last anyone saw of him. Fre's ancestors, and obviously Fre himself, had been trying to find out ever since what was written that day.'

'It would seem that maybe Fre worked it out then?' said Millie quizzically.

Felix nodded. 'Well yes maybe … *if* you believe the legend. Personally I think he had one too many beers and went walkabout.'

Arthur patted Felix on the back. 'Well, the world would be a pretty boring place if the odd legend wasn't knocking around the annals of history.'

'I guess so, Arthur.' Felix drew a long breath before continuing his tale. 'Every day for almost thirty years Fre used to go into one particular cave, the largest one as it happens. Some people were curious at first as to what he was up to in there, but after a while they left him alone and eventually everyone just stopped asking.'

'What did the other Aboriginal locals make of his behaviour?' said Arthur, who was obviously keen to get an insight into a part of the world he knew little about.

'Mostly they just let him get on with it. Some of them thought he gave them a bad name, but on the whole they weren't too bothered. They even let him have some input when Ayres Rock was handed back to the Aboriginal people and renamed. It's now officially called Uluru you know, which roughly translated means great pebble, or at least I think that's what it means!'

Felix looked at Arthur and Millie, who were more engrossed by his ramblings than he expected and said, 'Would you like to go there now?'

Millie sprang to her feet and dragged Arthur up to join her. 'Let's go!'

CHAPTER SEVEN

THE CAVES OF ULURU

Even from a distance the rock painted a stunning picture. As with the Taj Mahal, Millie was briefly rendered speechless when she approached it. The atmospheric conditions and afternoon sun were playing tricks with the light and the rock's colour majestically dipped in and out of varied shades of sandstone.

Their open top four-wheel drive came to a halt some way back and Felix pointed off in one direction. 'We'll stop here so you can appreciate the sight before we make our way over on foot to those caves.'

Millie scuttled off ahead while Arthur quizzed Felix. 'Fre said he'd already been inside the rock. Did he say what he saw in there?'

'Only what I've already told you. That he was in awe of whatever it was,' replied Felix, looking intently at Arthur. 'Hey this story has really captured your imagination hasn't it?'

Arthur realised that maybe he appeared just a bit too eager and waved his hand away in a nonchalant gesture. 'No not really. It just amused me, that's all.' He then held the same hand to one side of his mouth, pointed towards Millie with the other, who was now some way ahead of them, and whispered, 'I'm really only asking for her sake. If there wasn't a bit of mystery in the trip then she would just lose interest. This way it keeps us both happy.'

Felix stuck both thumbs up and smiled.

'THIS ONE?' Millie shouted back towards the others, as she pointed to the large cave in front of her. More thumbs up from Felix and she was inside.

The walls of the cave were covered with drawings of animals, weapons, and bold images of the sun and the stars. The floor was dusty and proved a great source of amusement for the children of some nearby tourists. They were quite happy playing noughts and crosses while their guardians got on with the serious business of filling the void with flashes of light from their cameras.

Most of the animals, although crudely drawn, were easily recognisable. One, though, drew Millie's attention above all others. It was a bird of some sort, but like none she'd seen before. She was standing before it scratching her head when Arthur and Felix finally arrived.

'My best guess is it's a churkey!' said Felix, as he passed through the entrance and walked towards Millie. His broad smile was a sure indication that he was making it up.

'A churkey! What's a churkey?' exclaimed a rather confused Millie.

'A churkey is a cross between a chicken and a turkey!'

She turned to her grandad who was a pace or two behind Felix and said, 'Does such an animal exist?' If anyone would know or at least give her a straight answer then it would be him.

'Can't say I've ever heard of one. I think Felix is having us on,' he replied, before coming to a halt beside Millie. 'Lend me your torch, Millie, so I can have a closer look.' She duly obliged and a beam of light woke up the dimly lit cave. Great shadows across the cave floor provided proof that the sun was well on its way down.

Somewhat miffed that his explanation had not raised a laugh, Felix said, 'All right, I made it up. There's no such thing as a churkey. To be honest, nobody is really sure what it is.'

Arthur's eyes followed the torchlight from side to side as he scanned the image. 'Well it couldn't possibly be what I think it is.'

'And what might that be Arthur?'

'Oh nothing, Felix. Let's just stick with churkey. I like the sound of that!'

Millie knew her grandad had an idea of what it might be, but his reluctance to volunteer the information meant he had a good reason for keeping quiet. Normally he would happily spout on about any subject of which he had knowledge. She made up her mind to ask him later when they were alone.

The cave went off in different directions and Millie was eager to explore further. Several more tourists, armed with a vast array of camera equipment and a local uniformed guide, emerged from the shadows.

Felix exchanged greetings – out of earshot – with the other guide and then motioned the pair to follow him as he wandered towards the largest cave leading off the one in which they were standing. 'Watch your step in here and stick close by me,' said Felix, as he pulled a huge torch from his backpack and flooded the area with light.

Arthur held Millie by the hand, sensing she was about to do the opposite and wander off alone. She shook herself clear. 'Don't worry, Grandad, I'm not going to run off.'

Felix and Millie shone their torches from floor to ceiling tracing out the pictures before them. The beam from Felix's torch hovered over a particular piece of artwork and he said, 'So tell me what's strange about that, then?'

Millie and Arthur peered upwards, almost in line with the ceiling, at a huge cluster of what looked like stars.

'Stars,' said a slightly unimpressed Millie.

'Yes, but how did they get there?' Felix responded. 'Think about it. They're some thirty feet up. These images were drawn hundreds, if not thousands, of years ago and there weren't many ladders around then!'

'I see,' said Arthur. 'They must have found another way, I guess.'

'Yes Arthur, but damned if I can think what it was. All the other artwork is at floor level.'

Arthur nodded.

Felix continued, 'Do you know, Fre once told me he thought these particular drawings were done by someone from another planet, who must have floated up there and merrily sketched away!'

Arthur felt sure that this statement would cause Millie to say something, but he was wrong. Her attention had been drawn to the area of wall about ten feet left of the stars. Her torchlight moved slowly from left to right across the surface and she appeared to be mumbling to herself. Felix noticed this too and moved his beam across to join hers. 'Found something interesting?' he said.

Millie didn't reply, as she was clearly captivated by what she saw.

Being engrossed by the secrets of Uluru wasn't unheard of. In fact most visitors could be seen standing, jaw open, at some point during their tour. The difference between what they were fascinated by and what held Millie's attention was that she stood staring at a blank wall. At least it was a blank wall to Arthur and Felix.

'Grandad, those birds were brought here for conservation,' she said as her torchlight continued to make its way back and forth across the wall.

The look on Felix's face grew more puzzled by the second and he was just about to say something when Arthur beat him to it. 'Ah yes Millie, the birds are still puzzling you. I thought it couldn't be this bit of wall because there's *nothing* on it.'

'For a second there, Arthur, I thought I'd gone blind and you could both read something on the wall! Millie, what are you looking at?'

It was then that Millie realised only she could see what was written next to the stars. She slowly pulled herself away and back to face Felix. 'Of course there's nothing written up there. I, er … was just daydreaming about the churkey and what it might be.'

'Well, young lady, a lot of people before you have tried to come up with explanations about what it is. I'll not bore you with some of the more fanciful ones. In fact I'll not bore you with any of them. Let's just call it a churkey and leave it at that!'

'Can we see the other cave now? The one on the left as we came in?' said Millie pleadingly.

'I'm afraid not, Millie. That one is out of bounds. It's no longer safe, because there have been a few rock falls recently.'

'But that's the one where Fre was?' she said without thinking.

'And how do you know that?'

Millie raised the light under her chin and pulled her best contorted face. 'Because you haven't mentioned him so far in these two caves and that's the only one left.' She was rather pleased with her spur-of-the-moment answer. After all, she couldn't say that she deduced it from the Zamorian writing that nobody else could see on the wall.

'You're correct in your deduction. The other cave was the one where Fre spent most of his time, but there's nothing to see inside it really.'

'Nothing really?' enquired Arthur. 'Which means there *is* something?'

Felix rocked back on his heels and moved his beam from Arthur's face to Millie's and then back again to Arthur's. 'You two sure ask a lot of different questions! Most people who come here do so to see the rock itself, its sheer magnitude and wonder, but you two are hooked on the mystery of a rather eccentric old man! Not to mention you,' he pointed the torch back at Millie, 'standing transfixed staring at a blank wall!'

Millie shone her torch back up towards the drawings of the stars and said, 'Well you would have a pretty boring job if everyone asked you the same questions. Don't get me wrong the rock is interesting, but the mystery of a missing man and an ancient legend – now *that* is something else entirely.'

Arthur stepped a few paces away from Millie and beckoned Felix to join him. 'You see, I told you before that by dragging out the mystery she will stay interested. I, of course, have no real belief in such mumbo-jumbo,' he whispered.

'No, of course,' muttered Felix unconvincingly.

'So what say we have a little peek in the other cave and then we can be on our way?' said Arthur imploringly.

Felix wiggled his head and torch in unison. An act Arthur took as meaning yes. 'Millie, Felix has kindly agreed to show us the other cave.'

'I have, but only briefly and we can't go all the way in as it's not safe. Just a quick peek and then out. OK?'

'Excellent,' exclaimed Millie as she bounced up to join them. 'Lead the way,' she said with her hand held out before her.

They all made their way conga-like back through the first cave and then off to the one as yet unexplored. As they stood at the entrance Felix held them back briefly to make sure nobody would see them climb over the rope that bore the No Entry sign.

A handful of paces inside the cave Felix once again stopped them in their tracks. 'That's as far as we can go.'

The first thing to greet Millie's torchlight was a pile of rocks about ten feet ahead of them. Other rocks were scattered randomly further afield. 'It's because of the rock falls that this cave is now off-limits,' said a slightly agitated Felix.

He fixed his beam on the wall furthest away. 'This is the only writing, if you can call it that, in here.' The light had exposed a series of dashes drawn into the stone.

'Six dashes. What does it mean?' asked Arthur, just as confused as Felix.

'A lot smarter minds than mine have tried to work that one out, I can tell you.' said Felix, who set about proving it was the only inscription by running his beam across the other walls.

Millie was still focused on the cryptic drawing. 'I know what we have to do to open the cave,' she said to Arthur in a hushed voice.

'How?' replied an equally hushed Arthur.

'It's written on the other cave wall next to the stars.'

BOOM!

A huge rock fell from the ceiling of the cave and landed close by, causing all three to jump. 'That was close,' stammered Arthur out loud.

'Come on, you two, we have to go. If I'm found in here with you I'll never be allowed back near the caves for sure.' The whispering was over – it was time to leave – and all three hurried to the rope and climbed over just in time to see several other people emerge to investigate the noise.

Felix raised his hand and said authoritatively, 'Nothing to

worry about folks. Just a little rock fall. Happens all the time. I was just telling these two here,' he motioned towards Millie and Arthur, 'how the cave with the No Entry sign is dangerous and bang, down came a rock.' Cover-up speech finished he wandered out of the caves, somewhat relieved to be in one piece, with the other two only a few paces behind.

The sunlight caused all three to shield their eyes from its fearsome glare. Once outside, they all took some time to collect their thoughts. Arthur stood gawping at the monstrous rock before him and Millie appeared to be doing the same, but was really thinking about the Zamorian writing on the cave wall inside. Felix, however, was just feeling sorry for himself, because a fragment had split away from the falling rock and wedged itself in his left shin.

Millie noticed the blood trickling down his leg and saw it as an opportunity to put the plan she'd been hatching into action. 'You should get that seen to, Felix. Why don't you go back to town? Don't worry about us; we can hook up with any of these coaches when we want to come back.' She pointed to a long line of tour buses.

'What about the rest of your tour? I've only shown you a few caves.'

Arthur had now cottoned on to Millie's desire to rid them of their guide. 'She is right, Felix. Don't worry about us. As for the rest of the tour, what we don't see today you can show us tomorrow. How about we meet at eleven, the same place as we met today?'

'OK folks, if you're sure, but promise me you're not thinking of going back into the dangerous cave.'

'Are you kidding? After that rock fall we would have to be mad!' Millie said this in such a convincing tone that, just for a split second, even Arthur believed her.

Felix retreated to his jeep and vanished into the distance

with both Millie and Arthur waving him off.

'OK, tell me. What did you read on the wall next to the stars?'

'It just said that the birds were brought here to save them from extinction. It doesn't say what they are, but it would appear that a traveller took pity on them on their way to Australia. The writing also seemed to imply that several rare species had been saved in this way.'

'Who was the traveller?'

'Aurora, I think.'

Arthur patted Millie on the head. 'It's a good job you can read Zamorian, my girl.'

Millie looked up and said, 'Well not really, Grandad. The writing doesn't actually mention anything but the birds. I think it's written as a diversion. I guess just in case a Belendrian happens to read it. It doesn't say what the dashes in the other cave mean, but I'm pretty sure it's hangman and the missing word is Aurora.'

Arthur crouched down beside her, 'What makes you so sure?'

'Got to go. I must dash.'

Arthur screwed up his face. 'You are not making any sense.'

'Those were the last Zamorian words written on the wall next to the stars.'

Arthur still stood crouched in front of her, his face all askew.

'Think about it, Grandad. "I must dash" was written and then in the next cave there are six dashes. It has to be his name. That's what we have to write on the wall.'

Arthur swapped faces. Out went the one with a grimace and in came the smiley one. 'Worth a try. Certainly worth a try. One question though. How did Fre work it out if he wasn't Zamorian?'

Millie was clearly taken aback by this question. She'd forgotten all about Fre, and Felix's inference that he'd already been inside the rock. 'You don't think Fre is a Belendrian, do you, Grandad?'

'That was my initial thought all right, Millie, but I'm not so sure now. If he is, then he must be a pretty thick one as he took decades to work out what you appear to have done in minutes!' The pair's laughter could not disguise their unease at the prospect of coming face to face with a much more powerful adversary.

Arthur wrapped his arms around Millie. 'When we go in, providing you're right about what needs to be written, you really must remain by my side at all times, because we don't know what we're going to face in there. If India is anything to go by then we need to be very alert. As soon as you feel the slightest effect of the curse then stop dead in your tracks immediately. I'll go ahead to check it out.'

Millie nodded and returned the hug. 'But only I can disable the curse.'

'I'm well aware of that, but at least I can clear your path of all dangerous objects, and this time I'll not be locked out as before.'

'OK, Grandad.' Her answer contained no reference to what she really thought – that a dead body might be lying around ready to spring back into life as it did in India.

'Hopefully, Millie, the key piece will be close to the entrance and we can beat a hasty retreat.'

Arthur rose to his feet, cursing his aching knees in the process, and led Millie by the hand back towards the main cave entrance. Once there they pretended to be ordinary tourists until the opportunity arose for them to nip back into the No Entry cave unnoticed.

Millie summoned her torch into life and they cautiously made their way across the cave until they came to rest in front of the six dashes – above which she used her fingers to scribe faintly the appropriate letters in the appropriate places. On completion of the final letter she took a step back and gripped her grandad's hand tightly.

They both watched the letters disappear one by one and as the final letter melted away the wall opened up before them.

Two deep breaths and two broad strides and they were in.

CHAPTER EIGHT

RAPHUS CUCULLATUS

Once inside they were faced with a huge cavern that had several dark passages sprouting off it in all directions. The natural light that splintered in through the rock way above them provided an eerie ambience to the place as it danced across the cavern floor in tune with the setting sun.

Arthur led Millie by the hand deeper into the main cavern. The light from her torch aided them greatly as they picked their way through the obstacles that were appearing all around them. Apart from rocks of varying sizes they were surprised to see an array of vegetation that had sprung up from the apparently barren earth.

With each stride they were presented with even more odd sights that seemed out of place in Australia, let alone hidden deep inside a giant rock in the middle of nowhere. Arthur grew more and more excited about the prospect that he was one of only a handful of people – Aurora, Fre, and of course Millie being the others – to feast his eyes on such an ecosystem.

The further in they went the more they found. Unusual trees, laden with a strange fruit like none even Arthur had seen before, stood proud and in great abundance. Seeds from the trees littered the floor and water could clearly be heard in the distance.

Other smaller trees, some even bearing berries, and rough vegetation could also be found scattered around. However, the sight of spiders and the telltale signs of snakes – like the discarded skin that Millie stood on, causing her to leap backwards – weren't such a welcome sight.

Their exploration came to an abrupt halt with the sound of the secret door they had come through thumping shut in the background.

'What was that, Grandad?' Millie's face conveyed the fear she was feeling within.

Arthur also projected a look of deep concern. 'I'm afraid, Millie, that might be the door.'

'But how do we get out?' Millie flicked her torch around the vast cavern in search of an answer.

'I'm sure there will be a way. Follow me.' Arthur took the torch from Millie and they walked tentatively back towards the door. Once there he pointed the beam at the wall and traced his fingers along the rock searching for a clue to the door's exact whereabouts.

'Grandad, we're trapped aren't we?'

'Millie, it will be OK. There has to be a way out.' Arthur scribed the word 'Aurora' on the wall and stepped back expectantly. After repeating this several times he calmly turned to Millie and said, 'You try it. I guess you need to be Zamorian to open it.'

She leant forward, but her attempt produced the same result as her grandad's.

Arthur placed his hand on her shoulder and said reassuringly, 'There will be another way. Aurora isn't going to trap us in here without an escape route. Check out the walls for any more writing.'

He handed the torch back to Millie, who used it to scan the walls from floor to ceiling.

Arthur hoped she wasn't thinking what he was thinking. That maybe Aurora *did* want to trap her – them – and somewhere where they couldn't escape. Maybe Aurora was really bad all along and left the book as bait to catch the only good Zamorian left alive on the Earth's surface.

'Nothing written in here, Grandad. Nothing at all.' Millie's hunched shoulders betrayed her feeling of despair. 'What have I done, Grandad? We're trapped and it's all my stupid fault.'

Arthur brushed the hair from her face and gazed deep into her eyes. 'Millie, there will be another way. I promise.'

They retraced their steps back into the depths of the cavern in search of clues to their exit. In their efforts to find a way out they almost forgot their real reason for being there.

Almost.

'Grandad, wait. Maybe the door closing is part of the curse. If we find the key and read the inscription, then the curse will be reversed and the door will reopen.' This very thought visibly lifted both of them for the first time in what seemed like hours.

Were it not for the rustle of life directly behind them they might even have stayed happy.

'Hello,' said a voice.

Arthur and Millie froze, unable at first to even turn around. When they did they could see the shadowy outline of a figure standing about six feet away.

Millie raised her torch. 'Felix?' she said, questioning her own eyes.

'Felix, you frightened the life out of us,' exclaimed Arthur. 'How did you get in here?'

'Same way as you,' he said as he looked around clearly taken aback by what he saw.

'I thought you were going back to town?'

'Yes Arthur … I know you did.'

A nervous chill raced through Millie's veins. What did he mean by that?

He stepped forward until he was face to face with Arthur and held out his hand. Arthur, although unsure why, took it. 'My name isn't Felix. It's—'

'But you said …' Millie interrupted before he could finish.

'I know what I said, but I was lying. At first I was just having a little fun with you, but once you showed so much interest in the legend of Ausvaldomic I thought I would carry on my disguise just to see what you came up with next.'

Millie stood silent and Arthur stared quizzically, still holding the liar's hand.

'It's not unusual for people to ask about the legend, but once their initial curiosity has been satisfied, they always move on to the more serious business of exploring the rock itself. You two were different.' He flicked his head back to clear his face of hair and looked at Millie. 'It was when we got to the caves and you went all mysterious on me, transfixed by the blank wall next to the star drawings, that I knew.'

Millie stared back, unsure what to say.

'So if you are not Felix, then who are you?' asked Arthur, still displaying puzzlement.

'I'm Fre Kles. Pleased to meet you.' Finally the purpose of the hand holding was explained as Fre shook Arthur's several times before letting go. 'Before you go on I have a question for you. How did you know how to open the cave door?'

'Lucky guess,' mumbled Millie, shuffling from foot to foot.

'People have tried for centuries to work it out and …'

'... And maybe nobody asked a kid to try. It was obvious straightaway to me it was hangman and to do with the stars. Once I told my grandad what I thought it didn't take him long to work out from the pictures which one it was.'

The splinters of light, not ten minutes ago so abundant, had now disappeared. The sun had set and Millie's torch was all that stood between the three of them and darkness. Fre remedied this by adding his own much larger beam to the proceedings. He was clearly spellbound by what he saw as he focused his torch on the surroundings, picking out the trees and vegetation as he went. Every now and then he would say, 'Amazing, just amazing,' before returning to silence. His question about gaining entry was obviously no longer at the forefront of his mind.

Arthur caught his attention by tapping his shoulder. 'You told us that Fre, I mean you, had already been in here.'

'I was just trying to build the story up. I've *never* been in here before.'

'So you lied?'

'Yes, Arthur.'

'You also mentioned a desire to "join them and become extinct". Another lie?'

Fre pointed his torch at the largest trees in the cavern, the ones that were most abundant and bearing fruit. 'No, not a lie really. I did want to join them. At least I wanted to see if they were real.'

'You wanted to see if trees were real?' said Millie, who was becoming increasingly concerned about Fre's sanity.

'Not trees, just that tree,' he replied, as he meandered over to inspect the object of his wonder.

Millie and Arthur looked blankly at each other before

Millie tapped a finger on the side of her head, indicating to her grandad that she thought their latest companion wasn't all there.

Fre crouched down on the floor, scooped something up and rejoined the concerned pair. 'You see these,' he said, shinning his torch in his palm, 'these are seeds from the Calvaria tree.' He looked up to see two blank faces.

'History, geography, and animals, yes. Trees no,' said Arthur, listing his specialist subjects.

'Television, computers, football, and junk food … oh and languages.' Millie didn't like being left out!

Fre dropped the seeds to the floor. 'It's very unusual to find such a profusion of wildlife inside a place like this, but if you account for the fissures in the rock that allow sunlight to sneak in, and combine that with the water I can hear, I guess it makes sense.' He refocused his torch on the fruit-bearing, seed-shedding tree. 'A Calvaria tree, however, could not possibly be here.'

'But it is. If you're right about its name of course,' said Arthur, now very intrigued by where this conversation was going. So intrigued in fact that he failed to notice Millie wander off.

'Oh, Arthur, I'm right. You see everything I told you about Fre – about me – spending the best part of thirty years scouring every inch of Uluru, its caves, and surrounding land in search of clues was true. One of my ancestors saw Ausvaldomic all those years ago vanish inside this cavern and I was determined to find some answers. A few hundred yards away from the rock there used to be a well that was sunk many centuries ago and used only for ancient initiation ceremonies.'

'What has that got to do with the Calvaria trees?' asked Arthur impatiently.

'I'm coming to that. As I said, the water from the well was used for centuries until one day, some fifty years ago, it dried up. This caused great concern amongst the community, as only water from near the rock was considered sacred enough for ancestral ceremonies. The government recognised this and some experts were brought in to sink another one. It turned out the underground water source had changed direction, but nobody was sure why.'

'Didn't anyone go down the first well to investigate?' asked Arthur.

Fre's face showed a look of horror. 'No, no, no. It was considered far too sacred to enter. Some thought the water drying up was a very bad sign. Going down the well would only have made it worse.'

'So the new well solved all your problems?'

Fre edged much closer to Arthur. 'Yes, Arthur, but the new well wasn't without its own share of surprises.'

'Like?'

'I raised the first bucket from the well and do you know what I found?' said Fre, now closer than ever to Arthur's face.

'Water?'

'Apart from water.'

'Tell me.'

'Seeds. Seeds from a Calvaria tree.'

'How did you know they were from that tree, and for that matter, what's so strange about them being here?'

'I know, Arthur, because I sent them off to be examined. You see I'm familiar with all the vegetation around here. For instance, this here,' Arthur nodded as Fre pointed to a stubby-looking bush, 'is an acacia bush and if you dig through its roots you'll find witchetty grubs. Not the most pleasant thing to eat, but good protein.'

Arthur winced; secretly hoping the large slice of cake he had eaten earlier didn't contain any.

Fre continued to point out and name a strange array of vegetation from desert raisins to wild tomatoes until Arthur raised his hand and said, 'I've got your point. You know the land well.'

Fre moved a touch closer and now Arthur could feel his breath brushing over his face. 'Arthur, when the results came back from the lab they thought it was a hoax and wouldn't believe my story.'

'Why?'

'Because this tree is only found in Mauritius, that's why.'

'Pardon me,' said Arthur, unsure if his ears had failed him.

'I said it's only found in Mauritius. Apparently there are only a handful left standing on the island, and they are knocking on three hundred years old.'

'Well how did they get here then, and how were they germinated?'

'Good question, Arthur. Good question.'

'Grandad, look what I've found,' said Millie, who'd reappeared from the trees holding a big white egg covered in brown speckles.

'Where did you get that from?' said Arthur, as he took it from Millie and offered it to Fre. 'Have you ever seen one of these before Fre?'

Fre shook his head, 'Never.'

They all stood, intently wondering at it, when Millie raised her hand, 'Quiet. Do you hear that?' The distant patter of feet that had initially attracted her attention soon became a rumble. There was more than one of them. A lot more.

Fre handed the egg back to Millie. 'Put it back right now.'

Millie shot back to where she found it, nervously twitching her torch from side to side as she went and pulled aside the tree beneath which was the egg's original resting place. Just as she did so she caught sight of two eyes squinting back at her through the undergrowth. Whatever it was it took off in fright when she let out an almighty scream that filled the cavern. Millie quickly put the egg down and retreated back to join the others, bumping into Arthur coming the other way.

'Millie, what was it? I heard you scream,' he said in a feverish tone.

He grabbed her hand and led her back to Fre. 'What was it, Millie?' he repeated, as they ran.

'Grandad, where's Fre?' Arthur hadn't noticed he was no longer there. His concern for his granddaughter had temporarily distracted him, but the whereabouts of Fre and what Millie saw staring back at her in the trees were just about to be answered.

'Over here, you two. You are not going to believe this. It's amazing.' The familiar sound of Fre's voice reverberated across the cavern.

Millie and Arthur walked towards him and soon discovered what the excitement was all about. Millie's torch picked Fre out sitting on the floor surrounded by dozens of very peculiar-looking creatures. 'Grandad, that's what made me scream in the trees.'

The creatures were smallish, about knee height, but their ample waistline made amends for this. They had two very stubby yellow legs, the same colour as their eyes, and a large, almost penguin-like, beak. Their tail was a plume of white feathers, very different to the downy ones that covered the rest of their body and the merest hint of wings could be seen tucked into their sides. Thick black clawed feet with one toe opposing the other three might have looked a tad intimidating if they weren't connected to such a bizarre animal.

'It's a bird all right. Well I think it is, but what's it called?' Millie threw the question out not really expecting an answer.

'Raphus Cucullatus,' said Arthur, as he bent down and ushered one over. Millie and Fre watched as first one, then several, waddled towards Arthur's outstretched hand almost tripping over as their large stomachs skimmed the floor and their inadequate legs beavered away.

'In English please, Grandad!'

'Dodo,' he replied as he knelt down to inspect the one nudging his leg.

Millie joined the others on the floor. 'Has everyone in here gone stark raving mad? First you,' she looked at Fre, 'talk about a tree that couldn't possibly be here, but it is.' She swivelled her head to look at her grandad, 'and then you think we're surrounded by a bunch of dodos!'

'So Millie, that leaves *you* as the only one in here that's *not* out of the ordinary. Am I right?' said Fre.

'Well, yes.'

Fre cleared his throat, 'Well then, would you mind answering me one question?'

'Shoot.'

'What exactly is a Zamorian?'

Of all the questions Millie expected Fre to ask that wasn't one of them. She tried to remain composed and not look at her grandad. 'A Zamorian?' she replied, playing for time. 'What makes you ask such a question?'

'I was standing in the shadows when you were trying to reopen the cave door from the inside. It was then that I clearly heard Arthur say that maybe you need to be "Zamorian" to open it.' Fre stopped stroking the birds, 'It was then that YOU stepped forward.'

Millie slapped the ground and fixed Fre with her bestest grin, 'Oh a Zam-o-r-ian. That was my grandad's poor attempt at humour. You see he has a sense of humour breakdown when faced with crisis. When I was a little kid I was convinced I was this funny character, called a Zamorian, from a television programme.' Her grin remained fixed, but Fre was having none of it.

'Good story. Rubbish, of course, but a good story anyway.'

'Fre.'

'Yes Arthur.'

'These creatures provide the answer to your tree problem.' Arthur's statement was meant to divert Fre's attention away from all things Zamorian, and it worked. Fre started to stroke the birds again and stared intently at Arthur.

'Explain.'

Arthur took a deep breath. 'OK. The Calvaria tree, you say, could only be found up until now in Mauritius.'

'Correct.'

'Well that's where the dodos lived up until they became extinct in the sixteen hundreds. Somebody brought them here, of all places, to conserve them – I guess late in the same century – and they must have had seeds still in their guts when they arrived. That's how the trees were germinated.'

Fre nodded. 'Well after what I've seen and heard

today,' he looked over to Millie and then back to Arthur, 'I would believe anything. Carry on.'

Millie picked up a few seeds from the ground to see what all the fuss was about. She examined them closely, but they just looked like plain old seeds to her. They smelt a bit funny, but apart from that they were nothing special.

Arthur continued, 'That's why the Calvaria trees left on the island were over three hundred years old. They obviously needed the dodo to prosper. The dodo ate the fruit, breaking the outer casing of the seeds down in its stomach, and passed them out the other end ready to germinate.'

Millie's fascination with the seeds was suddenly ended and she swiftly dropped them out of her hand. 'Yuck! Dodo poo!' she said, wiping her hands on the dusty floor.

'That leaves just one burning question then, Arthur,' said Fre. 'Who brought them here, and why?'

'That's two questions,' said Millie, still examining her hands. 'Ausvaldomic must have brought them.'

Fre turned to Millie; 'Yes, that's my guess too, but why?'

Millie offered no response.

'Hang on a minute, didn't you say outside something about the birds were brought here for conservation?'

Millie shrugged casually, 'Don't remember saying that.'

Fre shook his head disbelievingly.

While they were all engrossed in conversation they failed to notice that the dodo population had run into three figures. They were now appearing from everywhere. All harmlessly moseying along without a care in the world, curious to see what was going on.

'Why don't we split up and explore the rest of the caverns? Maybe we can find another way out. I'll go with Millie,' Arthur said, as he rose to his feet, scattering a couple of dodos that were comfortably nestling on his legs.

Millie jumped up and was quickly by her grandad's side, torch at the ready. She couldn't wait to get exploring again. Partly because she wanted to avoid any more of Fre's awkward questions, but mainly because she wanted to find the key piece and kill two birds with one stone – so to speak. Namely, get one step closer to completing the key and in doing so find a way out.

Millie's sudden movement in joining her grandad caused several dodos to fall backwards and briefly roll around with their legs in the air before righting themselves and ambling off into the darkness.

'I don't hold out much hope, Arthur, but let's look anyway,' said Fre, who started to shine his torch around the walls. 'There appear to be seven tunnels leading off this cavern. You two start from the left and I'll start from the right. Anyone finds anything, just holler, OK?'

Arthur nodded, took Millie's hand and headed towards their designated tunnel, and Fre took off in the opposite direction. The dodos, obviously worn out by their busy day so far, just wandered – occasionally bumping into each other as they went.

Out of sight and well into the first tunnel Arthur took the opportunity to quiz Millie about the Zamorian text from the other cave. 'What exactly did it say on the cave wall next to the stars?'

'Grandad, I already sort of told you. It seemed that Aurora tried to protect endangered species and would try to relocate them to somewhere safer. A sort of hobby, I suppose. I guess he used the movement of the dodos to shield his real reason for coming here.'

'I wonder how many other supposedly extinct creatures there are hidden around the world?' said Arthur, just before he jumped backwards, almost falling over Millie as he did so.

She steadied him as best she could. 'What is it, Grandad?'

'Spiders. Look,' Arthur said sheepishly. 'Can't stand the things.' His outstretched finger was pointed rigidly at a group of ugly-looking chunky-bodied spiders scurrying for cover out of the glare of Millie's torch.

'It's OK, Grandad, they're gone.' Millie brushed a rogue spider off Arthur's back as he composed himself and strode past her.

'What was that Millie?'

'Nothing. Just dusting you off.'

It wasn't long before they came to the end of their first tunnel and were on their way back. Apart from the spiders the only thing of interest was a couple of dodos apparently squabbling over a stone.

'What are they fighting over a stone for?' No sooner had Millie finished her question than one of the dodos, having knocked the other off balance, promptly flicked the stone up into its beak and swallowed it. 'Don't worry about answering that question, Grandad. All I can say is no wonder their bellies drag along the ground!'

They arrived back at the entrance to the first tunnel to see Fre appearing from his. 'Nothing down there but more dodos. Strewth! They sure are friendly fellas,' said Fre before he disappeared down the next tunnel leaving Millie and Arthur to venture down their second one.

'Can you hear the water, Millie?'

'Yes. I could hear it out in the main cavern, but the further down here we go the louder it gets. Sounds like a stream.'

'Watch your step, Millie.'

They both slowed their pace, carefully exploring the floor with the torch as they went.

CRACK!

Arthur was a couple of steps in front of Millie and holding the torch when suddenly he disappeared from sight. The tunnel was plunged into darkness. 'Grandad? Grandad, are you there?' The moment she heard the crack she stopped. Now in total darkness and with no sound from her grandad she was unsure what to do next.

She dropped slowly to her knees, the sound of running water now much more pronounced, and felt around in the darkness. Her fingers sifted through the sandy floor until she came across something familiar – her torch. She picked it up and knocked it back into life. For a split second she was elated to have regained her sight once more. However, her joy was to be short-lived, because just in front of her a huge hole had appeared where Arthur once stood.

Further investigation with the torch revealed water flowing freely through the hole. She looked up and into the tunnel ahead for any sign of life, but there was no doubt about it. Her grandad had fallen down the hole and been washed away by the water.

Surely this was a time to ask the book for help, but what if it couldn't? Then she would have to go in herself and try to find him, but that would mean leaving the book behind, as she couldn't risk getting it wet.

She buried the never-ending list of questions and answers and unbuckled her rucksack. She pulled out the book, hugging it close. 'Please help me save my Grandad.'

'You will not escape from here alive,' said a demonic voice in the distance.

Millie dropped the book in the water in fright, and watched helplessly as it too was washed away. 'OH NO!' she gasped.

All too quickly the shock of losing her grandad and then the book was overtaken by a searing pain which raged through her body. Her skin came alive and felt as if it was being blowtorched from within. This was a pain she'd felt only once before, when she was trapped in the secret room in India with the first key piece. It was all too much at once and she lost consciousness, falling forwards into the water hole.

CHAPTER NINE

THE TWO-WAY RIVER

The sudden shock of plunging head first into cold water immediately brought Millie round. She was being pulled along by the flow and was struggling to hold her breath. Somehow she'd managed to hang onto the torch, but light was of little help. What she needed desperately was air.

Her prayers were answered when, not a moment too soon, an air pocket presented itself in the form of another cave. Her head popped up out of the water and she eagerly filled her lungs, simultaneously stopping herself moving by grabbing some rocks.

Once she had got her breath back, she lifted the torch out of the water and used it to light up her surroundings. She appeared to be in another tunnel, not unlike the one she'd just left. Fortunately this one didn't come with the searing pain that the last one did. Unfortunately that was the only thing going for her, because there was no sign of life, apart from a spider or two, and certainly no sign of the book or her grandad.

Millie hauled herself out of the water. Apart from a few scratches on her legs and a cut forehead, she'd fared remarkably well, considering what she'd just been through. She couldn't, of course, see the gash on her head, but could feel the warm blood trickling down her face. A swift wipe from the back of her hand and the wound was quickly forgotten.

Cries of 'Grandad, are you there?' went unanswered.

Millie sat down beside the streaming water and rested her chin in her hands. In the space of a few minutes she'd managed to lose her grandad and the book, the things that were most precious to her. It was then that she realised she had something else to add to that list. The first piece of the key. It was still in the rucksack she left behind when she fell into the water. 'Great,' she muttered to herself, 'I came in here in search of the second piece and now I have none!'

The sound of approaching footsteps snapped Millie out of her bout of self-pity. The gradual building of pain in her head quickly dispelled any thought of them being friendly. The pain increased as the steps grew nearer, until she could bear it no more. She just had to retreat and scrambled on her hands and knees as fast as she could carry herself in the opposite direction.

Using the torch to guide her, Millie raced up the tunnel; but her escape wasn't going to be so easy.

'YOU MUST BE KIDDING!' she screamed, as the end of the tunnel greeted her torch. Frantically she looked around for another way out. Any way but the way she had come.

'You will not escape from here alive.' The distant demonic voice was back and as before it was soon accompanied by intense pain that ripped through Millie's body. This time, however, Millie had nowhere to run. Not even a water hole to fall down. This time she was going to have to face up to it.

Without the book.

Without her grandad.

Without anything.

Millie could feel the air being drawn from her lungs and the energy slowly draining from her body. She fell to her knees. Even though her eyes were starting to fail she could still make out a pair of legs that now stood before her.

'You will not escape from here alive.' She heard the

words, but felt powerless to respond. Each second seemed to drain her even more.

'You will not escape from here alive.' Millie could feel her life ebbing away, but still managed to find enough strength to lift her head and meet the eyes of the doom merchant.

'Yes, dear, it's me,' sneered Fre as he towered above her, clutching something in his left hand, 'and now you are going to die.' He reached down beside Millie and picked up a large rock with his other hand, lifting it high above his head. 'Now you are going to die,' he repeated, as Millie slumped to the ground.

'NOT IF I CAN HELP IT!' screamed another voice, as its owner came charging towards Fre.

Even as close to death's door as Millie was, she could still tell the sound of her grandad's voice and she was mightily relieved to hear it.

In the scramble that ensued both men fell to the ground. It quickly became apparent what was controlling Fre, when Arthur knocked the object he'd been so lovingly clutching out of his hand and it bobbled across the dusty floor. It was the second piece of the Key to Chintak.

The tunnel was suddenly filled with a deathly silence.

Millie could feel air returning to her lungs and she used it to power her legs back into life, but what she saw when she rose to her feet and pointed her torch into the tunnel sent shivers rippling down her spine. The key piece was far enough away to have little effect on her, but it was now being held by her grandad, and Fre was standing alongside him.

What disturbed Millie so much was that Arthur now shared the same sneering evil look as Fre. They were now *both* possessed by the curse emanating from the key piece.

'Grandad,' said Millie, 'can you hear me?'

Arthur and Fre stayed motionless; their eyes fixed on Millie.

'Grandad, throw it over your shoulder.'

'You will not escape from here alive,' was not the reply she was looking for, but nevertheless it was the one he chanted back at her.

'You will not escape from here alive,' repeated Fre.

Both of them started slowly forward towards Millie. Again, as before, the pain level increased as they grew nearer. There was nothing else for it. She had to run and hope she could split them up further down the tunnel. Maybe she would have a better chance if she could separate them.

Her running in their direction startled them enough for her to slip by and scoot off back down the tunnel. Fortunately she got up just enough speed past them to enable her to stay upright even though the pain being inflicted on her body was immense.

They didn't appear to be following in a great hurry and Millie soon found out why. Just as she rounded the corner, and a few paces short of the water hole through which she had entered the tunnel, a wall of glazed piercing eyes were there to meet her. She stopped, almost on the spot, and held the torch out in front.

'Dodos?' she said to herself. 'Surely *you* are not affected by the curse as well?' The way they all shuffled forward menacingly left her in little doubt of the answer to her question. They no longer looked like cute, harmless birds without a care in the world. Now they stood before her with eyes fixed, hooked beaks aloft and talons at the ready.

Millie could feel the pain returning and spun round to see Arthur and Fre step into the light of her torch. Their looks, as before, were those of madmen. She jumped backwards over the water hole as they neared her. Her action had moved her a few feet further away from them, but put her within striking distance of the dodos, one of which lashed out with its beak, tearing a deep gash in her leg.

'ARRRGG!' hollered Millie as she felt a second, then a third bird follow suit, each one inflicting more damage than the last. Millie frantically waved her torch in their direction, but it only seemed to make them more angry.

'STOP!' shouted Arthur. The birds did as ordered and withdrew a little.

Millie felt as if her legs had been ripped to shreds and she didn't dare look down. The feel of the blood streaming into her shoes was enough.

'She is mine.' If Millie thought her grandad had ordered the dodos to stop because he was trying to save her she was wrong. 'She is mine,' he repeated as he stepped forward holding the key piece out in front of him. Fre didn't move.

Millie slumped to her knees, gasping for air as her grandad drew closer. He came to a halt on the other side of the water hole, just a few feet away.

This was it. Millie knew this was probably her last chance. She didn't wait to find out what Arthur had in mind and with her last burst of energy she grabbed at the key piece. Arthur moved his hand out of the way, but as he did so he lost his balance and fell forward into the water and was swept away. Millie dived in after him just as Fre asked, 'Where am I?' Clearly the curse had worn off with the disappearance of the key piece.

As Millie was carried along through the water she felt the pain of the curse return only to disappear quickly again. The next thing she felt was a hand pulling her out of the water.

'There you are. I've been so worried.' It was Arthur and

he seemed to have returned to his normal self.

'Grandad, is that you?' Millie asked as she wiped her eyes free of water.

'Of course it's me. Who else would it be?'

Millie shone her torch in her grandad's face. His eyes had returned to their normal state all right, and his voice no longer carried a menacing air.

'Millie, what happened to your legs?' The shock on Arthur's face as he asked the question told Millie all she needed to know about the state of her lower limbs. Still she didn't look down at them.

'They happened,' Millie said as she pointed her torch down the tunnel.

Arthur turned to see a few dodos doddering harmlessly around, all of them startled by the glare of Millie's torch, and falling over accordingly.

'They did this?' Arthur enquired motioning towards her legs. Millie nodded.

'But how?'

'Grandad, what do you remember after you fell into the water?'

'What do you mean?'

'I mean you fell into the water and then you disappeared.'

Arthur nodded. 'That's right. I remember being pulled along by the current and struggling for breath and then finding myself in a different tunnel.'

'Then what?'

'Then you popped up and I pulled you out.'

Millie sat back on something and turned to investigate. 'My bag!' she exclaimed, pulling it onto her lap and foraging inside.

'What are you looking for?'

'This,' said Millie, plucking the first piece of the key out and waving it around.

'Millie, I don't understand.'

'Grandad, let me ask you a question. If you fell down a hole and were washed away to another tunnel—'

'This tunnel,' interrupted Arthur.

Millie frowned a don't-interrupt-me frown. 'Like I said. If you fell down a hole and were washed away to another tunnel, how come my bag is here?'

Arthur shook his head.

'I'll tell you,' and she did.

Arthur took some time to absorb all the information, and especially struggled when told how he'd behaved under the influence of the curse. It truly horrified him that he'd come so close to endangering his beloved granddaughter's life.

Once she'd finished telling the story they both sat quietly before Arthur said, 'You've missed something.'

'What's that?'

'How come we were washed in one direction the first time we fell in and then in the opposite direction the second time?'

Millie shrugged, 'I guess the curse is so strong, *it* must have done it.'

Arthur rocked his head to signal both yes and no. 'One more thing. The book. Millie, where's the book?'

He was right. She'd forgotten all about it, but she didn't have time to answer before they were both distracted by a beam of light making its way towards them down the tunnel.

'Are you there?' said the voice that accompanied the light.

Millie pulled Arthur to his feet and quickly tucked the first key piece back into her rucksack. 'That's Fre. We have to go,' she said, pointing to the water. She already knew the tunnel was a dead end and the water was their only way out.

'Hold on,' said Arthur. 'You said the curse controlled me when I fell into the water a second time.'

Millie nodded frantically in agreement.

'Well, I must have dropped the key piece in the water, which means he doesn't have it.' Arthur made sense all right, but Millie was so wary she still edged closer to the water hole. As she did so a mild pain made its way through her body and her face relayed it.

'What is it?' asked Arthur, sharing his attention between Millie and the fast-approaching Fre.

Millie moved back away from the water and the pain subsided. 'You're right, Grandad, I can feel the key piece is still in the water. When I go near it the pain returns.'

'Where have you two been?' said Fre as he came into view.

Millie and Arthur stared deep into his eyes and both of them breathed huge sighs of relief when they realised Fre too was back to his normal self.

'What are you two looking at and how did you get so wet?' As he drew closer yet more questions flowed. 'Millie, your legs are bleeding badly. How did that happen?'

Millie ushered him and Arthur away from the water. The last thing she wanted right now was for them to get close enough to be affected by the cursed key piece again.

'Follow me, you two. Follow me and I'll explain all,' she said, leading them away from the water and back down the tunnel and into the main cavern. Of course she'd no intention of filling in Fre's memory blanks as she'd done with her grandad's, but used the time gained as they made their way back to come up with a plausible explanation.

Once in the main cavern they sat on the floor and Fre wrapped some bandages around Millie's legs. 'You had a medical kit in your bag all along. I should have guessed it would have been standard issue and you'd no intention of leaving us in the caves alone.' Fre smiled to signify he agreed with Arthur's observation.

Once settled, and after being joined by a gaggle of curious dodos, Millie finally addressed Fre's questions with one of her own. 'What do you remember?'

Fre scratched the back of his head. 'How do you know I've forgotten something?'

'Because we both did,' she replied, puffing the hair out of her eyes and pointing at Arthur and herself, 'and we wondered if you experienced the same thing.' A lie of course, well for her anyway, but she figured the truth might just be a little hard to take.

'Yes, I do have a bit of a memory lapse,' Fre muttered, continuing to scratch his head. 'I remember leaving you and going down the first tunnel and finding nothing, but when I went down the second tunnel my mind went blank. I sort of remember picking up something a little odd and coming to tell you about it, but the next thing I know I'm staring down a water hole watching you disappear. What do you think could have caused it?'

Millie and Arthur shrugged in unison.

'What happened to you two then?'

'Similar thing, except we got wet,' said Arthur, sounding weary.

'Which leads me back to my last question. What do you think caused it?'

'Absolutely no idea,' said Millie rather unconvincingly.

She knew all right what caused it, as did Arthur. The same thing that Fre described as 'a little odd' – the second piece of the key, now lying in wait somewhere in an underground waterway.

'Why don't you two carry on looking for a way out and

I'll stay here?' ventured Millie.

'OK,' said Fre, who stood up and signalled Arthur to follow as he made his way to one of the few tunnels left to explore.

Arthur leant over to Millie and whispered, 'What are you thinking?'

'Grandad, I have to go and get the key piece and neither you nor anyone else can come with me. Once the curse is lifted I'll come and find you.'

'Easier said than done my girl.'

'I know, but it's probably our only way out of here. I still believe I have to lift the curse to reopen the door.' Millie could see Arthur was deeply concerned. 'Don't worry, Grandad, I think I know where the book might be. I'll find it before I tackle the key,' she lied.

'Be very careful, Millie.'

'I will.'

'How are you going to see under water?'

Millie tapped her faithful torch. 'It's waterproof, remember?'

'Are you coming or not?' hollered Fre impatiently. Arthur rose to his feet, joined Fre, and after a solitary glance over his shoulder the pair of them vanished out of sight down an as yet unexplored tunnel.

For the first time Millie looked at her legs, now clad in bandages with blood clearly seeping through. It was difficult to believe that the dodos gathered around her were most probably part of the pack that inflicted the injuries. She hauled herself up and headed back into the tunnel where she originally left her rucksack.

In everyone's haste to retreat down their respective tunnels nobody heard the door to the main cavern reopen.

CHAPTER TEN

WELL OUT

Millie checked around to make sure there was nothing about that could harm her. The sight of her torchlight and the sound of her hissing soon scared off a stray dodo.

She crouched over the water hole and leant forward to get a better look. That was a big mistake because she lost her handhold, slipped forward and was promptly washed away in the opposite direction to where the cursed key piece lay in wait.

The water flow eased as she was dragged further away from her entry point, giving her time to pinch a gulp of air along the way. She stuck out a hand and managed to grab hold of something to slow her pace, but the little oxygen available in the air pocket she was in was starting to run out. To make matters worse, her torch went out.

Feeling around in the water brought its just rewards when her free hand detected another pocket of air and she quickly guided herself into it. For once her luck had changed for it actually turned out to be another large cavern.

Only when her not so reliable torch spluttered back into life did she realise the magnificence of her surroundings. The cavern was grand enough, but all the walls were adorned with drawings of strange animals unlike any Millie had seen before. Beside each animal a few words were written. Zamorian words.

Millie dragged herself out of the water and wandered around exploring the drawings, awestruck as she went. She stopped beneath one and inspected it closely with her torch.

'Geechgot.' The picture she was referring to depicted a

huge bird with two wings either side of its enormous body, and a falcon-like head atop a long neck. An array of legs dangled beneath the giant bird, obviously drawn in mid-flight.

Millie moved further round and was soon attracted to another piece of Zamorian art. 'Snantav,' she mumbled to herself. The Snantav couldn't have been more different to the Geechgot. It was tiny by comparison, but its general features were hard to distinguish, because there appeared to be a herd of them all drawn together. If anything they looked as if they were lying down and asleep. 'Perhaps they have no legs,' said Millie to herself, 'or perhaps they sleep all the time. Now that would be my type of pet!'

Next was a picture of a person. Well, it looked like a person. An odd person, but definitely a person. If all the artwork was drawn to scale then the odd looking person must have been pretty short. Shorter than Millie even. Next to it was one word. 'Zamorian,' she said, tracing her finger around the outside of the drawing.

'AHHHHHHH!' screamed Millie as she leapt sideways back towards the water hole. Something had brushed her leg; something alive and her torchlight quickly revealed the culprit.

'A dodo! You frightened the life out of me. How did you get in here?' Not surprisingly her question went unanswered. Instead the dodo ducked its head down and fell over.

She scanned the cavern for any more signs of life, but none presented themselves.

Millie went over and knelt beside her new-found companion. The dodo had righted itself, but appeared to be sitting wearily on its stubby little legs. Its wet body a giveaway that it too must have fallen in the water and been

123

washed into the cavern. How it got out of the water was a question soon to be answered.

'You must have fallen in since the water changed direction,' said Millie, who was now stroking its soggy plume. The dodo responded by sidling a little closer and fixing her with its sad eyes.

'Well if you're looking at me for help, my funny friend, then I'm not sure you're looking in the right place. Everything I've done today hasn't quite turned out as planned!'

She went back over to the water hole, and explored it with her torch, this time making sure not to get too close to the edge. The dodo, however, was not so cautious. It waddled up beside her and straight on into the water after momentarily being blinded by Millie's torch. Before she could grab the flailing bird it was washed off, but it only went a few feet before it appeared to get stuck. Millie watched as the dodo wriggled out of the hole it found itself in and back onto dry land.

'Hey, a dodo water slide!' laughed Millie out loud. She couldn't help but laugh although deep down she really wanted to scream out in despair for the both of them.

'Wait here. I'll be back for you,' said Millie to the dodo as she stepped into the running water. The fear of being left alone again caused her feathered friend to fall into the water beside her and slide, as before, into the hole. This time he struggled to get his large frame out, but after a lot of effort he was once more on dry land. By the time he'd rolled upright Millie was gone.

She'd ducked underwater and, using the submerged rocks as levers, was pulling herself against the current, stopping periodically to make full use of the air pockets.

*

Back in the main cavern Fre and Arthur had finished exploring and found no sign of another way out. Fre wandered back past the Calvaria trees while Arthur went in search of Millie.

'Millie! Millie!' he shouted down each tunnel, 'are you there, Millie?' No reply was forthcoming. 'Fre, she isn't here,' he hollered in Fre's general direction.

'Arthur, come here. She has done it!' replied Fre.

'Done what?' Arthur said, running to see what had got him so excited.

'Done that,' said Fre, pointing to the open cave door. 'She has opened it.'

'How did she do that?'

'Beats me Arthur, let's go outside and ask her.'

They both walked through the door and quickly over to the No Entry rope.

It was pitch-black outside, but all the same Arthur was very pleased to be back out in the open air. Fre, by comparison, was not so happy.

'What is it, Fre?' enquired Arthur, who had caught sight of Fre's face in the light of his torch.

Fre ground to a halt and said, 'It's just that I've been waiting my whole life to find a way inside the rock and now I don't want to leave. It might sound weird, but I think I belong in there.'

He was right, to Arthur it sounded very weird indeed.

BANG!

The thud of the door closing was unmistakable and both Fre and Arthur turned just in time to see the last sprinkling of dust settle in its wake. A few loose rocks tumbling down from above removed any thoughts they had of going back over to it.

'Well at least we're all outside,' said Arthur. 'Let's find

Millie. She can't have gone far.'

*

Millie finally managed to heave her way back to the hole next to the key piece. She knew she was in the right place as the effects of the curse started to kick in. Her energy was sapped and she needed a few minutes to recuperate next to her rucksack.

'OK,' she said to herself out loud – somehow the sound of her own voice was comforting – 'if I go into the next tunnel up from this one and jump in the water there then I should flow back over the key piece. Hopefully I can grab it and throw it back into this tunnel when I pass by. At least then I can tackle the curse on dry land.' Not much of a plan, but it was the best she could come up with.

Millie left her rucksack on the floor and hurried to the next tunnel to put her plan into action, carefully tiptoeing through the main cavern so as not to disturb the others.

'Here goes,' she said to herself, as she moved alongside the water hole. 'Hang on a minute!' Millie looked quizzically into the hole. 'That can't be right.' The water was not flowing downstream as expected, but upstream instead!

She raced back to the other tunnel, slowing her pace briefly as she rounded the entrance, and slid to a halt next to the hole. Again she scratched her head in amazement. Inexplicably the water was flowing downstream. The curse was pushing the water in opposite directions away from itself.

There was nothing else for it. She would have to wade in against the tide and try to retrieve the key piece that way.

As soon as she plunged into the water the pain started to build. With each pull forward it grew and grew until she could feel her insides burning and her head pounding. She sucked in air whenever possible, but this was proving more difficult than before as the water tempo had increased.

The pain caused her to drop her torch and she followed her reflexes, grabbing it before it washed away. What she grabbed however was the second piece of the Key to Chintak. Immediately the water flow increased dramatically and she lost her grip. She was pulled downstream, whacking her head several times on the rocks, while she was dragged along. Her torch was nowhere to be seen.

Millie passed out with the pain, but somehow managed to keep hold of the key piece, as she was washed downstream into the cavern where the lone dodo was waiting. She regained consciousness when she crashed into the wall in which the dodo had previously been lodged.

'ARGGGG!' she yelped, when she felt her ribs crack on impact, spilling the cursed piece onto the dark and dusty floor.

*

'Millie! Millie! Where are you?' Fre said as both he and Arthur began to question their wisdom in leaving the cavern.

'I do hope she's safe,' said Arthur with more than a hint of doubt in his voice.

*

Millie could hear the onrushing dodo, now possessed by the curse, coming towards her and she tried frantically to free herself from the hole in the wall in which her legs were jammed.

THUMP! went the dodo as it replaced Millie in the hole. She'd managed to squeeze herself free but the dodo had now got itself well and truly stuck head first, with its little legs wagging furiously in the air.

The water that once flowed freely had stopped completely and the beam from Millie's torch, which had been washed downstream with her, now lit up the cavern.

Millie had fallen forward onto the key piece, which started to burn through her top. She grabbed it and read, '*to a far away place where the sky's painted blue.*'

*

She woke to see the dodo still flapping its legs vainly in the air and daylight clearly seeping through the rock from way above. 'I must have been out for hours,' Millie said to herself.

Slowly she stood up and dusted herself down. The first thing she noticed was her bandages that were previously blood stained were now as good as new. Her ribs no longer caused her to wince with pain and the cut on her head felt as if it had disappeared. The curse had caused the injuries. Now it was gone so had they.

Millie yanked the dodo out after a bit of effort, retrieved her torch, and lastly picked up the second piece of the key.

She led the way, dodo in tow, back up the dry riverbed to the tunnel where she'd left her rucksack. Before she climbed back into the tunnel she couldn't help but notice that the place where the cursed key piece previously lay hiding in the water was now full of rocks. A little water was seeping through, but nothing of consequence.

Millie scrambled back down the tunnel and called out for the others. 'Grandad! Fre! Are you there?'

She worked her way from tunnel to tunnel and then back into the main cavern until eventually she'd covered every inch of dry land she could find. Mentally and physically exhausted, she slumped to the floor and held her head in despair. Not even the crowd of chattering dodos that quickly assembled could distract her from how she felt.

*

Fre and Arthur had scoured the outside of the rock and even

returned to town in the vain hope Millie had somehow found her way back there. They too were sharing Millie's feelings of deep despair. If only they knew how close they really were – with just the small matter of the exterior of the largest monolith in the world standing between them of course.

Or was it?

*

'A torch, two key pieces, a rucksack, but no book and no adults and no way out. Great!' exclaimed Millie. 'But there must be a way out. There just must be,' she continued. 'Aurora wouldn't do that to me. Or would he? Maybe he wanted to trap me in here and has somehow made the adults disappear. After all I've lifted the curse, but the door has not reopened.'

Her rambling did little to disturb the assembled flock. They were still attending to their missing relative who'd returned with Millie. Clearly getting stuck in a hole with your legs waving about made you a hero in dodo land.

'Think. Think,' Millie said to herself.

She felt a nudge on her arm and looked up to see the dodo she'd rescued had waddled clear of its adoring crowd and had come to join her.

'Hello, my friend. Any idea of a way out?' Millie raised her eyebrows, but the dodo just wobbled a bit. 'Well I hope I like Calvaria fruit!' Millie often used humour to hide behind in times of great distress.

Then the dodo let out an almighty squawk and everyone else, including Millie, stopped talking. He turned and bobbled his way back towards the tunnel from which he and Millie had previously emerged triumphantly from. A glance back towards Millie and another loud squawk was all she needed to realise the dodo wanted her to follow.

And follow she did, all the way back along the dry riverbed and back into the cavern where they were first united. She stood for a second to marvel at the drawings before a third squawk centred her attention on the hole in the wall where the dodo was previously stuck.

They both stared through the hole and it was then that she saw it. There in front of them, some ten feet away and lit up by her torch, lay the book.

The hole still wasn't big enough for her portly friend, but a lot of wriggling and a hefty dodo charge was enough to see her through.

*

Once again the secret door to the main cavern slid open and once again nobody heard it.

*

'She must have found another way out,' said Arthur desperately, as he and Fre walked the perimeter of the rock.

'If she had I think we'd have met her by now. I don't want to rain on your parade mate, but I reckon she's still inside. Somehow we have to get back in,' Fre said, scrutinising the rock for clues of another entrance.

'Well, you know I wrote the word on the cave wall, just like Millie did originally, and you know what happened?' said Arthur.

'Yes. Nothing.'

'I don't understand it. I just don't understand it, Fre.'

'I do.'

'You do?'

'Yes.'

'Well tell me, then.'

'You are *not* Zamorian.' Fre stopped and faced Arthur as he delivered his line.

If Fre was looking for a reaction from him then he was

out of luck, because Arthur had got used to lying about Zamora a long time ago and just brushed Fre off. 'Oh don't be ridiculous man! Millie told you what that was all about.'

Arthur sped up and Fre followed behind.

*

Millie stood for a while relishing the feel of the book in her hands. 'I don't know why I'm so happy to see you. I thought you were supposed to help me fight the curse. Some help you've been!'

The tunnel she was now in stretched off into the distance and Millie followed its twisting path for a little while before she rounded a bend and stepped forward into a huge hole of light. Off went the torch and, using her hand to shield her face, she quickly became accustomed to the brightness. It didn't take her long to deduce she was standing at the bottom of a very deep well.

At last a way out, but impossible to climb.

A dodo isn't easily ignored and a distant squawk soon reminded Millie that one wasn't far away. After standing at the base of the well for a while she returned to the tunnel entrance.

'Hey, big fella.' Millie crouched down and looked through the hole. 'It seems we both have the same problem.' The dodo rocked from side to side. 'And that problem my friend, is that neither of us can fly,' said Millie, now reaching back through the hole and stroking the bird.

'This must have been the original well, the one that dried up,' she said, as she stroked away.

'Of course! Why didn't I think of it earlier? I've been so used to being without it,' she clutched the book harder to her chest, 'that I almost forgot it existed.'

'I need your help. I need to fly.' Millie felt nothing, but pushed off with her feet anyway. This caused two things to happen. Firstly she took off and whacked her head on the tunnel ceiling some five feet above. Secondly the dodo fell over in shock.

'I CAN FLY! I CAN FLY!' said Millie excitedly, now back on the ground and rubbing her head.

'I have to leave now, my friend. I'm going to fill this hole so none of your lot can wander down here and maybe be heard from above. I hope you understand I'm doing this for you. Take care,' said Millie to the bird, now fully upright.

Even though the dodo couldn't understand a word she was saying it still seemed to sense Millie's imminent departure and rocked unsteadily from side to side and let out a dull moan.

Millie gave it one last stroke and proceeded to fill in the hole with the many rocks at her disposal. The intermittent squawks on the other side grew dimmer and dimmer as she stacked more and more rocks up until several piles stood between her and the dodo.

Millie navigated her way back to the bottom of the well in no time at all. Once there she tucked the book safely back into her rucksack with both the key pieces, flexed her knees and pushed off.

There was no getting away from it. Flying was fantastic, if a little slow. Her ascent was gentle, far too gentle for Millie! She had visions of being able to streak upwards and across the sky at the speed of sound. Ambling upwards at walking pace did not match up with those dreams, but then again she could fly and it gave her a way out.

Her delight however was short-lived, as was it seems her new-found ability. As she approached the top of the well her ascent slowed to a snail's pace and then, horror of horrors, it stopped altogether only a few feet from safety.

Thoughts flashed wickedly through her mind as she hung

helpless in the air. If she ran out of steam now and the power suddenly vanished, then did that mean she would drop like a stone to the bottom of the well? She must only have had so much flying power, enough to get her out, but using some of it in the tunnel must have taken the extra bit away she now so desperately needed.

'HELP! HELP!' she cried out, but nobody could hear. Nobody came to the old well any more. An Out of Bounds cordon made sure of that.

Her body jerked suddenly, as if a cable had been cut, and her worst fears were confirmed. She was falling.

Millie picked up speed at an alarming rate, but she managed to get a hand to the book. 'I NEED TO FLY AGAIN. I NEED TO FLY AGAIN!'

Just a few feet from the bottom she stopped dead.

With her eyes closed she took a deep breath and raised one hand in the air. This time she took off skywards at greater speed than before, still slower than she desired, but any speed was good as long as it propelled her upwards.

A short distance from the top Millie reopened her eyes and instinctively lowered her outstretched arm to slow down. This had the desired effect and allowed her to gently draw level with the top of the well and grab on.

She pulled herself over the top and landed with a thud on the desert floor. At last she was back outside. At last she was free.

She ran back towards the rock in search of her grandad and Fre hoping that they'd somehow managed to find another way out and were waiting for her. The first place she checked was in the No Entry cave.

'I don't believe it. How long has the door been open? They must have got out, but I don't understand because when I looked it was closed.'

'MILLIE!' screamed Arthur, who'd just entered the cave behind his granddaughter.

It was a long hug, their longest ever. It was only broken up by the belated arrival of Fre, who said, 'There you are. We were worried sick about you. How did you manage to unlock the door again?'

'I didn't unlock it. I thought you did.'

'However it happened doesn't matter. You're alive and that's the most important thing,' said an extremely relieved Arthur.

'So how did you two get out then?'

'Same way as you – through the door,' said Fre.

'Yes, same way as you,' concurred Arthur.

They were both so relieved to see her she didn't want to complicate matters and tell them how she *really* got out. She would save it until later, until she was alone with Arthur. Instead she just nodded.

The door slowly started to slide shut, which interrupted the group hug. Fre raced into the opening and said, 'It's time to bid you two farewell. As I said, Arthur, this is the place for me. This is my destiny. There's nothing for me outside. I just know I belong in here.'

The door closed and Millie turned to Arthur. 'Is he nuts or what? I have to get him out.'

'No, Millie, he truly believes his place is within the rock. We've had many many hours together talking about it. There's a whole ecosystem inside there that can support life. There's nobody in the outside world for him. He has devoted his life to the rock, to Uluru, and this is what he truly wants.'

Millie was too tired to disagree. If Fre wanted it so much then who was she to disagree? She stood quietly for a few moments and then said, 'I guess the dodos will have company although I do hope he isn't a meat eater!'

During the journey back to the hotel, on one of the tourist buses, Millie quietly explained everything that had gone on since they last saw each other.

Exiting through the well or the door was something they couldn't agree on. Millie thought that Aurora put the ability to fly in the book and wanted her to get out through the well. Arthur thought the door must have been the way out all along and they should have been more patient.

Only one of them was right.

CHAPTER ELEVEN

SOUTH AMERICA

Journey to the original landing site of the first Zamorian explorers. Many landing strips were drawn out in the wastelands of Nazca. The ones that are important to you are the four nearest the native's depiction of our race. Walk in order from end to end and back again on each of the four lines to reveal the entrance that will lead you to the next part of the key. Only Aurora knew it was still there.

Discussing the meaning of the next clue while on board an aeroplane was now becoming the norm for Arthur and Millie. It had been revealed to them in the shadow of the rock, but neither had the energy then to speak about it at great length. Sleep and a good bath took priority that night.

Who knows how any of Millie's Earthly Zamorian ancestors coped travelling such great distances before the advent of flight, because the route to Lima, the capital of Peru, via Sydney and Santiago in Chile, was bad enough on board a plane.

'What does it mean, walk in order? Which end are you supposed to start from?'

Millie's ever-familiar shoulder shrug was in overdrive. She did it for the first two questions and the following one too.

'Only Aurora knew *what* was still there?'

'After all we've been through, Grandad, there's probably no point in trying to guess the answers,' said Millie, who was prodding her food with her finger, gingerly inspecting what delights were hiding under her grey-toned meat. 'Tell me more about Nazca.'

Arthur drew a long purposeful breath and Millie prepared herself for the long version. 'Nazca—'

'The short version please.' She thought she might as well ask.

'Nazca,' Arthur continued, 'is one the of the world's great mysteries. At least it was until yesterday!'

'Why what happened yesterday?' Millie muttered, still mostly engrossed in her food.

'What do you mean what happened yesterday? You read the clue and it told us the real reason for the lines. *That* is what happened yesterday.'

'Got ya.'

'As I was saying, the lines aren't too far south of Lima, maybe two hundred plus miles, and are one of this planet's great puzzles. Not to mention an ancient wonder of the world.'

'Why?'

'Because the drawings or patterns can only be appreciated from the air, but they were created a mighty long time before these babies were invented,' he said, leaning forward and patting the side of the plane. 'Many studies have been carried out on the lines, but apart from agreeing they date back between one and two thousand years, each study generally threw up a different explanation for their creation.'

'Like?'

'The most fanciful explanation being they were alien landing strips,' said Arthur, with a broad grin on his face.

'Yes, you have to watch out for those aliens,' said a hostess in a thick Aussie accent. She'd slid up beside them, and was clearing away their plates. Millie smiled an I-know-something-you-don't smile.

'Not like the food, dear?' she enquired, as she shovelled Millie's full plate on top of Arthur's sparklingly clean one, before dispatching both with consummate ease into her trolley.

'You haven't got any chocolate have you?'

'I'll see what I can do.'

Brake released and she was off.

Millie nudged her grandad. 'Carry on.'

Arthur looked up and down the aisle before saying, 'As strange as it sounds, because of their size they were not discovered, or rediscovered shall we say, until they were flown over by a local Peruvian pilot in the nineteen twenties. They've proved fascinating to mankind ever since and attract hordes of visitors each year who come to pay homage to a spectacle that pre-dates the Incas.'

'People travel from all over the *world* to look at lines in the sand?' The disbelieving tone to her question showed that Millie was fast losing interest in the subject.

'Not just lines,' huffed Arthur, 'birds, flowers, and all manner of other things are drawn out over a huge expanse of desert. There's also a picture of an astronaut which must be the drawing the book refers to as the natives' depiction of their race. The civilisation of that time must have seen them – Zamorians – and thinking they were gods, depicted their image in the desert.'

Arthur turned to Millie and was not impressed to see her gently snoozing instead of listening to his explanation of the astronaut, but once he too had closed his eyes it didn't take him long to join her in a peaceful slumber.

It took a few shakes to wake Millie from her dreams of sandy deserts and alien landings, but when she did so the sight of a huge bar of chocolate was greatly welcome.

'Here you go, dear. I bet you can't eat all that before he,' the friendly hostess had returned and was nodding her head in Arthur's direction, 'wakes up.'

Millie licked her lips and took the bar. 'I wouldn't bet on that if I were you!' she said, viciously disposing of the wrapper, breaking off a slab of exposed chocolate and stuffing it in her salivating mouth. 'Lovely,' she gurgled, between chomps.

*

What with sleeping, eating and jet lag, Millie had clean forgotten about her new-found power – flight, but the stopover at Santiago airport provided her with more than enough time to reacquaint herself with it.

She wasn't stupid. She knew somewhere quiet was needed to hone her aerial skills. The airport was teeming with people so the toilet seemed the most obvious place to go.

'Millie, did you know from Santiago you can surf and ski within a hundred or so miles of each other? Fascinating city don't you think?' muttered Arthur, who'd buried his head in the local freebie guide book.

'Yes, fascinating,' replied Millie, completely unaware of what Arthur had just said. She rose to her feet and slung her rucksack over her shoulder.

'You're not going anywhere without me by your side and I'm not moving. It was hard enough to find a seat in here as it was,' said Arthur, leaning back in the chair he'd fought so hard to find.

'Grandad, I need a wee. Do you really want to come with me?'

Arthur lowered his book and peered beyond Millie to the toilets behind her. 'Off you go then. I can see the door from here and I guess not even you could get into trouble in a toilet.'

Millie spun on her heels and was soon inside the toilet and carefully selecting her cubicle.

'Can I help you?' Millie had failed to notice that she was blocking the way of a woman who'd come in behind her.

'I was just … er …' said Millie awkwardly.

'I think you'll find they're all the same!' Millie stood, mouth ajar, as the very well-to-do woman brushed passed her and into a cubicle.

Millie sarcastically mouthed the words the posh woman said and took residence in the cubicle beside her.

She wasn't sure if she still needed the book or not, but a few futile arm raises and skips on the spot provided the answer. Book clutched to her chest she whispered ever so quietly, 'I need to fly. I need to fly.'

A gentle push was all that was needed, but Millie never did anything gently. Had her arms been raised she would have shot straight through the false ceiling and smashed her head on whatever supported it. As it was she rose up and nudged a tile out of place with her head and slowly descended again.

She did this a couple of times, smiling gleefully to herself, until on the third occasion she noticed another woman standing by the main door. Millie nodded at the woman, said, 'Hello,' looked left and right and casually drifted back to the floor. From the outside it looked as if she must have been bouncing up and down on the toilet seat. A weird vision indeed and the woman beat a hasty retreat. Millie just quietly giggled away to herself.

'With whom are you speaking? *Surely* you have parents somewhere who are worried about you?' said the snooty lady in the next cubicle.

If she could have seen Millie's scowl and tongue pointing from behind the partition then she would have said a great deal more. Any condescending statement involving Millie's parents was enough to make her blood boil. Who did the woman think she was? For that matter what was she doing in there anyway?

Millie came out and was about to leave when she noticed that all the other cubicle doors were ajar. The only person, apart from Millie in the toilets, was the stuck-up woman who was trying her hardest to annoy Millie.

Millie couldn't help herself; she *had* to have a peek and crouched down to see the back of the woman's legs.

How could she be seeing the back of her legs? Surely if she was on the loo she would be facing the other way?

There was only one thing for it. She pulled the book out again and whispered, 'I need to fly,' and pushed off from the ground.

She rose up above the cubicle door and saw the woman stuffing something in the toilet cistern. It was difficult to tell what, but whatever it was it was obviously something bad.

As Millie landed back on the ground the entrance door sprung open and she found herself standing face to face with a local security guard and the woman she'd earlier frightened off when she appeared to be bouncing on the toilet.

Millie quickly raised her finger to her lips to indicate silence. Her other hand pointed directly at the cubicle with the posh lady in it. Even though she was much smaller than the two people standing before her, her finger gestures had the desired effect and nobody made a sound.

Millie ushered the guard in and again pointed to the locked toilet door. Still taken aback by Millie dominating the proceedings, the guard reluctantly followed her hand gestures and peered under the cubicle. What he saw was enough to arouse his suspicions and he promptly knocked on the door.

'Hola?' said the guard, who'd now unclipped his gun holster.

Millie took this as her cue to leave, sliding out past the woman who had now forgotten about her complaint having, herself, become engrossed in the goings-on.

'What happened in there?' said Arthur, who'd come over to investigate. 'Can't you stay out of trouble for one minute?'

'It's nothing to do with *me*, Grandad. There's a woman in there up to something dodgy. I just happened to be in the wrong place at the wrong time.' Millie tried her best to look innocent, but Arthur wasn't buying it.

Fortunately for her the guard emerged clutching an armful of wet bags, contents still unknown, in one hand and a very well-dressed woman securely handcuffed to the other.

Millie smiled as the woman passed by but she didn't return the gesture.

'See, told you,' said Millie, leading Arthur away.

'I still can't believe I can fly. I wonder what else I can do?' she whispered to herself.

'Did you say something?'

'Er … yes I said, tell me more about Santiago.'

*

Lima airport provided none of the excitement of its equivalent in Santiago, although this was partly because Millie left the book safely tucked away in her rucksack. She vowed to find a less public place to practice her flying. Toilets were now strictly out of bounds.

Unlike the overland journey to Alice Springs, the trip from Lima to Ica, the transit town for travel to Nazca, didn't involve a modern form of transport or a tour guide. Instead they found themselves cooped up on a ramshackle old bus.

'Grandad, is this safe?' Millie was holding her rucksack for fear of it shooting off down the aisle when the driver carried out yet another of his last minute braking manoeuvres.

The bus was jam-packed with people of every description. Locals sat upon locals and tourists wedged themselves up against each other, occasionally knocking heads when the driver bounced over anything he could find in the road. It appeared that driving around something wasn't an option!

Arthur was made of stern stuff *and* he was British, which meant he was incapable of complaining about such things. 'It will be fine, Millie.'

A few whacks in the face from Millie's rucksack later, and they were there.

Ica looked a nice town but for the odd questionable character. 'Grandad, I have a funny feeling about this place,' Millie said, standing beside Arthur and inspecting the scene.

'Nonsense, Millie, this town seems fine to me. Very Spanish-looking and nothing like I imagined.' Arthur was interested in Spanish architecture and took great delight surveying the buildings around him.

Millie however had focused her attention on a group of men milling around a pick-up truck across the street from them. 'What about those guys, Grandad?' she said, subtly nodding her head to point them out. 'They don't look that friendly to me.'

'You get people like that everywhere. Don't trouble them

and they'll not trouble you. Besides, we're still about forty miles away from the Nazca Plains, so they'll soon be far behind us.'

Wise words, but all the same Millie couldn't help eyeing them up while she waited patiently in the searing heat for their next bus to arrive. Even the instruction from her grandad for her to 'stop staring' only diverted her attention away from them until Arthur wasn't looking.

They boarded yet another bus, this one more pleasant than the last mainly because the air-conditioning actually worked and it was not over crowded. A quick look around was all that was needed to confirm it was full of tourists.

Millie took a seat near the window and it wasn't long before her eyes gravitated back towards the group of men who fascinated her so.

'They look as dodgy as hell, wouldn't you say?' Millie twisted around to see a young lad about her age peeping over the back of her seat. Next to him sat an older man who was preoccupied with a local map.

'That's my dad. He loves maps!' said the boy, sticking his thumbs up and displaying a set of teeth a rabbit would be proud of.

'Malcolm, found yourself a girlfriend, I see.' Malcolm's dad's sense of humour produced not a smile between the objects of his derision.

'Sorry about that. My dad is *such* an embarrassment.'

Millie just screwed up her nose and Malcolm went red and slid out of sight, only returning to view once his dad had reacquainted himself with his map

After an age spent up front with the driver, Arthur plopped himself down in the seat beside Millie, 'Nice man. Very nice man. Lots of history in this town you know,' he said.

Suddenly Malcolm seemed much more interesting and Millie turned back to face him before her grandad could tell her any more.

'I agree they did look a bit dodgy,' said Millie to Malcolm.

'You aren't still talking about those men are you?' asked Arthur, who was dividing his attention between Millie and the same map that had Malcolm's dad so engrossed.

Millie left Arthur to his map and carried on looking at Malcolm, who was still bright red.

'Sunburn,' he said, sensing Millie was wondering how the girlfriend statement could cause him to change colour for so long.

'Hmmmm,' said Millie, almost parent-like, 'factor thirty all the time for me.'

'I wanted a bit of colour,' retorted Malcolm.

Millie smiled, 'Well you got greedy!'

Malcolm's dad chuckled to himself behind the map, much to the annoyance of his crimson son.

The bus chugged into life and pulled away. Both Millie and Malcolm watched the group of guys, now reduced to two, until they could crane their necks no more.

'So you agree with me?' enquired Malcolm of Millie.

'Sure do. Something's not right about them. Especially those two.'

'Murderers I reckon,' whispered Malcolm, now hunched up on his knees to get a better look at Millie.

'Not sure about that!'

'I reckon their pick-up was full of guns. OH! OH! Do you think they're going to hold up this bus?' said Malcolm excitedly, and in such a loud voice half the passengers glared at him.

Malcolm's dad and Arthur lowered their maps, exchanged

glances of pure pity, smiled, and returned to their studying. Malcolm went an even deeper shade of red and vanished out of sight.

Nothing else was said until they left the bus at Nazca. Needless to say no hold-up took place.

CHAPTER TWELVE

THE NAZCA LINES

The patch of greenery directly opposite their hotel in Nazca town seemed an appropriate place for Millie and Arthur to discuss the day ahead.

'You can't get a much better location than this,' said Arthur, who was tucking into a soggy mass that had once resembled a chocolate bar.

'So I did OK then? I told you there was nothing to worry about, booking the hotel on the Internet.'

'As long as *you* always drive the keyboard then I'm fine with the Internet!'

Millie's look changed from one of amusement to disgust. Amusement because she couldn't grasp the thought that a man as intelligent as her grandad was scared of something as simple as a keyboard and disgust at the chocolate that was fighting to escape his grasp. 'Grandad, you have chocolate running down both arms.'

Arthur finally conceded his battle – the heat had won – and wiped himself down. 'I've hired a car from the man at the front desk of the hotel. It should be here in a minute,' said Arthur, still discovering bits of chocolate with his hanky, 'That way we don't have to rely on anyone else.'

'Do you know where you're going then?'

'The Nazca Lines,' he said, smiling broadly, having finally finished his preening.

Millie shook her head, 'Very funny! Of course we're going *there*, but do you know how to find them?'

'I studied the map on our trip down and I now know this place like the back of my hand. No problem.'

*

'I'm sure this is the right road,' said Arthur, who'd been scratching his head at regular intervals for some time.

'I told you to follow the other cars, Grandad, but *you* wanted to take a short cut,' said Millie, who unfolded the map while Arthur pulled the car over to the side of the road.

A vehicle drew up alongside and the passenger tapped on Arthur's window. Millie fought with the map to see who it was, as Arthur wound his window down to talk to them.

She was happy someone wanted to help, but not happy it was the two men acting suspiciously she'd seen lurking opposite the bus station in Ica. Even though Arthur previously appeared to brush off Millie's comments about their demeanour, he still only wound his window down halfway.

'NAZCA LINES?' Arthur shouted. That was his way of dealing with foreigners, because for some unknown reason he thought that if they couldn't speak English then shouting would make them understand!

'My name is Diego and this is Miguel. My English not best, but OK. You lost, yes? Looking for Lines, yes?' said the passenger in a thick Spanish accent.

Diego was a slimy character. He had shoulder-length hair that looked as if it had been washed in cooking oil and skin that resembled the surface of the moon. How he ate with just a couple of stray teeth in his mouth was anyone's guess, and his blacker-than-black eyes were deep-set and menacing.

It was difficult to make out Miguel, but his ragged silhouette, picked out by the sun behind, was enough to make Millie think that he too shouldn't be trusted. The sight of Arthur's hand glued to the handbrake and his right foot hovering over the accelerator told Millie her grandad now agreed with her opinion of the pair.

Arthur nodded, 'Yes.'

Diego opened his door.

Millie felt for her rucksack.

Arthur clicked the button on the handbrake.

Diego didn't get out though, but merely held the door ajar with one hand and used the other to point back down the road that Arthur had just driven along. 'That way and left. Ten of minutes,' he said roughly.

A swift, 'Thank you,' and Arthur turned the car and drove off, checking his mirror more times than usual in the process.

'Scary pair, those two,' Arthur uttered, happy to finally see their pick-up vanish from sight.

'Told you,' said Millie knowingly.

'I saw a few shovels in the back of their truck. I wonder what else was lurking out of sight,' said Arthur.

'Bodies perhaps?'

'Let's not go too far Millie!' said Arthur, as he tutted loudly. 'I would say they're grave robbers.'

'WHAT?'

'I read in the guidebook that the police are trying to crack down on bandits stealing ancient artefacts from the nearby burial chambers. The civilisation that existed here two thousand years ago worshipped the Nazca Lines and many chose to be buried amongst them.'

'Along with their most valuable possessions?'

'Exactly, Millie, exactly,' said Arthur, at last back in the flow of traffic down the Pan-American Highway *en route* to the Lines. 'It's fair to say that the possessions are now valuable because they're so rare. We're only talking about pots and things like that, but so many have been stolen the authorities had to act.'

Arthur didn't tell Millie everything he'd read, because she

would only worry if she knew how ruthless the bandits could really be.

'We'd better make sure we avoid them and the police then. It will be hard to explain the nature of the artefact *we* are seeking.'

'Very true, my girl. I understand the fines are high and the sentences long in these parts.'

A sign was needed to tell the pair they'd arrived at the Lines because it wasn't obvious from the road. Cars littered the roadside, their owners wandering near by trying to fathom out their surroundings.

Millie ducked down in her seat as they passed Malcolm and his father. They were waiting in line to climb a tall roadside viewing tower. Even at speed Malcolm's strawberry cheeks were clearly visible behind the camera he had glued to his face.

'Keep your eyes peeled for a giant astronaut,' said Arthur lightly.

Millie looked at her grandad wondering if he, like Malcolm, had spent too much time in the sun. 'Grandad, are you feeling OK?'

'Millie, if you'd been listening to me on the plane, you would know what I'm talking about. The Lines, it would seem, were created as a result of early Zamorian landings, but the other artwork appears to have been done by the local people.'

'And they drew a picture of an astronaut?' asked Millie incredulously.

'A Zamorian astronaut according to the book,' said Arthur. '*That* Zamorian astronaut in fact.' Millie looked to where Arthur's finger pointed and sure enough there standing proud on the side of a gentle slope was a primitive portrayal of a person with one hand up in the air and the other clutching something.

'I've seen that picture before, or something very similar anyway,' Millie remarked, straining her eyes to make sure.

'Where?'

'In the underground cavern where I met the stray dodo. Don't you remember, I told you about the picture of a Zamorian on the wall there?'

'Oh yes, I remember now.'

'Well this one is similar, only a lot bigger.'

'So, Zamorians have similar features to us then?' said Arthur.

'Yes, except I don't think they've got noses!' said Millie, feeling her own one to see if it came off, making her a true Zamorian. 'We also know they're somewhere between the size of the cavern drawing, about three feet tall, and this one, which must be at least thirty times bigger!'

The astronaut drawing was some way from the road, and the flat plains of the arid Nazca desert weren't so hospitable when crossed by foot. It took the intrepid pair some time to reach it after leaving their car parked by the roadside. The aching heat of the plains made every step hard work, and Arthur let out a big sigh of relief when they finally arrived at the foot of the slope.

Unlike the wonders they'd encountered before in India and Australia, the arrow-straight Nazca Lines didn't have the same effect on the eye or the heart. It was impossible to appreciate from the ground the thousands upon thousands of shapes that had been carved into the plains twenty centuries earlier. A vast menagerie of animals also went unnoticed to those who ventured out on foot. Even the slope drawings, like the astronaut, were hard to pick out close up.

That's why so many flights buzzed back and forth overhead, no doubt crammed with people taking in the full glory of the pictures etched out in the shadows of the Andes Mountains. A hot air balloon could be seen in the distance, carelessly drifting across the skyline, its shadow playing hide and seek with the sun.

'Look, Grandad.' Millie was pointing at a small series of lines directly beneath the astronaut's right foot. Each line was five meters wide and about ten times as long.

'If they were landing strips then they must have had small spaceships!' said Arthur, who'd wandered over to the nearest line. He scanned the horizon from where he stood. 'I can only see two other lines from here,' he said, pointing off into the distance.

Millie trotted over to one of them and stationed herself right in the middle of it and then repeated this with the other two Arthur had picked out.

'You're right, Grandad. I can only see three as well. Where's the fourth?'

Arthur shook his head. 'Don't know.'

'You know what I need to do, don't you, Grandad?'

Arthur started to shake his head again, but stopped when he saw Millie reach for the book. 'Oh, no, you don't!' he said, realising what she was up to, 'you're *not* going flying around here.'

Millie stopped undoing her rucksack and puffed solidly. 'Why not? I can fly and we need to see where the fourth line is, don't we?'

'Two reasons. Firstly, you don't know how to control it. You said yourself how close to death you were when you flew up the well in Australia.'

'But ...' Millie was about to say that she'd practiced a little more since then, but thought better of it.

'No buts, young lady. Anyway, just imagine how many cameras and pairs of binoculars there are trained on this slope.'

'What was your second point?' said Millie, arms firmly crossed.

'That was it. We can't chance you being seen hovering around the sky out here. We're going to have to find another way.'

Millie reluctantly agreed to climb the slope on foot while her grandad paced off in varying directions – both of them in search of the nearest line to the three they'd already discovered.

As she walked up the left side of the drawing it quickly became evident that her route took her parallel with a line that appeared to run the full length of the slope. Another line greeted her eye to the left of the astronaut's head when she reached the top.

Millie could see lines running off in all directions from the summit, but none so close as the two she'd just discovered, and she scurried back down to tell her grandad about them.

'The nearest lines to these three are all about five hundred feet away,' said Arthur, his face awash with sweat.

'Well, I've found two that are nearer than that. One runs all the way up the side of the astronaut,' Millie waved her hand to indicate its location, but Arthur couldn't pick it out even through squinted eyes. 'The other is right at the top next to its head. It could be either of them, they're both pretty close.'

'OK. Start by pacing out the three lines at the bottom and then try the one up the side, and let's see what happens,' said Arthur.

Side by side they wandered over to the nearest of the small lines. Arthur motioned Millie to start walking. 'I'm going to stand aside because no doubt only you can reveal the entrance so it would be pointless me trying. I'll just wait here.'

Millie was sure her grandad was right, but knew his decision was partly based on his desire to rest. He must have felt tired out because she sure did, but now was not a time for Millie to put her feet up. Now was a time to find the next part of the key and so off she traipsed, back and forth along the three lines at the base of the slope.

The lines were small by comparison to some of the other monsters that criss-crossed the desert, but under the vicious glare of the afternoon sun they were more than long enough.

After the three lines were completed Millie stood beside her grandad contemplating which one to tackle next. A big puff of dust streaming across the plains towards them looked set to put their decision on hold.

The word *Policia* was written across the front of the off-road vehicle that skidded up beside them.

'What do the police want with us, I wonder?' enquired Arthur to himself.

'Inglish?' probed the policeman in an accent that rather reminded Millie of a cartoon character. She sensibly contained her urge to laugh.

'Yes. Arthur Jarman. Pleased to meet you.' Arthur held out his hand, but slowly withdrew it when his gesture wasn't reciprocated.

'Iz your car?' said the policeman, now out of his vehicle and gesturing towards their car, parked on the side of the main road.

'Yes, that's my car. Is there a problem?'

'No park there. Park in park place. Danger there,' said the policeman, slaughtering the English language with every breath.

Arthur bowed his head apologetically. 'So sorry, I didn't

realise. I'll move it straight away.'

Taking the policeman's nod as his cue Arthur held Millie's hand and made to leave.

'Wait!' said the policeman suddenly, 'what in here?' His words might have been jumbled, but his eyes were not and they were looking straight at Millie's rucksack.

Millie dropped it to the floor. 'Nothing, just a few girlie bits and pieces,' she said twirling her feet nervously in the dust and hoping he would take his curiosity no further.

'What in here?' he repeated, stepping forward to take it from Millie. Her instinctive reaction to snatch it away only fuelled the policeman's suspicions further and he grabbed the rucksack to investigate.

'I say,' howled Arthur, 'there's no ...' his sentence faded away when the policeman popped open the stud on the gun holster that was strapped to his side.

'Problem?' enquired the policeman menacingly.

Arthur took a step back, 'No, no problem.'

Arthur and Millie stood and watched as he emptied the contents of Millie's rucksack onto his bonnet. Some manky old sweets, a bottle of now very warm water and a personal stereo were quickly shoved back in. The book and the two key pieces however, were not.

He riffled through the pages of the book, his brow becoming more furrowed as he did so, and said, 'No words.' He continued to flick back and forth and then repeated, 'No words?' Only this time it was directed as a question towards Millie.

She edged a little closer to the policeman, greatly suppressing her desire to snatch the book and key pieces back off him. 'I plan to draw in the book,' she said, using her hands to demonstrate, 'pictures. You know ... art?'

The key word seemed to be art. Until then the

policeman's expression was one of mystery. 'Art … OK,' he said, closing the book and sliding it to one side of the bonnet.

Next up were the two key pieces, which he examined intently, turning them over and over in his hands. There was going to be no easy answer to his next question. In fact it wasn't a question, but a gesture. He held both pieces aloft and raised his eyebrows, so much so his cap moved back on his forehead revealing a bald spot that shimmered in the sunlight.

'Ah yes, those,' said Arthur, 'they are mine. I work in a museum and they are from there.'

The policeman shook his head.

'A MUSEUMMMM,' Arthur shouted, now reverting to his deaf foreigner theory.

'Si, museum. I know museum,' said the policeman, still rolling them around in his hands. 'You take from here?'

'No, no, no. Absolutely not. *They are mine*,' Arthur's forward motion was stopped by the policeman palming both pieces into the same hand and using his spare one to remove his gun and lay it on the book.

'Si, you take from here. Now take I,' said the policeman, who tucked the two pieces into his shirt pocket.

Arthur and Millie exchanged frantic glances.

'I check,' muttered the policeman, 'move car now.'

Millie stepped forward and pointed to the book and her rucksack. 'May I?' she enquired. The policeman slowly nodded and Millie quickly retrieved her possessions. Dismay at having the key pieces taken away was temporarily masked by her delight at getting both hands back on the book. At least with that she had power and a plan was forming in her mind about how best to use it.

Arthur grabbed Millie and led her away to the car.

'What are you doing? I was going to use the book to get the pieces back.' she muttered loudly.

Arthur's pace quickened and as he had a firm grip on Millie, so did hers. 'Don't shout,' said Arthur lightly.

'Why? He can't understand.' Millie again spoke far too loud for Arthur's liking.

He pulled her up just short of the car and bent down to draw level with her face. A sure sign a lecture was coming, but in defiance Millie still held on to her angry look. 'How do you know he can't understand? Maybe he really can speak perfect English and is just having us on to see what we say.' Arthur looked back at the policeman, who was still standing watching the pair, 'and another thing. How do you know the number of powers the book can give you?'

'What do you mean?' said Millie, her look of displeasure still in evidence.

'I mean maybe, just maybe, you'll only be granted the power you need to retrieve the key pieces.'

'Yeeeessss, that's what I want to use it for, to retrieve those two key pieces,' Millie said, rolling her eyes sideways towards the policeman.

Arthur was not amused. 'Let me finish. For each new piece you may only be given one power so if you'd asked for a new power back there it might not have been the one you needed to find the next piece. Get it?'

She got it. Her expression told Arthur so.

'STOP!' shouted the policeman, now on his way over to join them, drawing to a halt within shouting distance. 'You station morning. I talk museum Nazca.' He stopped and turned back towards his off-roader as soon as Arthur acknowledged him with his customary nod.

Not a word was said as they set off on the road back to Nazca town. The air-conditioning was on full blast and the cool breeze emanating from the dusty vents was a welcome change from the blazing heat of the plains. Even though it was on its way down the sun still kicked out gas mark ten.

Arthur had contemplated stopping at the viewing tower and maybe backtracking, but the tower was empty, the sunlight fading, and Mr. Policeman was right behind him, remaining there until they pulled into the hotel and parked up.

'Do you know where the police station is?' Arthur asked at the reception.

'Yes sir. Out of front and two blocks down on right.' The receptionist, wholly engrossed in his reading matter, refrained from asking the reason why.

'Let's go and have a look shall we?'

'OK, Grandad.' These were the first words Millie had said since her dressing-down. She had time in the car to contemplate Arthur's lecture and he was right. What if she did only have one power per key piece and she'd wasted it back on the plains? She could have ruined the only chance the Zamorian children had of escaping. Sure, she might have been able to get by with the book allowing her to breath, as in India, or by using her flying skills, but who could tell? Her grandad was right. She needed to think more about the consequences of her actions.

The police station really was only a few hundred yards from their hotel and just across the road from a roundabout. Arthur and Millie stood out of sight and watched the policeman saunter up to the door, fiddle with his keys and then go in. It was easy to tell where he took up residence, as a light suddenly spewed out into a dimly lit street to the right side of the building.

Arthur and Millie waited until there was nobody around before they crossed the road together, walked past the main entrance to the station, and disappeared into the side street. Their hearts had started to pick up speed by the time they'd come to a halt beneath the lit window. They couldn't risk Millie being seen flying, so Arthur gave her a leg-up. She peered nervously through the rusty bars that chequered the window and into the room below to see the policeman fast asleep and clutching a bottle. The two key pieces were piled neatly on the desk in front of him.

Safely back on the ground Millie told her grandad what she had seen. 'He's sleeping like a baby. The key pieces are on the table.'

'Let's get back to the plains and try to recover the next piece,' said Arthur, who was rubbing his back – it had been a long time since he'd hoisted someone up with his hands and his aged bones were none too pleased. 'It will be better if we do it by night. There should be nobody, including our friendly sleeping policeman, around. Then we can find out if you have another power to add to your arsenal, which may serve us better in getting back the first two key pieces.'

Millie stuck her thumbs up.

'Whatever happens we have to get them before they find their way to the local museum. I don't know what they're forged from, but I would guess it isn't found on Earth,' said Arthur, as he led Millie back towards the hire car.

CHAPTER THIRTEEN

AURORA'S SECRET

Their journey to the plains was uneventful and, unlike the last time, it didn't involve any wrong turns! The solitary car they passed was full of youngsters, arms flailing and screaming, as they shot off in the opposite direction.

Arthur pulled off the side of the road and bounced slowly across the plains.

'Grandad, I can't see the astronaut. How do you know we're in the right place?'

'Trip meter,' he said, tapping his speedo. 'I checked it just before we left here last time and when we drew up outside the hotel.'

That was one of the reasons why she loved her grandad so much. He always seemed to think of the things she didn't – practical things.

'I want the car as close to the drawing as I can get, I've no desire to wander these plains at night any more than I have to. Besides if we're off the road then we'll attract less attention. I hope the car can take it!'

The car rocked on until the familiar shape of the astronaut's foot showed them they'd arrived. Arthur drove as close as he could and then turned the lights off, condemning them to darkness. He switched on the interior light and said, 'We'll use the torch from here, but if you hear any sound or see any lights that you don't expect then switch it off at once and don't move from where you are.'

Millie nodded, stepped from the car, and retrieved both the torch and the book from her rucksack. One was held close to her chest and the other led the way to the lines.

There was little reason to bring her rucksack, now hanging loosely off her back, but somehow she felt lost without it.

Millie retraced her earlier steps over the three lines at the foot of the slope before trudging up and down the one to the left of the astronaut. Even at night, without the sun to contend with, the air was still unbelievably hot and humid, and the walk to the top of the slope and back down again was already causing Millie to sweat buckets. Arthur waited patiently for her halfway up the hill, because Millie had instructed him to stand back in case the key piece suddenly appeared and he became affected by the curse.

Their efforts were in vain, however. Nothing unusual revealed itself to Millie's probing torchlight.

'It has to be the other one then,' said Millie, as sweat dripped steadily from her forehead.

'Yes, but the book said they must be done in order so it still could be the four you've just done, but in another order,' said Arthur, with both hands on his knees – evidently struggling with the oppressive weather.

Millie sighed deeply. 'Why can't they just be hidden in a more accessible location?' Arthur didn't need to answer the question. Millie knew they needed to be well hidden from prying eyes, human, as well as Zamorian. They were cursed against Zamorians, but so far Millie had been able to overcome that. True enough she was only part Zamorian and a full-blooded Zamorian would probably die instantly, but Aurora saw fit not to take any chances and had hidden them well. Just too well that's all!

Over half an hour ticked by. Millie trudged back and forth along the lines, trying stacks of permutations, until she finally struck gold.

Arthur could tell the latest route had unearthed something, but he could never have guessed in his wildest dreams what that something might be.

'What is it?' he shouted, from his position halfway up the slope to Millie at the summit.

Millie just stood there, moving the light from her torch back and forth towards something that was out of Arthur's line of sight.

'What is it?' he asked again. Millie remained riveted by what she saw and apparently unable to hear or speak.

Arthur climbed the slope much quicker than his body really wanted him to, but his need to find out what had struck his granddaughter dumb was far greater than his need to rest his aching limbs. He reached the summit and repeated his question. 'What is it?

This time Millie answered. 'Can't you see it, Grandad? It's magnificent.'

Since she got to the top of the slope she'd remained staring in one direction. The only trouble was when Arthur looked in the same direction he saw nothing. For a brief moment he feared she was under the control of the curse, but as he felt normal, apart from a tired body and screaming lungs, that notion was quickly cast aside.

'You can't see it, can you, Grandad?'

'See what?' he gasped.

'That,' said Millie, who was now running her torch in circles as if tracing out something in the air.

'That?' he said quizzically.

'Yes that,' said Millie. 'The spaceship.'

'THE WHAT?'

'The spaceship, Grandad. It's amazing.'

Arthur now took his turn to look dumbfounded.

'This must be what the book was talking about. The thing only Aurora knew was still here. He must have kept it from the others. It was his secret. It must have been left behind somehow when the Zamorians first explored Earth. Maybe it was broken and they had to abandon it.'

If Millie expected Arthur to say something after that explanation then she was wrong. Instead he remained agog.

'The next piece to the key has to be inside,' said Millie, who, having taken a few steps forward, now appeared to be standing underneath the ship, as her head was tilted back and her torch pointed upwards.

Finally Arthur broke back into life. 'What does it look like, Millie?' He came over and stood beside her, but for him looking up proved fruitless.

Arthur had always believed in life on other planets and thought sceptical people were just ignorant. How could they possibly be so stupid as to think that in such a vast universe our solitary planet was the only one to foster life? And now here he stood next to a spaceship that had travelled great distances and he was unable to see it! How unfair was that?

'It's completely round, Grandad. It looks as though there are lots of places for things to pop out from, though. Do you think we can fly it?' said Millie, who was now jumping up and down at the prospect.

'Maybe we should take one thing at a time, don't you think? For a start, we don't know if it still works and then there's the small matter of having to retrieve the key piece first. If, of course, it's actually in there.' Nobody was keener to give the ship a blast than Arthur, but first things first.

'You think it might not be in there, Grandad? Maybe you're right and we have to fly off to another planet to find it!'

Millie grew more excited by the minute.

'What did I just say about taking one thing at a time?' Arthur laid a calming hand on his granddaughter's shoulder, which appeared to do the trick, because she immediately stopped jumping around.

Millie continued to inspect the ship with her torch. 'Can't see a way in.'

'How big is it?'

'Not that big. Maybe twenty, thirty feet around.'

'Maybe it's not a ship we can get in to. The book said the original Zamorian exploration was carried out by probes, didn't it?' Arthur enquired.

Even though he couldn't see anything he still felt compelled to look up to where Millie was shining her torch.

'I'm sure they said ships too.'

'Come to think of it you're right, Millie. This must have been part of a manned flight, because it would appear we're standing on the head of an astronaut who took part in the mission. His ship – this ship maybe – must have broken down, forcing him to hitch a ride with another one, but the locals must have spotted him in the process. Hence the drawing,' said Arthur, now itching to get inside.

Millie walked a few more paces to get a look from another angle.

'How far away from us is it?'

'It's about ten feet above our heads, just hovering,' said Millie, still keenly looking for a way in.

'The first manned flights here were thousands of years ago. How come they never sent anyone back to retrieve it, I wonder?'

'Maybe they did, Grandad and the mission failed somehow. We may never find out why, but I'm just glad it's here, that's all.'

Arthur plonked himself down to rest his weary feet and contemplated what his peers might say back at the museum if he pulled up in a spaceship! 'Yes, Gerald, you may have discovered an ancient dinosaur fossil to go with all the others, but come outside because I want to show you what *I've* found,' he chuckled to himself. 'Oh, and did I mention that the dodo is still alive?' More chuckles.

He was broken out of his little dream world by Millie asking, 'Who are you talking to?' Her torch lit up his face and he shielded his eyes.

'Just rambling Millie. Just rambling. After what we've been through recently I'm entitled to the odd ramble!' His weary expression still contained traces of a grin.

'I've looked all around. Of course I can't see the top, but from what I can see there's no obvious way in,' said Millie, dropping herself down beside her grandad.

'Try the book,' said Arthur.

Millie squeezed the book tightly. 'I need the door open,' she whispered. If it had obeyed her instruction and opened a door it wasn't one on the ship above.

'Right now there could be someone in Nazca wondering how their front door had sprung open!' said Arthur, still apparently in grinning mode.

Millie laid a few more requests on the book, but each of them failed in turn.

'You'd better get up there and have a closer look then, my girl, and see if you can find a way in.'

This was exactly what Millie wanted to hear. She was going to suggest it, but after her lecture about errant air travel earlier in the day she was hoping her grandad would come up with the idea first.

'You can go up, but do NOT, on any account, enter,' he warned.

'OK!'

'I mean it, Millie. We don't know what we're contending with here. We have no idea what might be lurking inside that ship.'

'OK! OK!'

Millie checked the horizon for activity, but nothing was in sight. 'Hold this please,' she said, as she passed her rucksack to her grandad and clutched the book to her chest. 'I want to fly,' she whispered, and pushed off. The motion of pushing off took her a few feet from the ground where she hung unceremoniously until she remembered her lesson in the toilet. She needed to raise her arms, but was it one or two and how fast would she go? She slowly drifted back to the ground.

'Is that it?' said Arthur, most disappointed by what he saw. 'That's not flying, that's meandering!'

Millie didn't rise to the comment. Instead she whispered, 'I want to fly,' to the book and dropped it in her grandad's lap. This time she flung both arms in the air and was propelled upwards at great speed.

Arthur tried to track her with the torch, but lost sight when she veered violently off in one direction. He could hear her screams of joy breaking up the night sky, but apart from that his eyes were blinded by darkness.

A minute or so later her feet appeared in mid-air before him, swiftly followed by the rest of her body as she made a graceful and soft landing. Her face was a sight to behold. She had the biggest grin you could ever imagine that wavered only slightly when she discovered that her forehead was party to an insect windscreen moment. Arthur peeled the bug off and asked, 'Well?'

In her excitement at finally being able to fly freely she'd actually forgotten what she went up for. 'I'm right on it,' she said, taking the book from Arthur, issuing another flying request, and passing it back to him.

Before he had time to say another word she was off again. This time she drifted gently up towards the ship with her arms not directly above her head as before.

Her hand placed on the ship's hull turned out to be all that was required. Millie watched as the ship lowered itself down towards the ground and a doorway appeared near to where she was hovering. 'OUT OF THE WAY, GRANDAD!' she yelled, as it continued its descent – remembering just in time that he couldn't see it coming.

Arthur felt a tad silly leaping aside to avoid something he couldn't see, but he was keen to get inside an alien spaceship and not be the first human to be crushed by one!

Millie stayed airborne. 'Look, Grandad. Over there.' She was pointing far out across the plains to a set of headlights that were bounding towards them.

'Come back down here now,' said Arthur urgently, quickly extinguishing the torch.

This time Millie landed with a thump and fell to her knees. 'I must practise that a bit more,' she said, leaping to her feet and brushing dust off her legs.

'If we saw them, then the chances are they saw our torch,' said Arthur, who was still nervously staring towards the fast-approaching lights.

'Damn!' he muttered to himself, 'I should have been more alert.'

'What are we going to do? By the time we get to the bottom of the slope they'll be on us. Apart from the ship, we've nowhere to hide,' said Millie, knowing they had little choice, but to climb aboard.

'How, oh how, do we get ourselves into such fixes?' groaned Arthur wearily.

Millie scooped up her belongings and said, 'Let's go inside, Grandad. If *you* can't see the ship then they'll not be able to either.' She took hold of his hand and guided him forward into the entrance. It was almost more than he could take, because once he stepped inside he could see everything Millie could and it was an amazing sight.

The ship was crammed full of a wondrous collection of instrumentation. Several seats stood about ten feet away from their position, all facing away from them, and in front of the seats was a huge panel laden with a vast array of lights and controls.

Even though the image was slightly blurry, it was still easy to see through the hull to the outside. The ship appeared to be completely transparent. The only place where the blur was not in evidence was the doorway they'd just stepped through.

'Don't go in any further, Millie, in case you activate the curse. Let's just wait for whoever this is to go and we'll take it from there.'

'OK, but we have to close the door because they might be able to see us if it's open,' said Millie, placing her hand on the inside of the hull hoping that would do the trick. It didn't. Nor did her limp request that followed. 'Door close,' she said hopefully.

Arthur stood with his eyes fixed on the base of the slope where the approaching vehicle had stopped. The sound of two doors slamming shut prompted him to say, 'You have to try something else, Millie. This ship doesn't understand English. You're going to have to think Zamorian, and quickly because I can see torchlights coming up the slope towards us.'

The footsteps drew nearer and Millie's thoughts became more and more jumbled. How was she supposed to think Zamorian? How should she know how a Zamorian thinks?

She had no choice but to try and find out because she reasoned that being part Zamorian she would possibly be shielded by the ship's invisibility, but she felt for sure that her grandad would be spotted – through the open doorway – hovering just above the ground.

She closed her eyes and concentrated really hard, squeezing the book for inspiration.

'How did you do that?' whispered Arthur.

Millie opened her eyes to see her grandad patting the closed door. Now the whole ship had the same blurred view. She didn't know how she did it. All she knew was that she found the right word from somewhere. The door was closed and that was all that mattered. Millie didn't answer her grandad. Instead she just closed her eyes and concentrated some more.

Arthur tottered backwards a little as the ship gently responded to Millie's command to rise upward ten feet. She did this to stop the approaching people from bumping into the side of an invisible ship. She wasn't sure if being invisible meant that people would just ghost through it, but she didn't want to take the chance. The only problem was that the move caused Arthur to bump into Millie, who in turn staggered backwards and into the range of the curse.

The ship lurched forward and the door sprang open. Millie was just able to grab hold, but Arthur was not so fortunate and he tumbled out to the ground below, slamming into it with a tremendous thud. Millie felt a sudden pain come and go as something knocked past her, and watched helplessly as the next piece of the Key to Chintak, the book, and her rucksack, spilled out of the open door landing directly beside her motionless grandad, stretched out on the ground below. The door closed as quickly as it opened and Millie stood watching the events unfold below.

She racked her brains to try to think of a plan, but before she could come up with one things took a turn for the worse.

The two guys with the torches were looking down the

slope when Arthur, and everything else that was so precious to Millie, fell out of the sky, but they soon turned around when they heard the noise and it was then that Millie got a good look at their faces.

It was Diego and Miguel, and they raced up to investigate the noise as Arthur suddenly sprung to his feet clutching the cursed key piece and pointing frantically towards the sky. Diego shone his torch up in the air, but like all non-Zamorians before him, he couldn't see the ship that was now hovering above his head.

'What have you there?' enquired Miguel, anxious to relieve Arthur of his treasure. He too, like Diego and Arthur, was now consumed by the power of the curse, and all three of them were sporting a demented look in their eyes. The curse must have been strong, because Arthur did not appear to notice that his left arm was broken and hanging limply by his side.

'IT'S MINE,' hissed Arthur, who lunged forward and smacked Miguel straight in the face, knocking him clean off his feet.

Diego pulled a gun out of his pocket just as Arthur was charging him down.

BANG! BANG!

The sound of the gunfire echoed far out across the Nazca Plains – unlike Millie's heartfelt cry of, 'NOOOOOOOOOOOOOO!' that remained within the confines of the ship.

She sank to her knees at the same time as her grandad. Only she didn't drop down dead.

He did.

CHAPTER FOURTEEN

MIND POWER

Millie watched in horror, tears streaming down her face. She felt incapable of doing anything except crying. Her only living relative was dead and it was all her fault. All her stupid fault. The whole adventure smelt of danger, but in her heart of hearts she truly believed they would come through it together. Bashed and bruised maybe, but not dead. Never dead.

How could it possibly happen? Surely the book should have done something to help? Now Millie came to think about it, the book was often missing when she needed it most. It was washed away in Australia and now in Peru it lay worthlessly beside the dead body of her beloved grandad – a true gentleman who had a heart laced with gold and had always put Millie before himself. How could the children of Zamora allow such a thing to happen?

Millie watched, paralysed by guilt, as Diego revived Miguel and they both set about collecting up the belongings beside Arthur's body. Only when their car sparked into life did Millie start to compose herself.

'OF COURSE!' she said at the top of her voice. 'Why didn't I think of that earlier?' She rose to her feet and took a good look at her surroundings and closed her eyes.

'Door open,' she said. Out loud Millie spoke English, but in her head she was speaking telepathically to the ship in Zamorian. Somewhere buried in the depths of her body was a whole other language and when she concentrated hard enough she could see it spread out before her mind's eye as clear as day.

The door slid open and Millie barked, 'Down to ground level.' Again the ship duly obliged, coming to rest beside her motionless grandad. She stepped out of the ship and confirmed her worst fears when she felt Arthur's wrist for a pulse. 'It's OK, Grandad. Everything is going to be all right,' she said, stroking his hair and valiantly trying to fight back yet more tears. 'I promise.'

Millie found the strength, from somewhere deep inside herself, to drag Arthur's body onto the ship. She needed him near her. It was the only way her plan would work.

Meanwhile Diego and Miguel were haring across the plains towards town, their actions controlled by the cursed key piece.

'Door close.'

'Hang on, I must have been doing this all along,' she said to herself, suddenly realising she was speaking in English, but thinking telepathically in Zamorian.

She hurried to the front of the ship and looked at the writing on the instrumentation panel. 'Speed, distance, fuel, autopilot,' she recited out loud, and there were more, lots more. In fact she could read everything around her. Some words just didn't translate, but that was the whole point. Millie could read Zamorian all along. The words in the book were *not* written in English. Nor were the ones on the walls of the caves in Australia. Somehow she automatically translated Zamorian to English.

Any lingering thoughts she might have had about her true Zamorian roots were dispelled there and then. She was part Zamorian all right. Although that might not give her an edge over a fully-grown adult Belendrian, it sure did over pond life like Diego and Miguel. Now they were about to find out what happens if you mess with a part Zamorian and part feisty human child.

'I can open and close doors and drift up and down, but how the blazes do you fly this thing properly?' she asked herself. Millie thought she'd made the enquiry in English alone, but it seemed that anything she said in the ship worked in two languages automatically. One out loud and one in her head. Her request on how to fly was answered immediately.

'Autopilot on,' said a voice, and Millie watched in amazement as a holographic image of a Zamorian pilot appeared in one of the seats next to the main console. The pilot sat motionless with his back to Millie, who in turn was a little freaked out by being able to see right through his head to the lights beyond.

She walked up beside the pilot, who looked at her and said, 'You fly this ship with your mind. Once you have mastered the speed and distance rules you will find it very easy to navigate. Listen to my mind and you will learn. I listened to your mind and learnt this language. I thought it would make you happy to converse in it, but you must instruct the ship in Zamorian. Where to?'

If Millie had more time she would have used it to ask countless questions, but the sight of her grandad's lifeless body on the ship's floor dictated otherwise. She didn't know how much time she had, if it wasn't already too late.

'There,' said Millie, pointing to the only road below, 'follow that road.'

'Sit down, please,' said the autopilot.

Millie quickly took her seat and the ship sprang into life. The outer skin seemed to be rotating at unimaginable speed and could turn in any direction, but the inner shell remained motionless. It almost felt as if she was on a multi-directional hamster wheel!

'No! No outside lights,' Millie hollered.

'As instructed,' said the autopilot.

It was then that Millie realised that no lights had actually come on. She'd picked the thought out of the pilot's mind that he was about to switch them on and stopped him.

Millie was learning fast.

'Lights no problem. This planet sparsely populated. Locals have no means of powered light,' said the autopilot.

'Things have moved on a little since you were last fired up. This area has a lot more people now, the whole planet does, and we've mastered the powered light thing as well,' said Millie knowingly.

'Speed?'

'Show me the speeds,' was Millie's response. The speed range was something that didn't translate too well. The Zamorian numbers that Millie could read flashing across the pilot's mind seemed to go up to millions. Surely that couldn't be right?

'Seventy,' Millie said, and the ship pulled away at a gentle speed. 'Faster,' she commanded.

'As instructed. Tell me when to hold speed.'

Millie sat back as the numbers started to rack up in the pilot's mind and in what was no more than a few seconds they were hurtling up behind the only car on the road.

'Hold speed,' said Millie.

'Cruise control on,' responded the autopilot.

'Cruise control off,' said Millie, as the ship overshot the car. 'STOP!' she cried, now looking backwards as the car became a distant pinprick on the horizon. 'STOP! WHY DON'T YOU STOP?' she howled, turning back to face the empty seat where the autopilot once sat.

'THIS CAN'T BE HAPPENING,' she screamed to herself. The car headlights had now disappeared completely from view. 'Compose yourself Millie, you can do it,' she said out loud, 'we're probably going too fast to just stop.'

She closed her eyes. 'Slow to half speed,' she said, and the ship obliged. It also followed her instructions to slow more, turn, and speed up again. Within the bat of an eyelid she was hovering along directly above Diego and Miguel's car, travelling at exactly the same speed, but careful not to get too close, because she didn't want the ship to be affected by the curse again.

Some time back she had posed a question to herself about the ship being able to ghost through things because it was invisible. That question was answered when she flew through the top of a tree scattering leaves everywhere and frightening the life out of its resident bird population. Without the lights on it was difficult to see far ahead, but fortunately the full moon, which hung majestically in the night sky, provided some useful background light.

The car she was tailing eventually came to a halt outside a house on the outskirts of Nazca and one of its two occupants bailed out and went inside.

'Reference point,' Millie said to the ship. Her handful of minutes on cruise control afforded her a little time to investigate more of the flight controls and she took Reference Point to mean just that. It was either learn more about the ship or dwell on the fate of its other human inhabitant.

The car pulled away, but stopped after another twenty feet or so where it sat for a short while and then pulled off again. She continued after it and watched as it wound its way through the town and drew to a halt outside an official-looking building just opposite a roundabout, the police station that she and Arthur had visited earlier.

Unlike the movies she couldn't find any reference on the ship to a 'Transporter' of any kind. She would have just loved to beam into the police station, grab her belongings and then beam out again. On second thoughts the cursed key piece would no doubt have caused havoc to the system and beamed her to somewhere like the bottom of the sea, so it was probably best no such system existed.

Other gadgets abounded though, including a most useful voice amplifier that was built into the ship and with a little tweaking Millie was listening to the goings-on inside the station.

'Hola!' said the policeman to the car driver.

A heated conversation started between the station's only two occupants, none of which Millie could understand because it was in Spanish.

'Translate to English,' she said, but still the conversation flowed in Spanish. She pulled her mini Spanish-to-English dictionary out of a pocket in her shorts and held it in mid-air. 'Here.'

The pages of the book were suddenly riffled.

She hoped the dictionary would come in handy, but never imagined when she bought it from the hotel shop in Nazca how useful it would turn out to be.

'WHAT DO YOU MEAN YOU DON'T REMEMBER?' blasted a voice over the speakers. It was the policeman's voice, and it was now in English.

Millie was beginning to like this ship more and more.

'I remember phoning you. You promised to make yourself scarce for us tonight, and I remember being out near the astronaut and seeing a torchlight,' said the car driver hurriedly.

'Diego, I was here all along as I told you I would be,' said the policeman.

The mere mention of Diego's name made Millie's blood boil. She knew when he killed Arthur he was under the control of the curse, but what was he doing with a gun in the first place?

She was going to make him pay.

Oh *yes*, she was going to make him pay.

'Yes, yes, but the next thing I remember is calling you five minutes ago,' said Diego haphazardly.

'Where were you when you called me?'

'Near Miguel's.'

'And what does he have to say about things?'

'I don't remember.'

'You don't remember or you are keeping something back from me? Need I remind you, Diego, that if I ever find out you are holding back on giving me my share of anything you sell then you'll be behind bars before you know it.' The policeman's voice was now calm, but it had a definite menacing air about it.

'I'm not holding back, I promise.'

'YOU promise … huh! Let's go to Miguel's and get his side of the story, shall we?' said the policeman.

'If Diego can't remember then he must be free of the curse, which means that Miguel has the cursed key piece,' said Millie quietly to herself. 'I'd better get there before them. The less people around when I tackle the curse the better.'

The ship did as commanded and flashed back to the Reference Point above Miguel's house. She brought it down to roof level and opened the door.

'Leaving?' said a voice from behind, which turned out to be the missing autopilot.

'Where did you disappear to?' said Millie, stepping back into the ship.

'Ship malfunctions. Ship needs repair. Awaiting repair,' the autopilot replied. 'My Holographic Replicator needs repair as well.'

'Your what?'

'Holographic Replicator. It is what drives me. It reflects an image of my inventor.'

'Can anyone use one?' said Millie, hatching a plan as she spoke.

'Of course. Would you like to try? There is one by the door. Feel it for instru—' the autopilot vanished again, this time in mid-sentence.

'He must mean instructions,' said Millie to herself, as she unclipped the small object the autopilot had directed her towards. Once in her hand the instructions on how to use it flowed through her and she left the ship with a smile, closing the door behind.

The instructions told how a person could be replicated in various shades of realness. The pilot was created in transparent mode so that anyone else on board would get a clear view of the instrument panel from anywhere on the ship. However it was possible to create an image of something, or someone, that looked and felt just like the original. Just what Millie wanted.

She clipped it to her shorts and turned it on.

Gazing at herself in the flesh caused Millie to stand open-mouthed until her double said, 'And what do you think you're looking at?' and promptly crossed its arms and shuffled its feet.

'Amazing,' said Millie, now inspecting herself from behind and making a mental note to get her hair sorted at the back.

'What's amazing is that we're standing here when we have very important work to do. So if you're finished inspecting,' said her twin, who'd obviously inherited not only her looks, but her lack of patience as well.

'*Well*, excuse me.'

'*Well*, that means I have to excuse myself then!'

'Hmmm … this could get complicated … OK … Follow me,' said Millie to herself, and Millie number two wandered side by side with her creator through the roof stairwell door and then quietly down the stairs to the first floor hallway.

They could hear somebody frantically pacing up and down in the room below. Millie angled herself so she could see what was going on in a mirror that hung on the downstairs hall wall. Miguel, who was talking frantically on the phone with his hands flailing wildly, was alone in the house and the key piece was sitting on a table not far from him.

'OK, you being me you know what I'm after. I'm going to go down, knock on the door and get Miguel out into the street. As soon as I do that you run down the stairs and shut the door, grab the key piece, and read the inscription. Do you understand?' whispered the real Millie.

'Of course I understand. I'm you, aren't I?'

Millie made another mental note to stop being so smart! 'I'll meet you back by the ship.'

'OK!'

'Good luck,' said Millie to her fake self, before making her way quietly back upstairs to the roof.

Although she was rather pleased with her plan, she did feel a little guilty sending someone else to do her job. Mind you that someone else was technically her and any plan that involved the real Millie not suffering agonising pain was fine by her. After all, nobody could deny that she'd suffered enough for a while and was due a break.

Millie didn't want to be spotted flying so she descended a fire escape at the back of the house and crept around to the front door.

KNOCK! KNOCK! She rattled the door loudly and Miguel flung it open. If she was hoping to avoid the pain of the curse completely then she was out of luck. She grabbed a startled Miguel and fell back with him into the street. Immediately the door slammed shut, and the pain vanished. Miguel, now free of the curse, stood up and stumbled off down the street in a daze.

Millie peered through an open window at the front. The second Millie was not there and neither was the key piece. 'Excellent,' she said, 'that solves my problem for the next two pieces.'

She ran back up the fire escape and saw her double patiently standing by the ship.

'What took you so long?' said the double. Millie was now beginning to tire of her own self and looked forward to shutting her down for a while.

A car screeched to a halt outside and a heated debate ensued when its two occupants, the policeman and Diego, came face to face with a dazed and confused Miguel.

Millie stepped towards the ship, but as she did so she felt her body twinge with pain. Another step brought still more pain, but how could that be if the curse had been lifted?

'Interesting object wouldn't you say,' said fake Millie, holding her hand out to display a gently glowing key piece. 'Shame you're not going to live to appreciate it,' she continued.

The pain Millie now felt as her double strode purposely towards her was undeniable proof that her plan was falling to bits before her eyes. The irony was that Millie number two appeared to be suffering no pain at all, safely cocooned from it by the curse that was driving her on.

If that wasn't enough, Millie could hear the front door slamming shut and footsteps coming up the stairs behind her.

Fake Millie jumped at her creator, grabbing her round the neck with her spare hand. Millie tried vainly to wrestle her loose, but was overcome by the pain that engulfed her entire body. She felt herself stumbling backwards towards the roof edge and grabbed her attacker's arm for support, but it was too late. They were both about to go over the side.

Millie's other hand knocked something on her belt, the Holographic Replicator, and she scrambled to turn it off. As soon as she'd done so fake Millie just vanished and the key piece fell into her outstretched hand, '*my mind often wanders to lazy summer days*,' she yelled as she fell backwards off the roof.

The curse was lifted, but she was falling fast. 'I NEED TO FLY,' she screamed, and threw both hands in the air. She stopped inches short of the ground and shot back up to the roof and landed a few feet away from the policeman, Diego and Miguel. The sight of a young girl flying up to his rooftop was too much for Miguel to bear and he fainted.

Millie stood looking at them and they stood looking at her. It was time for her to get some revenge and teach them all a lesson.

'You have stolen from the gods and we have been sent down to retrieve what's ours,' she said huskily.

'You make magic. Me think trick you appear?' said the policeman, now over his shock of seeing Millie arrive in style and convinced some sort of trickery was at work.

'Who is we?' ventured Diego, slowly summoning back his courage.

'THIS IS WE,' shouted Millie, pointing with one hand to distract them away from what she was doing with the other, which was pressing the Holographic Replicator many times. Seven times to be precise, because that's how many Millies appeared next to her on the rooftop.

Grandad would have nightmares, faced with eight Millies, she thought to herself.

Thinking of her grandad was enough to concentrate her mind on the task in hand.

Miguel, who'd just regained consciousness, again crumpled to the floor at the sight of the gaggle of Millies. The other two just froze, with absolute fear running rampant through their faces.

'If any of you venture anywhere near the Nazca Lines for anything other than, she looked directly into the policeman's eyes, 'law and order,' and then deep into Diego's, 'to admire the view ... then you'll feel our true wrath come down upon you.' She couldn't speak for the other seven, but Millie was beginning to enjoy this.

'DO I MAKE MYSELF UNDERSTOOD?' she bellowed at them.

They were frightened all right, but it was clear they didn't comprehend all that she said, because it was in English. 'Translation,' Millie whispered in English, and thought in Zamorian.

Instantly an exact translation into Spanish of all she had just said came from the ship. A foreign voice plucked out of mid-air was the icing on the cake. Both of the Spanish-speakers had now got the message. Their faces were a picture of horror. To compound their terror still further the ship also translated everything she said to them afterwards.

'Si, si, yes, yes,' they both quivered.

'Now,' she said, as she paced over to the policeman, 'I believe you have something that's ours?'

'Er ...' he mumbled forgetfully, but the sight of the other seven Millies moving forward soon refreshed his memory. 'Oh yes, these,' he said, gasping for breath and reaching nervously into his pocket to retrieve the two key pieces he'd taken from her when they first met.

Millie revelled in drawing out the drama of the moment, taking ages to pluck them from his quaking hand, all the time fixing him with a forbidding glare. She'd practiced the glare on her friend Ted when he got her to eat his sandwich spread filled chocolate delight, but *this* was much more fun.

She turned to Diego, 'My bag and book, if you will.'

'Down,' he said pitifully, pointing to indicate it was downstairs in the house.

'GET IT THEN!' she ordered loudly, and motioned some Millies to follow him.

Fear certainly carries you much faster than any other emotion, because Diego and the Millies returned in moments. During their time away Millie just stood and stared at the policeman, clicking away on the Holographic Replicator for fun, scattering yet more Millies around the rooftop.

She took the rucksack and book from Diego and announced theatrically, 'Now be gone and remember *we* are watching your every move.' These were the last words she said to them and the last words to be boomed out in Spanish from the ship.

They didn't need to be told again. Each of them grabbed an arm of Miguel's and unceremoniously bumping him face first down the stairs.

'Thanks!' said Millie to the other Millies.

'You're welcome!' they replied in unison. 'Most welcome.'

Millie didn't wait to see if they'd anything else to say, powering them all off before they had a chance, because she'd much more important business to attend to.

'Door open,' she said to the ship.

'Millie, there you are, I've been so worried!' Her grandad's voice rang out and it was music to her ears. She'd hoped and prayed the book wouldn't let her down and it hadn't. The curse was the cause of his death, and as the book said, counter the curse and everything it perpetrated would be undone.

'Grandad,' she yelped, running over and unleashing the type of bear-hug that was commonplace when she was little. This continent had made her keep a number of mental notes and she added another – extra bear hugs required!

'I guess more went on than I realise,' said Arthur, somewhat taken aback by Millie's show of emotion.

Millie let go and led him further into the ship, closing the door behind her, 'I have a lot to tell you. An awful lot.'

CHAPTER FIFTEEN

EUROPE

The next piece is buried on the highest peak of the British hunting grounds on the tip of southern Spain. Use your Nazca discovery to get you there. Be careful to monitor the amount of Ref ...

'Ref?' said Arthur curiously.

'This book has been scribbled in! I can't make out the rest of the clue,' Millie proclaimed. She flicked through a few pages and then back to the one she was reading from. 'Look!' she said holding it open for Arthur to see. 'I was going to say something about it before, but I was hoping I could still read the clue,' she said crossly.

Arthur inspected the page closely and the few either side. His face was screwed up exposing a mass of wrinkles as he pored intently over the scribble that was strewn across several pages. For the first time he could actually see something in the book – unlike Millie who was of course, a whizz at reading invisible Zamorian writing. The only trouble was he couldn't make out many of the words.

The ones he could read led him to declare, 'Spanish!'

'Yes I know,' said Millie, 'the tip of southern Spain. I just said that to you.'

She sat up, a little more attentively. 'Hold on, are you saying you can read the Zamorian text now?' Her voice was laced with just the merest hint of self-pity. She wouldn't begrudge her grandad the ability to read Zamorian, but she felt special being the only one able to do so.

Arthur sensed this, but his answer soon calmed her fears. 'Don't worry, Zamorian will always be your speciality.' Millie wriggled shyly in her seat. 'What I'm talking about is the other, appallingly messy, writing on these few pages,' he said, flicking through the pages in question. 'As far as I can make out the words are Spanish. My foreign language skills aren't good, and whoever wrote this text appears to have done so blindfolded!' Arthur now had Millie's Spanish phrase book open. 'It looks as if someone took notes about the astronaut in Nazca.'

'Miguel. It must have been Miguel. I clipped a pen inside the book when the policeman gave it back to me to make it look as if I was going to draw or write in it. Miguel must have written those notes when Diego was driving him back to his house.'

'Makes sense,' said Arthur.

'The idiot. The absolute idiot,' whined Millie, still shaking her head. 'I knew I should have left half a dozen Millies there to ruin his life!'

'*Nobody* deserves that much punishment!'

Millie looked up at her grandad's smiling face and couldn't help but join him in the act.

'Seriously Millie, what's done is done and we just have to move on. We know where the key piece is; we just have to be careful, that's all. I mean, even more careful!'

Millie nodded, 'I just had a thought.'

'What?'

'If you or anyone else gets possessed by a key curse in the future I'll just shoot the lot of you! You're all going to come back anyway.' Millie grinned devilishly.

'Charming!' said Arthur.

'I'll just shoot *you* in the leg, Grandad!'

'Well, that makes it better then,' he said. 'Actually I have a question. Everyone, including your supposed doubles, becomes evil when they're possessed by the curse—'

'And only I feel pain?' interrupted Millie, finishing the question for him. 'I have thought about that too.'

'And?'

'And I don't know! It must be that I'm neither full human nor full Zamorian. The former goes mad, or extra mad in your case, and the latter drops down dead.'

'Holographic doubles of you also turn bad,' Arthur chipped in.

'You can say that again, Grandad, but I have to say that being possessed by the curse seems a lot less painful than the alternative!'

'I guess so – from what you've told me about the pain.'

'It seems, though, that I have to trigger the curse first. Otherwise, if you think about it, everyone around a key piece would be demented already. If you find one first, like you planned to before, then you have to make sure I'm nowhere near it.'

'Easier said than done, I think, but we can always hope.'

'As we're on the subject, I would like to know why Aurora didn't just kill the other Belendrians with a curse. If he could curse the key pieces then why not them?' The question had obviously been preying on Millie's mind for some time.

Arthur shook his head. 'I don't know, Millie. Maybe they were never all together at once and he was afraid to pick them off one at a time. The others must have been more powerful and he was just too scared to take them on.'

'That must be it, I suppose,' said Millie.

'Now I've another one for you,' said Arthur. 'Why didn't

they give us this ship to start with? It would have made life much easier.'

Millie nodded in agreement. Slowly at first, and then at more speed once the question had properly settled in her head. 'Good question. There must be an answer, but I sure don't know what it is!'

'We should, I guess, be grateful we have it at all,' said Arthur, who was now off exploring the ship, careful not to touch anything.

Millie watched him scour every surface with his eyes and said, 'It's OK, Grandad, you can touch things. You aren't going to evaporate. He took her advice and cautiously prodded something hanging from one of the walls. 'Except *do not* touch anything on the walls!' she said, pretending not to notice what he was doing.

Arthur yanked his hand quickly away and looked at it closely, presumably to ensure he still had all his fingers! Only when he saw Millie suppressing a great urge to laugh out loud did he realise she was playing with him. 'Ha, ha, very funny,' he said.

Millie came over to inspect the gadget her grandad was so intrigued by.

'What is it?' enquired Arthur, nervously peering over her shoulder for a better look.

Millie unclicked it from its position and rotated it in her hand. It was black, pen-like in shape, and had a small switch on the side. Millie clicked the switch and a Zamorian word appeared on the device. Four clicks displayed four different words. On the fifth click she was back at the first word again. 'I see,' said Millie, 'if I select one and hold the button down then … BLIMEY!'

'What?' said Arthur, springing back away from Millie, 'are you OK?'

'Yes I'm fine, but this thing is unreal,' she replied excitedly, all the time looking around the floor of the ship, 'just unreal.'

'Why what does it do?' said Arthur eagerly.

'It's a Sense Enhancer,' said Millie matter-of-factly. 'It accelerates a chosen sense many times. I've just picked *Sight* and I can see at least ten times further than before. Everything is so much bigger.'

'Can I have a go?' asked Arthur, hand outstretched.

'Of course, here you are,' and Millie passed it to him. 'Oh!' she said as she let go of it.

'What is it?' said Arthur, wondering if he should just put it down or not.

'My sight is back to normal. Must only work if it's in your possession.'

Arthur was pleased with that explanation and proceeded to click away merrily on the switch. 'You need to pick one then hold the button down,' said Millie, 'just pick any one and see what happens.'

'Nothing,' said Arthur downheartedly. Millie looked at the Zamorian word. She reached into a small pocket at the front of her shorts and retrieved a wrapped toffee.

'Try this,' she said, shaking it in front of him. 'Go on, try it,' and unwrapped it and stuck it in his mouth.

'WOW!' he said, 'that's amazing!'

'Taste,' said Millie, 'you chose taste.'

They each played with it a little more before Arthur said, 'Zamorians must have only four senses. Smell is not here.'

'Must have. If you think about the picture of the astronaut, it has no nose,' said Millie.

Arthur took a seat at the control panel. 'Where's the autopilot you told me about? We could look at him and check out his features.'

'I never thought of that, Grandad. However, I think he's on the blink. He said the ship needs repairs.'

'That must be why it was stranded here then. Try and summon him anyway,' said Arthur, bouncing on the seat like a little boy about to open a big present.

'Autopilot on,' said Millie hopefully, but as she expected he didn't make an appearance. 'It's a shame, but you may not get to meet I'm afraid. It doesn't matter, though, because I know how to fly this thing,' she said, before murmuring quietly, 'at least I'm pretty sure I do.'

It may have pleased Millie that she could now add spaceship flying to her ever-growing list of skills, but Arthur felt deflated at not seeing a Zamorian for the first time and he did a poor job of hiding his disappointment.

'I'll try again later, Grandad. Maybe he's having his lunch,' said Millie cheerfully, detecting her grandad's mood and attempting to lighten it. It worked and a smile gradually crawled its way across his face.

'On to more important matters. *If* you know how to fly this thing then we had better get going,' said Arthur, pointing to the controls.

Millie sat down next to him. She didn't need to because, thanks to her telepathic skills, she didn't have to touch the controls, but it somehow felt right to be sitting at the helm – as she was the captain! 'Where to?' she enquired of her co-pilot and navigator.

'First the hotel to pick up our things, and then on to … Gibraltar,' replied Arthur thoughtfully. 'The book must be talking about Gibraltar,' he said, reassuring himself.

'Hunting grounds?' questioned Millie. 'Gibraltar is not a British hunting ground?'

'Of course not now, but it used to be, or at least the area surrounding it used to be, when it was first ceded to them as part of the War of the Spanish Succession.

'The what?'

'The War of the Spanish Succession happened when Britain joined up with a few other European countries in the early seventeen hundreds to fight against Spain and France. You see they were worried about France becoming too powerful in Europe and Britain fought to stop that happening,' said Arthur, happy to be back on familiar ground.

'Yes, but if they were scared of France then what had Spain got to do with it?' said Millie, almost afraid to ask.

'I thought you would ask that. They got involved because when the King of Spain died around the turn of the eighteenth century he had no natural heir to the throne, so he left the crown to a French Prince.'

'Why would he do such a thing?'

'I don't know,' said Arthur, scratching his head.

In a way Millie was happy to hear him say that. It was great having a walking encyclopaedia for a grandad, but it was reassuring to hear, every once in a while, that he didn't know everything!

'But what I do know is soon after the crown was handed over the Prince's father took it upon himself to declare Spain part of France. They would be united—'

'There was a lot of fighting, the French guy never got the crown in Spain, but we got Gibraltar,' said Millie hurrying him along.

'Not exactly.'

'Oh!'

'We got Gibraltar yes, and incidentally Newfoundland, Nova Scotia and a few other bits and pieces, as part of the treaty of Utrecht, but the French guy, as you so eloquently put it, *was* eventually crowned King of Spain.'

Millie shook her head and started playing with her feet. 'OK, stop. I've lost the plot. Didn't you say Britain went to war to stop that happening, and I'm assuming we won, as we got a handful of countries?'

'I'll keep it short,' said Arthur impatiently.

'Please.'

'We won yes, but the French Prince was crowned King of Spain because the only other alternative, an Austrian I think, turned out to be a worse option. As part of the deal France also agreed that they would never be united with Spain.'

'How do you know all this?' asked Millie, clearly impressed by his depth of knowledge.

'I read a lot,' Arthur replied coyly. 'Have you got any more toffees?'

'Nope, but I have an idea,' said Millie tapping her stomach.

Arthur sat dumbstruck as she commanded the ship to start the journey to Europe. She repeated her Zamorian thought commands out loud in English so he could hear what she was up to. His face was a picture of delight as they zoomed along, although he did have to berate her when she decided to fly low over some unsuspecting animals that were happily grazing away, until a great whoosh of air sent them scattering in all directions!

In no time at all they'd left South America and were following the Florida coastline up to a place Millie always wanted to visit.

'Disney!' she yelled excitedly, pulling the ship to a swift stop over the Magic Kingdom. 'Do you have any dollars on you?'

'None!' said Arthur, peering below him at the heaving crowds.

'I know we haven't got time to spend here now, but I

want to buy something quickly,' said Millie eagerly.

'What?'

'It's a surprise,' she replied, setting the ship down in an out of bounds area behind one of the rides. 'Stay here, I'll be back in a flash.' Before Arthur could say anything Millie had quickly scuttled out of the door and closed it behind her. He jumped to his feet when the ship started rising, but calmed down when he surmised it was Millie sending it upwards in case someone accidentally bumped into it at ground level!

Millie slipped unnoticed through a gate marked Staff Only and into the thronging crowd. The sight of so many people, all happy and carefree, made her yearn a little to return to normality and be a regular kid again.

She purposely landed near a place to change money and quickly swapped hers for dollars. Correct money in hand, she took her place in the queue for what she really came down to get.

'I WANT ONE OF THESE TOO!' bawled a huge circle of fat with podgy little arms and legs.

'Duncan, you can't eat everything. You just had a great big turkey leg *and* a hot dog,' said his equally rotund mother.

'I WANT ONE AND I AM GOING TO HAVE ONE!' blasted the unrepentant Duncan as he bounced off Millie in his attempt to get closer to the food.

'Your eyes will be bigger than your belly,' said the mother, joining his side, and temporarily eclipsing the sun from Millie's world.

This gave Millie an idea. She'd always been a practical joker, but since she'd started reading the book, she'd had little opportunity to practice on anyone. Duncan was perfect, and she overcame her guilt by telling herself it was for his own good.

She pulled the Sense Enhancer out of her shorts, clicked it round to *Sight*, and lent over to whisper something to Duncan. 'She is right, you know.'

'About what?' he slobbered.

'If you eat too much your eyes *will* be bigger than your belly!' she replied, and unbeknownst to him held the Sense Enhancer against his rippling flesh, causing him to gurgle a little and then rub his eyes.

'What is it Duncan?' asked his mum. 'You've gone all white.' She was trying to sound concerned, but her flickering glances towards the front of the queue and the food told their own story.

When he stopped rubbing his eyes Millie had taken her hand away and his sight was back to normal.

'Come on, Mum, we're going,' he said meekly. 'I need to diet.'

Millie smiled wickedly to herself and tucked her little Zamorian plaything away for safe keeping.

Moments later she was back on the ship. 'Here you go,' she beamed, handing Arthur something. 'It's a chocolate Mickey Mouse ears ice cream. I saw someone eat one on a holiday programme and I've wanted one ever since!' she said, as she watched her grandad peel back his wrapper.

'Aren't you going to eat yours too?' he asked, realising she was still sitting there with hers neatly wrapped.

'I thought we would take it in turns,' she said, handing him the Sense Enhancer with a smile.

'Of course. Excellent,' he said, excitedly pressing the button down. 'Oops, Hearing,' he whispered, before clicking away again. 'Oh fantastic. Absolutely fantastic,' he said, tucking into both mouse ears with great relish and obvious delight. 'Fantastic,' he repeated.

Millie just sat there, salivating.

When her turn came she too revelled in the delight of feasting on the scrummiest thing she'd ever tasted.

'Not sure why they invented this thing, but it sure is brilliant,' she said, polishing off the last piece of ice cream and licking the stick clean.

'I CAN FLY!' she screamed suddenly, and dropped the Sense Enhancer.

'Er … I know Millie,' said Arthur, scooping it off the floor and tucking it in his shirt pocket.

'No you don't understand. I can fly without the book. I have only just realised,' said Millie, with a look of amazement.

'How do you know that?'

'When I fell off the roof with the key piece I called out that I needed to fly and I did, and I didn't have the book on me at the time.' Millie was visibly taken aback by this.

'Well, maybe the book gives you the powers and after that you can use them when you want. Very handy I would say.'

'Very handy indeed, Grandad. I wonder what other powers the book has in store for me.'

'Let's not get too far ahead of ourselves. Now, I would like to have a look at that thing, please.' Arthur was pointing to the Holographic Replicator. 'Do you think I can use it?'

'There's only one way to find out. Just stick it on your belt and switch it on, but please only press it once, Grandad!' said Millie, handing the device over.

Arthur studied it closely and then clipped it to his belt and fired it into life.

'My, my,' said Arthur to himself, 'you *do* look tired.'

Although Millie quivered at the prospect of spending time listening to two Arthurs chatter away, she couldn't help being fascinated by seeing her grandad in duplicate.

'Maybe I should try and find another Replicator, Grandad, or should I say Grandads? Then I could make another one of me and we could all play Ludo!' she said, trying to break them up as they argued about the name of the French Prince who was crowned King of Spain. It didn't work, so Millie left them to it and got back to the serious business of flying the ship across the Atlantic to Gibraltar.

'Which way is Gibraltar?' she enquired.

'That way,' they both said in unison, pointing to indicate, and then returning to their argument.

'Surreal,' she muttered to herself, 'surreal,' and adjusted course accordingly before searching the ship for more goodies. Nothing new presented itself, so she sat back down at the console and watched the sea race by.

'I wonder what happens if I ...' she muttered playfully.

The ship dropped down to sea level and skipped along the top of the waves. 'Excellent,' she said to herself, but at that level and speed she didn't have time to adjust course to avoid a large breaking wave that suddenly appeared pulling the ship under water.

'Oh!' she said, as the ship ploughed on below sea level.

'What have you done now?' asked the real Arthur, or was it the fake one? Millie found it almost impossible to tell.

'Yes, what have you done now?' echoed the other one.

Millie raised her hand to indicate she had it all under control and the ship lifted out of the water and resumed its position above, only this time it was a safe distance away from the crashing waves.

Millie decided to leave underwater exploration for another time and just sat back, watching the world go by while the two Arthurs moved on to the subject of their favourite football player for the team they both supported.

'How can you disagree with me? You're me!' said one.

'I'm just being opened-minded, that's all,' said the other indignantly.

'So you're saying that I'm not?' replied the first.

And so it went on.

She couldn't understand how it was possible to argue about it. After all they'd both seen exactly the same matches, but argue they did until the Rock of Gibraltar appeared on the horizon. Still, it broke up the time and gave Millie something to smile about.

CHAPTER SIXTEEN

GIBRALTAR

'What did you do that for?' moaned Arthur, as Millie switched off the Holographic Replicator, plunging the ship into relative silence. 'We'd just moved on to dodos and were trying to guess what other animals Aurora might have hidden away around the world.' Arthur had obviously become wrapped up in the engrossing conversation he'd been having with himself.

'Do you realise how mad you sound?' said Millie, shaking her head and pointing towards Gibraltar.

'Well, yes, I guess I do,' said Arthur, composing himself. 'We got here quickly,' he said, looking out towards their destination, but still mumbling about sabre-toothed tigers.

Millie clicked the Sense Enhancer into life and chose *Sight*. 'There's military personnel up the top of the rock – loads of them – and they appear to be guarding a radar station,' she said, squinting to make out as much as she could through the billowing cloud that was straddling the top of the rock. 'I don't understand, Grandad, there's no cloud anywhere else except over the rock.'

'Yes, I've read about this and if I can recall correctly the cloud only appears when the wind is blowing in a certain direction,' said Arthur vaguely.

'Let's take the ship up to the top and get a closer look.'

Arthur shook his head. 'Can't risk that. The building right at the top looks like a radar station.' *He* was now holding the Sense Enhancer and exploring the rock's summit as best he could through the streaming cloud. 'Levant, that's what I think they call it here,' he said, relieved it had finally come to him.

'Call what, Grandad?'

'The wind that brings the cloud on top of the rock.'

'Oh … that.'

'The book said the next piece is hidden on the highest peak, but it looks as if the radar station is built right on top of that point,' said Arthur, still clutching the Sense Enhancer.

'How are we going to get it then, Grandad?'

'Not sure. Let's take the ship down to the end near that big tower,' he said, pointing off to the right, 'We can explore on foot from there. Maybe something will come to us when we're on the ground.'

Millie took the Sense Enhancer back and looked at the rest of the rock. 'Hmmm … there's a cable car that goes up near the summit. That's probably our best bet.'

They set down near the big tower, which turned out to be a splendid-looking mosque that was somewhat marooned at the end of the isthmus. Once outside, Millie returned the ship to a safe height overhead and walked side by side with Arthur back towards the town in the direction of the cable car.

'Tour of the Rock?' enquired a friendly taxi driver who'd pulled up alongside them, as they stood at the roadside and debated the best way to go.

'Good idea!' exclaimed Arthur.

'What about the cable car?' said Millie, tugging at his sleeve, trying to discourage him from getting in.

'I'll drive you around the rock and then take you to the cable car. I'll give you a good deal.' The driver was eager not to lose his fare.

'Come on Millie, we need to explore, and we can ask a lot of questions.' Arthur fell into the minibus, apparently commonplace on the rock as several trundled past them as they spoke, and pulled Millie in beside him.

He wasted no time in getting started with the questions. Millie, however, said very little while the van tottered its way up the narrow roads that were carved into the rock. She was none too pleased to be sitting in the seat nearest the edge as the driver was continually flirting with it.

'What's that thing on the very top of the rock?' enquired Arthur, straight to the point for once.

'The radar, you mean?' said the driver, craning his head to hear Arthur and drifting a little closer to the edge.

'It's a radar?' said Arthur, throwing the question back.

'Yes, it's an approach radar for the airport. I'm not sure how long it has been there, but I would guess it was installed during the last war.'

'Can we go and have a look at it?' said Millie hopefully, trying her best to ignore the oncoming cars on a road that must surely have only been built for one way traffic!

'Why would you want to do that? There are plenty of more interesting things to see, like Saint Michael's caves,' Millie rolled her eyes at the thought of entering any more caves, 'the upper rock, and not to mention the famous Barbary Apes, the only wild monkeys in Western Europe.'

'I'm just interested in aircraft. I'm a plane spotter,' Millie announced, trying to find a cover for her interest, but wincing at the thought of what she had just said.

Arthur looked at her and mouthed the words, 'plane spotter,' and smiled to himself.

'You can't go up there even if you wanted to, my love. It's off-limits and guarded by the Military Police. Gibraltar airport is still run by the military, and you wouldn't get within two hundred yards of the radar before you were arrested,' said the taxi driver, as he drew up next to a group of monkeys loitering by the side of the road. The monkeys were taking the opportunity to relieve a small child, unwittingly pushed forward by his parents for a photo opportunity, of his prized bag of crisps. With the daylight robbery complete they scuttled off in search of their next victim, while the child threw a tantrum and sat down in front of the taxi.

'Of course, when I said they were wild monkeys I meant they steal by day and party by night,' said the driver, chuckling to himself. He didn't wait for the child to be scooped up, instead he swerved round him with consummate ease, causing Millie to slide a little further away from the window.

Arthur actually quite enjoyed their little tour, which took in all the places the driver mentioned. Millie, however, didn't get so much out of it, but what she was told about the tunnels intrigued her most. She waited until the tour had finished and they were back on level ground outside the cable car station before she asked the driver, 'Tell me a little more about the tunnels. Are there war rooms hidden inside, full of secret agents like in the movies?' She thought she should at least try to do an impression of an excitable twelve-year-old.

'Oh ... lots of agents ... yes,' said the driver, tapping his nose to indicate he had inside knowledge, and then laughing out loud. 'You kids have such imaginations these days. There are, or at least were, war rooms inside, yes, but who knows what they're used for now? I do know there are about thirty miles of tunnels running through the rock and most of them are out of bounds to tourists. The main tunnel in everyday use, though it's not open to the public, is the Admiralty tunnel, which runs at ground level from one side of the rock to the other,' said the driver, who was now relieving Arthur of the fare.

'Thanks,' said Arthur as the driver pulled away. 'Well, what do you think then?' he said to Millie.

'Not good. Even if the key piece is still in place there's a giant radar on top of it, guarded by armed police,' she said despondently.

'Well, if you put it like that,' said Arthur, who was equally pessimistic about their prospects.

Millie didn't give him time to comment further. 'Grandad, let's get ourselves up to the top. Maybe things will look better from up there.'

They both climbed into the cable car and peered out enviously at the people splashing about in swimming pools below while they sweltered in their cramped confines along with a throng of tourists *en route* to the top of the rock.

'The only way I can see of getting a closer look at it, Grandad, is for me to fly over there at night,' said Millie once they'd left the cable car and were safely out of earshot.

'Too dangerous,' rebuffed Arthur, who was trying to put the Sense Enhancer to good use. Actually he was looking through the public telescope, but using his own bit of Zamorian wizardry as well. 'The only thing I can say is the radar *does* appear to be on top of the highest peak,' he said, before adjusting the telescope slightly. 'Hang on a second, there seems to be an entrance below it. Yes, someone is coming out. Millie, there must be a tunnel underneath.' The one problem with his entire conversation was that it wasn't directed at Millie, because she'd wandered off to check out another vantage point. No, Arthur was inadvertently chatting away to the waiter who'd come out of the café next to the cable car station.

'Are you talking to me sir?' he said to Arthur.

'I'm so sorry,' he replied, slipping the Sense Enhancer

into his pocket and refocusing on the man before him, 'I thought I was talking to my granddaughter.'

'That's OK, sir. Funny how most people seem to get bored with the rock and direct the telescope up there,' he said, pointing over to the radar station, 'but I've never heard mention of the door below it before!'

An embarrassing silence hung between them, before the waiter said, 'Never mind … can I get you a drink?'

'No thanks. I'd better find my granddaughter.' Arthur hurried off in search of Millie, just in time to stop her climbing up onto the café roof.

'Millie, you can't just wander off. I thought I was talking to you and it turned out to be the waiter. I made a bit of a fool of myself,' he said, wagging a finger in her general direction.

'Well you should be more careful then!' said Millie, still eyeing up the roof. Arthur felt sure he was the one supposed to be lecturing her, but all the same he didn't say anything else on the matter.

Millie fixed him with her best stare. 'Grandad, we've no other choice. I have to fly over there tonight and check it out.' She had both hands on her hips and she meant business.

'There may be another way rather than going directly up to it,' he said.

'How?'

'There's a door below the radar. I think there may be a tunnel underneath and maybe you can come up from below.'

'No,' she replied, hands still firmly glued to her hips.

'What do you mean no? You haven't even considered it!'

'I don't mean no, I'll not consider it. I mean no as in *oh no*. If there's a tunnel below then the summit of the rock has been disturbed and the key piece may be lost for ever!'

Millie dropped her hands by her sides and stared at her grandad hoping for some inspiration, but his face didn't provide any.

'*Now* I'm saying no to the tunnel idea anyway.' Arthur started to open his mouth, but Millie continued, 'because you heard the taxi driver. There are over thirty miles of tunnels in the rock. How do I know where to begin? I *have* to fly over. We have no other choice,' she said determinedly.

In just thirty seconds Millie had shot down Arthur's suggestion of coming in through a tunnel, and more damagingly had highlighted that he didn't even consider the ground below the radar being disturbed as a problem. Arthur looked downbeat and Millie attempted to make him feel better by saying, 'I'll try tonight and I'll take the book for help. If it looks too dangerous we can think about your tunnel idea. Is that OK?' she said, holding his hand.

'I don't like it, Millie, but you're right. If we're to do this then it's the only way.'

They both hung around until the café closed and the last cable car descended for the day, but only one of them went down on it. The other remained hidden up top keeping the monkeys company until well after sundown.

Millie certainly couldn't be accused of going into battle unprepared. The Holographic Replicator was on her belt, the Sense Enhancer tucked safely away in a pocket, and the book was close at hand in her rucksack.

Apart from the obvious worries about the curse and being spotted, she also had a nagging doubt about how long she could fly for. She rather hoped that now she could do it without the book, staying airborne wouldn't be a problem, but the memory of the well in Australia still sat heavily on her mind. However, her aerial worries proved unfounded, because all she had to do was raise her arms and think about flying and she was up. All the same she hovered close to the top ridge, which led to the radar station, just in case.

The Levant cloud provided her cover as she drifted stealthily up to and over the perimeter fence. She was all eyes and ears, thanks to the Sense Enhancer, but even with its help she still failed to see a transmitter mast that appeared from nowhere out of the mist.

'OUCH!' She wished she hadn't said anything, but it was too late.

'WHO GOES THERE?' said an unfriendly voice below, as Millie clattered into the mast, snagging her rucksack on the rigging.

The sound of several pairs of booted feet coming from all directions only served to increase her heart rate enormously as she tried despairingly to free herself.

How was she going to explain this if they found her? She could maybe bluff her way through being found on the ground, but twenty feet up in the air hanging from a mast surrounded by barbed wire was asking a bit much, even from someone with Millie's aptitude for lying.

The same mist that caused the accident was now buying her some time, but the sound of a metal ladder clanking against the mast below did not bode well. Try as Millie might she just couldn't get herself free.

'WE ARE ARMED OFFICERS OF THE GIBRALTAR MILITARY POLICE. SHOW YOURSELF NOW!' roared the voice ascending the ladder directly below her.

Millie reached into her rucksack, loosened the straps and managed to get one hand on the book. 'I want to move things with my mind,' she whispered.

CRASH!

She'd got her wish – her new power – and had used it

immediately to move the ladder the policeman was climbing, sending him crashing dramatically to the ground below.

It bought her just enough time to wriggle free and fly off out of range of the guns she could hear being cocked.

Millie landed next to the now unguarded radar tower – all of the policemen had assembled about thirty feet away under the mast. She went through the open door directly below into a huge concrete bunker, which had a tunnel leading off it down into the rock. All of this confirmed her fear that the earth beneath the summit was well and truly disturbed and anything that had been buried there was gone for sure.

'Blast!' she said to herself, 'now what am I supposed to do?' She couldn't think about the answer because the policemen were returning, giving her no time to get back out of the door. She had no option but to venture further into the tunnel.

As she stood some way inside the dimly-lit tunnel, Sense Enhancer on *Hearing*, she picked out two voices coming into the room above.

'Sounded like a nasty fall, Michael. Are you sure you're OK?'

'Few bruises, I suspect, but I'll be fine.'

'What do you think it was then, Michael?'

'Sounded like a voice, but maybe it was a bird after all. Can't explain it,' he answered. 'I think I need a break. I'm going down below to get a coffee. Do you want anything?'

'No thanks. Oh … Watch out for the big birds,' he replied jokingly as Michael started down the stairs, leaving Millie with little choice but to continue down herself until she came across an apparently dozing cat, which promptly leapt up and rubbed against her legs.

'Of course,' she whispered to herself, reaching for the book. 'I want to be invisible.'

Millie flew forward a few feet, but the cat followed – it was clear she was still visible. It hadn't worked and Michael was almost upon her.

In panic Millie stood on the cat's tail and it hissed its disapproval.

'Who's there?' said a voice further down the stairs.

Now Millie had no way forward or back and her request for invisibility had failed.

'It's only me,' said Michael, passing the cat, who was staring straight up into the dark stairwell ceiling wagging its fluffed-up tail in displeasure.

'Oh!' said the voice below, 'did you step on the cat?'

'Not me,' said Michael. 'You know that cat, it was probably scared by a mouse or something!'

If the cat could talk it would have told them exactly what had made it cry out. The shivering little girl pinned to the ceiling with the one power she could really rely on – flight.

Millie hovered silently hoping that her flying power would hold out and she wouldn't drop onto Michael's head. Snagged to the transmitter pole was bad enough, but falling out of thin air onto a military policeman inside a top secret base was probably worse! She waited until Michael, complete with a steaming hot coffee, had returned to duty in the radar station, and the guard further down the stairs had gone, before she felt safe enough to come back down to earth. The sight of her doing so was more than the cat could take and it scurried off into the shadows, brandishing its bushy tail in disgust.

Her route up was most definitely blocked so she cautiously headed down the steps in hope of finding another way out. 'Looks as if I'm going to have to use the tunnels after all, Grandad,' she whispered to herself.

The Sense Enhancer was invaluable with *Hearing* getting the most use as she slowly picked her way further and further down the plunging stone staircase. Every time she heard a voice she retreated up into the shadows until she felt sure the coast was clear to come back down again. It took Millie several minutes to work out that the noises coming from a drinks machine, which was balanced precariously between two expansive steps, were not, as she originally thought, those of a dozing guard!

Eventually she arrived at a door that led into a huge room that was unlit except for the myriad of flashing computer lights that were in abundance as far as the eye could see. Millie switched the Sense Enhancer to *Sight* and stared intently through the glass panel in the door. She was undecided whether to go in and investigate or continue her descent when somebody else made the decision for her.

'Come in,' said a voice that seemed to be drifting lazily through the air.

CHAPTER SEVENTEEN

THE GUIDING VOICE

Millie quickly rotated on the spot, her heart thumping wildly, but nobody was in sight.

'Come in.' There it was again, even more muffled this time around, more distant, but whoever delivered it somehow knew she was there.

She squinted through the glass at the same array of lights as before, but there was no one looking back at her. Nobody she could see, anyway. The hairs on the back of her neck were now dancing to their own tune and she was certain she could feel the blood running colder through her veins. Who was speaking to her and how?

She didn't have any longer to dwell on the question because the stairwell suddenly came to life with noise, only this wasn't the sound of a melodic voice drifting through the air, this was the sound of feet clattering from both above and below the place where she stood.

Up until that point the stairwell had been dimly lit by meagre wall lights which provided Millie with ample shadows in which to hide. Now, for whatever reason, ALL the lights were on, leaving nowhere for Millie to take refuge except the dark computer room that seemed to be the source of the mysterious voice.

Millie tried the handle, but it was locked. By now panic had well and truly set in and she was fast running out of time. The footsteps grew louder and louder as she fruitlessly tried the handle several more times.

It was then that she remembered her latest power and concentrating hard, she unlatched the door with her mind.

This time, when she flexed the handle the door opened and she had just enough time to duck inside and relock it before the footsteps came to a halt on the other side.

The sound of keys jingling told her she needed to hide, and quickly.

By the time the group of fully armed military police had entered the room and switched on the lights she'd managed to hide herself inside the base of a huge computer racking system. Fortunately for Millie the cabinet she was hiding in had enough ventilation slots for her to peek through and see what was happening in the room. The first thing she saw was Michael being addressed by someone who was obviously of a higher rank, because everyone stood to attention as soon as he came in.

'I can only tell you what I saw, sir. The warning light came on in the radar station and we immediately called you and alerted our American colleagues. It may be the first time this has ever happened, but we still followed the procedures to the letter sir,' said Michael, who was bolt upright standing to attention.

'At ease. I am not questioning what you did. In fact everyone seems to be here in record time, which shows that our regular drills have been useful.' Millie could tell that not all those assembled were so keen on the drills, because several shuffled at the mention of the word. 'I guess what I'm questioning is the alert system itself. As you say, this is the first time it has ever gone off for real and if it turns out to be working properly, and not a malfunction, then the implications – well – they don't bear thinking about.'

'No sir,' said Michael.

'OK, let's do it. Open the doorway.'

'Yes, sir,' said another officer, who was standing only a few feet from Millie.

210

She could hear him typing away on a keyboard, but she couldn't see what he was writing. Whatever it was it did the trick, because as soon as he stopped, a seemingly immovable bank of computers descended into the floor leaving an exposed wall with two large silver doors in it.

'OK, team. We only have authorisation to proceed to level two, which means we're here just to establish if this alert is for real. Everything, I repeat everything, from here on MUST be done by the book.'

'I have waited a long time,' said the distant voice. The same distant voice that Millie had heard earlier outside in the stairwell. This time there were others present and surely they must have heard it too.

Michael suddenly raised one hand to his ear and the other in the air.

'Yes, Michael.'

'Sir. I just got word that the alarm went off again.'

Michael's statement caused considerable unease amongst the men present. Several of them removed their headgear and mopped their foreheads.

It was then that Millie realised that nobody heard the voice except her, although it seemed to trigger an alarm of some sort back up in the radar station. If no one else heard it then that meant there was only one possible explanation.

The person speaking to Millie was doing so telepathically, which meant they must be Zamorian.

Panic poured through her like never before. She wanted to be out of the cabinet and away from the rock – and NOW. She suddenly found it difficult to control her limbs, which were shaking badly. In an effort to stop them she inadvertently banged the side of the cabinet with her elbow.

'What was that?' said one of the exceedingly twitchy officers.

'I realise the gravity of this situation, men, but let's not overreact. That was probably nothing more than the air-conditioning system playing games with our nerves.' After he'd delivered his calming speech the commander walked purposefully over to the two large silver doors and punched a code into the keypad on the wall beside them. 'You four come with me,' he instructed. The silver doors spluttered into life revealing two more doors behind them, gold this time. In turn these slid apart to expose an antiquated lift. Four men duly followed the order and nervously boarded while their commanding officer trotted over to Michael, who along with one other hadn't been selected as part of the lift team.

Millie had by now regained enough control of herself to switch the Sense Enhancer to *Hearing* – just in time to hear the commander's next set of instructions, which he delivered in a hushed voice. 'Stick someone on the door and sweep this room after we've gone.'

Millie felt her new-found calm drain away when she saw Michael nod in agreement.

The commander then joined his men in the lift and sparked it into action by pressing one of the buttons inside, causing it to descend slowly out of sight. The space left behind was no doubt supposed to be filled by the two silver doors, but they ground to a halt before they'd completed their task, leaving an inviting gap that someone of Millie's size could squeeze through.

Michael made a few hand signals to his colleague, who got the message and took up residence by the glass-paned door with his rifle at the ready.

Even though she was riddled with fear Millie knew she would have to go down the lift shaft and try to find out to whom the voice belonged. Maybe the owner knew where the key piece was.

Millie was now unsure exactly where Michael was in the room, because she could no longer see him from her hiding place. She could, however, hear him as he methodically worked his way down the cabinets, no doubt with his gun readied, opening and closing each door as he went.

It was now or never. She concentrated her mind on the light switch on the inside of the door and using her new power she turned it off, causing both officers to scream out for each other. As they both stumbled around in the dark Millie switched the Sense Enhancer to *Sight* and used it to guide her out of the cabinet and through the darkness into the lift shaft.

When the guard by the door finally managed to locate the switch Millie was gone.

She floated down and down for what seemed like a hundred floors until she eventually came to rest on top of the lift. Millie slowly prised up the escape hatch and checked to see if anyone was inside. On finding it was empty and that the doors were closed she turned to her Sense Enhancer – set to *Hearing* – for help.

'So any life or not then?' said one of the guards outside the lift.

'Nope. Apparently the sensor that detects electrical activity keeps going off, but there appear to be no signs of life,' replied another.

'I don't know about you, but all this gives me the creeps. I'm telling you, if anything odd comes anywhere near me I'm going to keep my finger on the trigger until the smoke clears,' said the first.

And then all hell broke loose.

Millie lost her grip and fell down into the lift. What followed happened so quickly she had no time to react. The noise alerted a guard who was standing nearby. He in turn flipped a switch to kill all power to the lift. As a result of this action the escape hatch slammed shut and the lights inside went out.

Try as she might she couldn't budge the escape hatch either with her mind or by flying into it. Her frantic button pressing efforts also went unrewarded.

In the end all she could do was sit and wait in the darkness and listen to the sound of more and more guards as they assembled noisily outside the lift doors.

'They are too close and too many for you right now. Come no further. You are a Belendrian – use your powers,' said the voice in her head.

'What does that mean?' said Millie desperately to herself, as she rose to her feet. She didn't have much time to work it out, because no sooner had she posed the question to herself then the lights came back on and the doors opened.

Millie had only seen five men go down from the computer room in the lift, but there were at least ten times more assembled in the red strobe-lit corridor that led off from the lift and all of them had their guns raised and pointed at her.

Clearly there was at least one other way down. In normal circumstances that might have proved useful in her quest to find her way out, but these were anything but normal circumstances.

The guards slowly lowered their guns and made way for the commander Millie had seen back up in the computer room. He strode through the mass and came to a halt within touching distance of her.

'I can explain,' said Millie to the commander.

'I'm listening,' said the commander to Michael.

Millie had got it just in time before the doors opened. The voice said to use her Belendrian powers and she remembered the one power that the book had told her all Belendrians had. The power to take the human form of another and she, with the help of the book, chose Michael.

'I thought I caught sight of someone on top of the lift when you went down, sir. I called it back up again, got in, and rode it down – all the time listening for movement above. When it reached the bottom I undid the hatch and jumped up to look,' said Millie, aka Michael.

'And?'

'And there was nobody there, sir, but it was so dark I misjudged the distance to the hatch and rather embarrassingly slipped and fell through it.'

The commander seemed to take an age to respond to Millie's quick explanation until he said, 'What's that?' and pointed to her rucksack on the floor.

She'd clean forgotten about it and was struggling for an answer when the commander gave her some help. 'Did you find that on the roof? It looks rather old and dusty.'

'Yes sir. That was the only thing up there when I looked. Someone from … maintenance … must have left it there.'

'What's in it?'

'Nothing. Just a few tools and a book.'

The commander looked keen to finish the conversation, because in-between questioning Millie he was constantly glancing back over his shoulder. Clearly he had other things on his mind.

'OK, take it back up in the lift and get yourself checked out. By all accounts you must have hit the ground with an almighty thud.'

For the first time in a very long time Millie had actually got a break and she wasn't about to hang around to see if her luck was going to change back again. 'Yes, sir,' she said, as he pressed one of the lift buttons and stepped back into the busy corridor just as the doors closed.

The lift made its way lazily back up to the computer room, but when the doors opened the *real* Michael was there waiting to greet its occupant.

'At ease,' said Millie to Michael.

'Yes, sir,' said Michael to his commander.

Exactly what the fallout would be to Millie's chameleon-like changes from her to Michael and then to the commander was anybody's guess, but she wasn't going to wait around to find out.

'Wait here, I need to check on something up in the radar station,' she said, brandishing the rucksack as if that was the 'something.'

'Yes, sir.'

Millie raced up the stairwell and out through the radar station, setting a couple of men 'at ease' as she went, and was extremely relieved to get back above ground again. However, it was then she realised that her ability to change appearance was *not* entirely foolproof, because she suddenly reverted to her normal self. Luckily she was out of sight of the guards and able to fly away from danger and down the side of the rock to a road below.

She was so pleased to be out she hadn't noticed the young man sitting by the side of the road.

'Nice trick!' he said, clapping his hands.

Millie jumped backwards in shock.

'Wish I could fly,' he said, flicking his ponytail.

His starry-eyed appearance allowed Millie a route out of a potentially tricky situation.

'Have you been drinking?' she enquired coolly.

'One or five!' he replied playfully, apparently struggling to focus on his inquisitor.

'Too much drink can make you see things, you know,'

she said, as she pressed the Holographic Replicator a few times.

The sight of four Millies leaning over him did the trick. He leapt up and staggered off down the road, holding his head.

Millie dispatched her three copies and decided it was probably best for her to walk the rest of the way to meet her grandad, who was waiting nervously by the lower cable car station.

'I'm so glad to see you,' he said, wrapping his arms round her to display his joy that she had actually made it to their prearranged meeting point.

Millie wriggled free and said breathlessly, 'I'm glad to see your friendly face too, Grandad. It was a wee bit hairy up there. I have an awful lot to tell you,' and she proceeded to relate her exploits of the previous hour. It was difficult to gauge Arthur's precise feelings, because he said almost nothing as she rattled her story off. His facial expressions, one of shock at the mention of the voice being the most profound, did, however, shed a little light on his thoughts.

Once she'd finished he took some time to digest it all before offering up an explanation for the voice.

'It must be a Belendrian, but I don't understand because I thought that if they found out you were alive they would try to kill you. Yet this one seemed keen to help you out.'

'I'm just as baffled as you, Grandad.'

'Hold on a second. Maybe it was Fitar you could hear, because you were far enough underground – closer to the hidden continent in the Earth's core – for him to contact you directly.'

'Hey! You could have a point there.'

They batted some more ideas around about the owner of the mysterious voice, and Arthur delivered a lecture telling

Millie not to use her shape-changing power for fun. Then they moved back on to the subject of their reason for coming to Gibraltar in the first place.

'After all is said and done, Grandad, it seems one thing is clear. The key piece is no longer where Aurora left it, so I've no idea where we go from here,' said Millie, with a downcast look plastered across her face.

'I do!' said Arthur triumphantly, much to Millie's obvious surprise.

'You do?'

'Yes … well it's a guess, but it's a pretty well-educated one.'

'What … I mean where?' said Millie, puzzled.

'On the way down in the cable car it was just me and the operator and we got talking about the top of the rock. He told me that a specialist American company was brought in, specifically to do all the preparation work for everything up there including the radar station, and when they excavated the land they found lots of interesting objects: all of which are now on display in the local museum. Of course, by the time I found all this out it was too late to tell you!' Arthur said, rubbing his head and displaying a look of anguish.

'Well, it would have been a lot easier to check out the museum first. To think we had the answer to our search in the cable car on the way up, but didn't ask!' said Millie, eyes rolling in her head.

'At least you're back in one piece.'

'Good work, Grandad. I don't suppose the museum is open right now?' she said hopefully.

'Nope, but let's not let something little like that stand in our way,' he replied with a sly grin. 'I went down to look at it. It's small and only protected by a high gate, which leads into an open compound just big enough for a Zamorian

ship,' said Arthur, eyebrows at full attention.
    'Let's go get it then, Grandad!'

CHAPTER EIGHTEEN

NO PAIN, NO GAIN

Getting back into the spaceship proved to be a little trickier than expected. It would seem that late at night the place where they'd parked it – Europa Point – was frequented by gaggles of people just sitting in their cars and taking in the fantastic views across the Straits to Africa. It took a great deal of co-ordination and extra Millies to make sure everyone was distracted enough not to notice the real Millie and Arthur effectively disappear into thin air.

The sanctuary of the ship was most welcome. The discovery of a large rip in the bottom of Millie's rucksack was not.

'What is it Millie?'

'The key pieces,' she said, horrified.

'What about them?'

'They're gone!'

'WHAT?' said Arthur, loudly.

She emptied the contents of the rucksack on the floor and sure enough everything was there – minus the three key pieces. 'They must have fallen out when I got caught up on the mast.' Millie was beginning to feel she couldn't take much more of this. How unlucky can one girl be? The children of Zamora, if ever they get there, had better be pleased to see them!

'The mast.' Arthur repeated in disbelief.

Millie didn't reply. She just stayed sitting on the floor with her head buried in her hands.

Arthur also fell silent. He too couldn't help thinking that nothing else could possibly go against them.

Wishful thinking on both their parts …

'OK!' proclaimed Millie loudly, jumping to her feet, 'back up to the top, then. Let's take the ship up from this direction and follow the ridge to the café.'

'That's a bit risky, Millie. As I said before, what about the radar? Maybe we should wait until we can get back up in the cable car tomorrow.'

'We can't wait that long. The longer they're up there the more chance they'll be found. The café will provide our cover from the radar. I'll fly solo from there AND without my stupid rucksack,' said Millie, kicking it along the floor for good measure. 'I'll just take the Sense Enhancer and the Holographic Replicator with me.'

'Not the book?' Arthur had never felt so much worry in such a short space of time as he'd done today and he was keen for Millie to take as much protection as she could muster.

'No. I don't need it. I'm not fighting the curse and I have more than enough powers now to retrieve the pieces. Setting the Sense Enhancer to *Sight* should be enough to help me find them in the dark.'

She was pretty determined all right.

'And your new power to move objects might prove handy if you encounter any unfriendlies, but it's a shame you can't become invisible.' Arthur had secretly hoped all along that invisibility might be one of the powers the book granted her and was most disappointed to hear that wasn't the case.

As if to demonstrate she could cope without it and to test her movement power minus the book, Millie held her hands out in front of her and trained her mind on the rucksack that lay on the floor.

'Impressive!' cooed her grandad as the rucksack leapt into her outstretched hands. Millie just smiled.

'One power you can't use, because it just can't be trusted, is your ability to morph into the shape of another person.'

'No I've already decided on that, Grandad. It's too risky. The last thing I want is to change bodies unexpectedly!'

As planned she guided the ship along the top ridge and came to a halt next to the café.

'I'll be back in no time.'

'Take care,' said Arthur, as the door closed behind her.

Once again Millie found herself drifting through the mist caused by the Levant towards the radar station, but this time she was crawling along, careful not to repeat her earlier mistake. The Sense Enhancer was on *Sight* and at the pace she was travelling it worked well in the near zero visibility. She could see the guards scurrying around below her feet, but *they* couldn't see her.

She stopped just short of the mast and looked directly downwards, and there on the ground lay two of the three key pieces both within a foot of each other. Off in the distance she could see another guard and a man in plain-clothes heading in her direction.

'Show me exactly where you found it,' said the smartly dressed man, who appeared to be clutching something in his hand.

The guard came to a halt a few feet short of where Millie hung in the air and pointed at the ground. 'There,' he stated. 'My colleague heard a noise from the mast that turned out, we think, to be a bird, but in the process of my follow-up investigation I came across the thing you're holding. I reckon that when my colleague fell off the ladder he must have disturbed the top layer of dirt and exposed it.' That explanation wasn't as implausible as it sounded, because Michael was a veritable man mountain and if he fell over you would definitely expect the ground to know about it.

It was only a matter of time before the plain-clothed man discovered the other two pieces with the probing beam of his torch. 'Well would you look at that – two more. They all look very shiny. Glowing almost,' he said, as he bent down and added them to his hoard. 'I've no idea what they are, but I'll take them to the museum tomorrow and ask the curator if he can throw any light on them.' He rose to his feet and dusted himself down.

Millie just hung there hopelessly, but not for long.

'Well, we've the birds to thank for this little find,' said the plain-clothed man as he flicked his torch skywards.

It was a good job that Millie could move things telepathically, because she wouldn't have had the time to actually say the words out loud that were being processed by her brain. Inches before the beam settled on her she made the torch fall out of his hand and when he picked it up and tried again she was gone.

The door to the ship reopened and Arthur felt at ease to breathe normally again. 'What happened?' he asked.

'Grandad, the guard found the pieces,' Arthur's face dropped, 'but it's OK, we can get them back.'

'How?' Arthur was glad she had a solution because he was all out of bright ideas.

'There was someone else with the guard, some official looking bloke in plain clothes who plans to take the pieces to the museum tomorrow for the curator to identify. We can make our move then and hopefully pick up the other piece at the same time.'

Millie and Arthur looked absolutely exhausted and were both happy to exchange nods in agreement that Millie's plan was the way forward.

'Let's get some sleep and crack on in the morning,' he said, sinking back into his chair and closing his eyes.

Millie played with her rucksack for a minute, lifting and dropping it onto the floor with her mind, before curling up beside it and dozing off.

*

'What time is it? What time does the museum open?' asked Millie, when Arthur woke her.

'Calm down, we've plenty of time. The museum doesn't open until ten and it's only just gone nine.'

'Oh,' groaned Millie, her eyes flickering into life.

'I was going to suggest we make our way down there in the ship and hover above the enclosed courtyard.'

'OK,' said Millie wearily, and, even though she was still sleepy, she guided the ship to their destination with relative ease.

She then came up with the ingenious plan of leaving a Holographic Millie on guard while they both went back to sleep!

People trickled in and out of the museum for the next few hours until the man in the plain-clothes arrived, carrying a large padded envelope.

The plan was for fake Millie to wake the real one so she and her grandad could go in after the plain-clothed man, retrieving the three key pieces he had in his possession and then, if it were there, the cursed key piece. That was the plan, but fake Millie was bored and she wanted a piece of the action, so she came up with her own plan and it only involved her.

She exited when the coast was clear, jumping down away from the tables and chairs that had been laid out in the enclosed area, and returned the ship to hovering height before casually strolling into the museum in pursuit of her prey. She didn't have far to go because he was standing just inside the main doorway with his envelope resting on top of the souvenir display counter.

The curator, who was sporting a tight collarless white shirt that was buttoned to his neck, accompanied by undersized trousers that his belly was fighting to get out of, and casual shoes, appeared in another doorway. His face matched his belly and was a rosy red. Clearly this man enjoyed indulging himself.

'Hello, Douglas,' said the curator. 'When you spoke to me on the phone you sounded very excited. So tell me what has the Ministry of Defence unearthed today that you think might interest me? More shell casings perhaps?' He was evidently indifferent to the meeting, but his mood changed to one of delight when he saw what was in the envelope that Douglas was holding open in front of him.

'Still not interested, David?' probed Douglas.

'Well, well, well,' muttered David, scratching his chin, 'very interesting. Go and take a seat outside I'll be back in a minute,' and he scurried off into the main part of the museum.

'Can I help you?' enquired the lady behind the souvenir counter.

'Just browsing, thanks,' said fake Millie, who was trying not to draw attention to herself while she listened to the conversation between Douglas and David.

'Are you on your own?' said the lady.

'Err … no, I'm waiting for my grandad who has gone to get a paper … oh and my twin sister,' she said mischievously. 'When they return we'll probably come in.'

'I see,' said the lady, who was straightening the souvenir tea towels and place mats.

Fake Millie wandered outside and stood by the gate. She had the Sense Enhancer and switched it to *Hearing*. It appeared she'd thought of everything and was rather proud of herself. 'Anything the real me can do, I can do too,' she murmured contentedly to herself.

But there was one thing she hadn't thought of in her eagerness to outdo her creator – the cursed key piece. When she saw David carrying it out to place it alongside the others that Douglas had laid out on a table, she just froze in fear until it dawned on her that was all she was feeling – fear. Not consumed by the curse in any way, not in pain, just fear. How could that be, because she was close enough to be affected?

'This is the piece that Aidan Conor sent over to me about five years ago,' said David, who was comparing his piece to the other three. It appeared to be similar, at least in size and weight, but didn't exhibit the faint glow of the others.

'Who is Aidan Conor exactly?'

'Aidan Conor is the son of Peter Conor, the man who originally led the American team who excavated and prepared the land for the building of the radar station and cable car café, just after the war. He smuggled this thing back home with him, even though he knew it was rightly ours,' said David, waving his key piece.

'Why?'

David shook his head, 'I don't know exactly, maybe he took a shine to it and wanted a souvenir. It was sort of forgotten about until I became curator. One day I was flicking back through some old paperwork when I came across a photo of it and some accompanying documentation. That was twelve years ago and it took me seven of those to persuade his son Aidan, who had inherited it, that its rightful place was back in Gibraltar. Eventually, after a bit of legal arm-twisting, it turned up in the post and it has been on display ever since.'

'And now I arrive with another three pieces sixty years

after the original was found,' said Douglas, scratching his head. 'I can only think that when the mast they were found under was put up a few years back it disturbed some land that Peter Conor's guys never touched, and a bulky policeman rolling around in the dirt was all that was needed to bring them to the surface!'

'Your one feels lighter than these three,' said Douglas, comparing the weight of all four before laying them back on the table.

David shrugged.

'Now let me show you something you wouldn't have known with just one of them,' said Douglas, eagerly rearranging the pieces in front of him. 'There!' he said triumphantly, 'they all fit together.'

He was right, of course, and fortunately for him there was one piece missing otherwise they would both have been sucked into oblivion.

'We seem to be missing a piece.' said David, with a crumpled face.

Douglas put all four pieces into the envelope and handed it to David. 'Come by my office later and I'll give you authorisation to go up to the radar station to try and track down the missing one,' said Douglas, rising to his feet.

David got up with him and they both walked back inside where David placed the envelope on the souvenir counter. 'There's no time like the present, Douglas. I just need to find Janine and tell her where I'm going.'

David swivelled his head round in search of his missing assistant before wandering into a back room while muttering, 'She is always roaming off from her post, that girl.'

This was fake Millie's chance. Douglas had his back to the envelope and was typing out a text message on his phone, and the shop was empty behind him. She concentrated on the envelope to try and lift it past him and away somewhere where she could retrieve it later, but her telepathic powers didn't work. She might be the image of Millie, but evidently that's as far as it went.

Janine came out into the shop alongside David, who scooped up the envelope and said to Douglas, 'Just a second, I'm going to stick this in my office for safe keeping.'

'See you later Janine ... and don't leave the front desk,' instructed David purposefully, as he emerged from his office and locked it behind him.

She responded by pulling a faint smile.

'I hope you put them somewhere safe?' enquired Douglas.

'Oh yes. I put the envelope in an alarmed presentation case.'

'You have one of those in your office?'

'It's useful for the petty cash. We can't afford a safe!'

Both men laughed out loud as they passed fake Millie who was pretending to read the notice on the museum gates.

*

'Wake up, sleepyheads,' said fake Millie.

'Is he here?' asked Arthur, as Millie slowly awoke from her slumber.

They sat quietly, listening to fake Millie tell her story.

'Is that it?' said real Millie calmly.

Fake Millie nodded.

'Are you sure?'

Fake Millie nodded again, waiting for the earbashing, but there was no need, or no point, in Millie shouting – *she* had an off button.

'Bit harsh,' said Arthur, as fake Millie disappeared.

'Bit harsh? That stupid girl could have blown everything,' she scowled.

Arthur knew the time wasn't right to point out that the 'stupid girl' was an exact replica of her!

'We have to be a lot more careful from now on when we use the Holographic Replicator,' said Arthur.

'We sure do.'

'I wonder why the key piece wasn't cursed. I reckon it's a fake,' said Arthur frowning.

'You may be right, Grandad. Fake Millie said that according to Douglas, the piece in the museum felt lighter than the others. It could very well be a copy, but there's only one way to find out; we have to steal them.'

Arthur winced at the mention of the word 'steal.' 'It's OK, Grandad, we're not *really* stealing. We're just reuniting the pieces with their rightful owners. I'm sure the Gibraltarian people would be happy if we use their key piece to help a race that has been so heavily persecuted.'

'You're right, Millie, and do you know what?' Millie shook her head. 'This time I have a plan and it involves an old friend of yours.'

'Who?' said Millie curiously.

'You, Millie. It involves you,' said Arthur knowingly.

Fortunately for them the museum wasn't busy, but all the same they felt, unlike fake Millie before them, they would be chancing their luck too much getting out of the ship in broad daylight. They both agreed it was safer to move it somewhere quieter and return on foot, which is exactly what they did, and it wasn't long before they returned to the courtyard and sidled over to the barred window that led to David's office. Janine was nowhere to be seen when they breezed past the entrance.

'Grandad, we're close enough to the supposed cursed key

piece for it to have an effect and I feel fine,' said Millie.

'I was thinking that too. It seems more and more likely that it's a fake. Let's find out shall we?'

'What now, Grandad? Apart from knowing that it involves me in some way you still haven't told me about your plan.'

'When you switch on the Holographic Replicator the first projected image always comes out a couple of feet to your left?'

'Correct,' said Millie, nervously scanning the courtyard.

'Well, if you stand with your left hand side against the wall and switch it on then by rights your double should appear on the other side of the wall, which just happens to be David's office.'

'Good idea, but why not just use my mind power to lift the piece out?'

'Aha! Because we need someone in there to look through the paperwork for anything on Aidan Conor – in case we need to pay him a visit.'

'Brilliant, Grandad!' said Millie beaming, but not quite as much as her grandad was.

'Once she's inside, speak to your copy telepathically and tell her what to do. Then, once she has done it, just switch her off – simple! We'll be half-way down the street by the time the office door has been opened.'

'Like I said, Grandad, brilliant,' enthused Millie, taking up her position and switching on the Holographic Replicator.

Millie and Arthur hadn't had a plan come together so far on their world tour, and this one might have been the first to break the mould were it not for Janine who'd gone into her manager's office to browse the Internet.

Fake Millie materialised right behind her chair, casting a

reflection on the screen Janine was hunched in front of.

Millie's fast telepathic reactions were enough to save the day because when Janine looked back from the door, having shot out of her chair, fake Millie was gone. Janine scrambled a key into the lock and left the room, hurriedly locking the door behind her before sliding sheepishly back to her counter. There was little chance of her mentioning the incident, as David's office was strictly out of bounds and she wasn't even supposed to know where he hid the spare key. Besides nobody would believe she had seen a ghost anyway!

'Phew!' said Millie and Arthur in tandem.

The second time around they peeked through the window to make sure nobody was there before Millie sent a double back in.

'How's she doing?' whispered Arthur, as he watched fake Millie rifle through the filling cabinet.

'She's got something.'

Fake Millie found what she was hunting for, but in her haste she slammed the cabinet shut instead of doing as real Millie instructed and closing it quietly. The noise alerted Janine to the presence of someone in the office, but understandably she was reluctant to enter. Instead she stood fidgeting at the counter mumbling to herself. The sound of the alarm forced her to take action and she ran screaming round the counter and out into the courtyard. A second earlier and she might even have seen the backs of Millie and Arthur as they left clutching the four key pieces and some paperwork.

Back on the ship they examined their haul and it wasn't long before Millie placed the latest key piece on the book and, as they suspected, nothing happened. It was a fake.

'America it is, then,' said Millie.

'Oh boy!' sighed Arthur, 'Away you go, then.'

Before they went they posted the fake piece through the museum's letter box as it was of no use to them, and at least the museum would be no worse off than it had been a day earlier.

CHAPTER NINETEEN

NORTH AMERICA

'I've never been to Chicago before,' said Arthur, flicking through the few bits of paper they had on Aidan.

'Me neither!' said Millie light-heartedly, as she steered the ship low across the ocean.

The sea was much busier than their last Atlantic trip. Towering waves rose and fell into the ocean, rhythmically in tune with the wind. Rain lashed down and the clouds from which it came were of the type seen on a typical English summer's day!

Millie never thought grey clouds blanketed across the sky would make her feel homesick. Travelling the world had always been one of her dreams, but right then, in that moment when she was transfixed by the weather, she really missed her cosy home, complete with it's blazing log fire. She even missed her grandad's sticky rhubarb crumble that he used to murder in the oven!

Arthur had grown tired of reading about Aidan and was now occupying himself by playing the countries of the world game with a Holographic Replica of himself. They'd already got to the letter C and real Arthur was bursting to have a go.

'It's not your turn, so shhh!' said his copy.

Arthur tapped his foot and strummed his fingers impatiently.

'Cambodia!' said fake Arthur triumphantly.

'Stupid game!' said real Arthur, switching off his clone.

'Grandad, do you miss home?' asked Millie; stuck between thoughts of picking rhubarb out of her teeth and the fact both Arthurs had missed Canada.

'Yes I do. I've travelled a lot, but I always like to go home,' said Arthur thoughtfully. 'Canada! Of course! Do you think I can get him back and win the point? How did *I* not come up with that before?'

More aimless questions came and went before Millie sighted land. 'America!' she shouted, as if she'd just discovered it!

Arthur, who was now sitting alongside Millie at the front, pointed off to the right and said, 'You see that bit of land sticking out over there?' Millie nodded eagerly. 'Well, I've no idea what it is!'

Millie screwed up her nose. 'A fat lot of good you are, then!' she said, half-jokingly.

'Of course I know what it is. I was only kidding. That, my girl, is Long Island. To get to Chicago from here you need to head directly inland until you pass over the second big expanse of water, which should be Lake Michigan. Chicago borders its south-eastern edge,' said Arthur, coolly proving his point.

'What's the first?' retorted Millie, trying not to look too impressed about his never-ending geographical knowledge.

'The first what?'

'Lake.'

'Oh …' he mumbled, playing with her, 'now let me think.'

'Aha! I caught you at last!' said Millie triumphantly.

'Erie,' said Arthur, nudging her and grinning.

'One day I'll catch you out, Grandad. Surely you can't know *everything* about the world?'

Their banter was brought to an abrupt end when the ship suddenly shuddered to a stop.

'Quit messing about Millie!' Arthur looked down below

to the forbidding sea and then back to Millie. His brows were up and his nostrils flared – both signs that he was not amused.

Millie was equally unamused because *she* wasn't the one who'd stopped the ship. More worryingly it wasn't responding to her thoughts any more, but just hanging in mid-air a few hundred feet above the sea.

'I didn't stop the ship, Grandad,' said Millie, frantically trying to reconnect hers and the ship's thoughts.

'If you didn't, then …' Arthur paused because not only had they ceased flying, they were now slowly descending toward the sea. He was trying to remain calm, but his voice was one of barely contained panic as he pointed at an enormous tanker that was being thrown about by the waves. 'If you can't stop us falling then we're going to end up in the path of that tanker.'

Millie however felt no such urge to suppress *her* panic. 'I AM TRYING!' she screamed. 'Silence for a minute,' she said, closing her eyes.

Whatever she was asking for it certainly wasn't to continue their descent, but suddenly they ground to a halt just above the reach of the waves.

The huge tanker that was making its way perilously out to sea was edging ever closer. Below it was a very angry expanse of water that was tugging and slapping the boat from all angles causing it to pitch and toss severely in and out of the murky depths.

'We may miss it, Millie,' said Arthur, now on his hands and knees watching it approach. Millie opened her eyes to see the tanker just lurch by, but its wake created a huge wave that literally snatched their ship out of the sky and plunged it deep into the frenzied ocean. Millie should have knelt down next to Arthur as then she wouldn't have been thrown around so much as the tips of the waves clawed the ship under.

She tumbled forward, smashing her head on the console. Just as that happened the lights went out.

The water became calmer as they sank until the ship finally came to rest some way below the surface of the water. They may have stopped falling, but it was of little consolation, because they were now a long way down and sitting in complete darkness.

'Millie, are you OK?' whispered Arthur. He didn't need to whisper, but it seemed appropriate in the circumstances. No response from Millie prompted him to dispense with his hushed approach and do the complete opposite. 'MILLIE!' he shouted.

Again silence.

'This can't be happening.' Light wasn't needed to know Arthur's feelings. The despair in his voice revealed all.

He felt his way along the floor until he stumbled across Millie's rucksack and delved inside for her torch. As soon as he filled the void with light he could see straight away why his granddaughter had not replied.

She was gone.

The only trace of her existence was some blood splattered on the console that she'd been thrown into.

'Where can she be?' he said to himself, slumping down into a chair.

The sound of the sea is often used to help people relax. The rhythmic movement of water and its accompanying creatures convey a peaceful aura that little on this planet can equal, and those sounds were now reverberating through the ship.

'I can hear the sea? First I lose Millie and now I can hear what's going on outside?'

Before this point nothing outside could be heard at all. Not the wind whistling past as the ship cut through the air or the noise of busy cities full of people leading busy lives – nothing at all.

Now Arthur could hear clearly the sound of water gurgling around him, the distinctive cry of a passing whale, and shoals of fish sweeping by. The rumbling of engines surprised him most, because the tanker they'd passed was way above on the surface and surely the rough sea would drown it out?

Arthur sat and watched in trepidation as a huge dark object came towards him. The engine sound he heard wasn't from the tanker. It was from a submarine. 'MOVE, SHIP!' Arthur shouted, as the submarine grew ever closer. The spaceship didn't obey his order, but the submarine did and it slowly skimmed by. It didn't do so because Arthur requested it. It did so because the captain of the submarine had so ordered.

'Status report,' demanded the captain of his sonar operator.

'I don't know what it is, sir. Its size and density doesn't compare to anything we've encountered before,' came the puzzled reply.

'What about thermal?' asked the captain.

'Yes, sir. The Thermal Imager picks up signs of life and Sonar reports sound and movement on board.'

'I don't like this,' said the captain. 'We're only ten miles off the East Coast and sitting five hundred feet astern of an unidentified vessel. Open all audio frequencies. Let's see if they want to talk to us.'

'Audio open sir,' said the radio operator.

Arthur's ears pricked up when he heard a couple of clicks and then a voice boomed out.

'THIS IS THE CAPTAIN OF THE USS *FREEDOM*. YOU ARE IN UNITED STATES WATERS. PLEASE IDENTIFY YOURSELF.'

Arthur had no way of responding. He could only sit there and wait for the next message, which wasn't long in coming.

'YOU ARE IN UNITED STATES WATERS. PLEASE IDENTIFY YOURSELF.'

Nothing came back over the submarine tannoy.

'IF YOU DO NOT IDENTIFY YOURSELF WE WILL CONSIDER YOU TO BE AN AGGRESSOR AND WILL BE FORCED TO TAKE APPROPRIATE ACTION TO DEFEND OURSELVES AND OUR COUNTRY.'

Arthur got out of his chair, went over to the wall of the ship and placed both hands and his face against it and stared out. Never had he felt more helpless.

'Load tubes one and two with depth charges and fire just short of the target when ready. Let's stir them up and then maybe they'll talk,' said the captain.

His instructions were carried out to the letter and explosions rang out around Arthur as he was tossed mercilessly from side to side. 'STOP!' he shouted, but they couldn't hear. Nobody could.

Eventually the waters around him calmed and another message boomed out.

'YOU ARE IN UNITED STATES WATERS. PLEASE IDENTIFY YOURSELF.'

'We're going to have to fire on them. Inform command of our plans,' said the captain.

'Aye, aye, sir. Stand by.'

Back on board the ship a couple of lights flickered into life and for the first time in what seemed like hours Arthur didn't need the torch. The available light was no way as bright as before, but the ship's one occupant appreciated it all the same.

'YES!' he cried out, 'at last. Now let's get out of here.' His moment of joy was to be short-lived, however, because the lights went off again and darkness returned.

'Launch when ready, sir. Central command in agreement.'

The captain swept the deck with his eyes. 'Load tubes three and four with torpedoes.'

'COME ON, COME ON,' begged Arthur, now slapping the console with both hands.

'Tubes loaded,' said a voice from the launch bay.

'Fire one,' said the captain without hesitation.

'Torpedo one in the water.'

As soon as it was away Arthur could hear it droning towards him and then, out of the darkness, he saw it coming and closed his eyes in preparation for the worst.

'Autopilot on. Force field up and set to Magnetic Impulse,' said a voice from inside the ship. Arthur opened his eyes and sitting in a console seat was the same autopilot that Millie had met in Nazca.

Arthur just stood there dumbfounded as all the lights burst back into life. The torpedo which was previously heading straight for him was now looping at great speed round and round the ship.

'Stand by,' said the autopilot.

'Stand by for what?' asked Arthur.

'Stand by,' repeated the autopilot.

Arthur just shook his head and stood by.

'Report,' said the submarine captain.

'I don't understand it, sir. The torpedo appears to have malfunctioned. It's still active, but the direction finder has gone haywire,' said the radar operator.

'Fire two,' said the captain calmly.

'Torpedo two in the water,' said a voice from the launch

room.

'Second approaching. Disposing of first,' said the autopilot, and the first torpedo shot off into the darkness in the opposite direction to the submarine. 'Unjamming,' continued the autopilot, and instantly the ship rocked back and forth as the first torpedo exploded.

'First torpedo exploded, sir,' said the radar operator. 'Target vessel still intact.'

'And the second torpedo?' asked the captain.

'Three hundred feet and closing sir. Five seconds until impact.'

'Four!'

'Three!'

'Two!'

'One!'

Silence.

'Report,' prompted the captain, but he got no response. 'DAMN IT MAN, I SAID REPORT!'

'Torpedo two malfunctioned as well, sir. I can't explain it,' said a very puzzled radar operator.

'Well, find an explanation and fast!'

'Yes, sir.'

'Load torpedoes into tubes five and six!' said the captain abruptly.

The second torpedo was doing exactly the same as the first – going round and round the ship at great speed.

'Just what is going on?' said Arthur.

'That should be enough,' said the autopilot, and the second torpedo fired off into the darkness and exploded. 'Take a seat,' he continued, and Arthur quickly obliged. A moment after he sat down the ship was back above water again and zoomed along until it sat over the tanker, which was still being beaten up by the waves.

'Good cover,' said the autopilot.

Arthur breathed a huge sigh of relief and said, 'Can you please tell me what happened back there – and do you know where Millie is?'

'This ship's fuel supply was damaged, leaving it stranded on your planet. Power was switched to its backup device – The Reflective Energy Cell.'

'And that is?'

'Reflective Energy works by taking the energy of another energy-giving product and redeploying it into its own cells. It's very primitive technology, and is only used as a last resort. Out in the desert the Reflective Energy Cells on this ship were charged by your sun and used to power basic evade and protect manoeuvres. Not enough energy was stored to fly the distances you required. I shut myself down before to conserve the little energy that was left in the cells,' explained the autopilot.

'Solar power,' said Arthur, nodding his head.

'I do not know this,' said the autopilot.

'Why didn't you warn us?' said Arthur angrily.

'Warning system also damaged. Aurora was to give warning.'

Arthur slapped his forehead and looked to the sky. 'Reflective Energy … *of course*! That must have been what was written in the book when Millie read the last clue. She said the word began with "Ref".'

'I don't understand,' said the autopilot.

'Never mind. So we just ran out of power over the ocean and that caused us to drop below sea level?'

'Almost out of power. All power over and above that required for minimal evade and protect manoeuvres was exhausted. The self-defence mechanisms came online and dropped the ship to the minimal safe level to wait for your sun to recharge the cells enough to move to safer territory.'

'How long would that have taken?' asked Arthur.

'Twenty-seven of your Earth years.'

'Why didn't the ship just stay up in the air where it was? Why drop it to sea level?'

'Wind less strong at sea level. Fundamental objective was to save energy.'

'OK, enough of that. Why did we sink and where's Millie?'

'The ship did not have enough power to pull up out of such strong water after the waves had pulled it under so it dropped to a sustainable level until water calmed.'

'And Millie?'

'One of the other self-defence mechanisms built into this ship is to save Zamorian personnel on board at all costs and so she, the one you call Millie, was placed in a Time Bubble just at the point she was about to be severely damaged.'

The autopilot kept the answers coming and Arthur kept firing the questions and all the time they continued to track the path of the tanker below.

'I expect you can guess my next question?' said Arthur, wearily rubbing his head.

'I am not programmed to guess,' said the autopilot, matter-of-factly.

'Fair enough! What's a Time Bubble?'

'A Time Bubble is used to transfer a Zamorian being to the nearest available land mass in times of absolute peril. All of the energy left in the Reflective Energy Cells was used to initiate that transfer. Only there was not enough to get her to dry land.'

'So where is she?'

'Below us on that vessel,' said the autopilot, pointing to the tanker. 'All of the ship's energy, even that required for evade and protect, was drained when the Time Bubble was created. Only the audio link to the Time Bubble, which has its own power source, was left, but not even that could function properly.'

'Why?'

'It was not designed for water.'

'That must be why we got audio from outside the ship and heard the submarine hailing us,' said Arthur. The autopilot didn't respond. 'So when the submarine—'

'What is submarine?'

'The submarine was the vessel that fired on us under water,' he explained. 'So I'm guessing that when it fired, the Reflective Energy Cells were able to divert the energy from the torpedoes, and Bob's your uncle!' said Arthur, happy at last to be piecing everything together in his mind.

'Who is Bob?'

Arthur smiled. 'It doesn't matter. Just an expression.'

'Hmm, Bob,' said the puzzled autopilot.

'Without the small explosions that preceded the torpedoes, this ship would not have survived as it was those explosions that provided just enough power to bring me and the self-defence systems back online,' said the autopilot.

'So how much power have we got exactly?'

'Enough to bring Millie back and travel three Zebnons.'

Arthur shook his head and just stared down at his feet. 'So how do we get Millie back, and what the heck is a Zebnon?'

'A Zebnon is about the same as three hundred Quadclicks I think, or about two thousand miles – give or take,' said Millie.

'MILLIE!' Arthur leapt up. 'Where did you come from?'

'Down there. I have been in telepathic communication with the autopilot since you came overhead, but he said he couldn't concentrate on bringing me back because you wouldn't stop talking!' said Millie, before unleashing a huge grin.

'I saw your blood on the console, but I can't see any on you,' said Arthur, as he looked her up and down.

'The Time Bubble has healing powers.' She replied in such a manner as to give the impression that a Time Bubble was a common thing!

'You know about Time Bubbles then?'

'Oh yes, I heard your conversation through the autopilot. Now I think we should get out of here. We've already ruined one sub commander's day and we don't want anyone else after us!' Millie took her position at the console. 'Thanks!' she said, smiling to the autopilot.

'Bob's your uncle,' he replied, and then disappeared.

CHAPTER TWENTY

AIDAN CONOR

Millie followed the route as Arthur had previously instructed, skilfully skimming the ground to stay out of radar range until the imposing city of Chicago rose up from the distance.

'Where to from here?'

'It should be easy to find our next destination, Millie. The Sears Tower is one of the tallest buildings in the world. Follow the lake around its borders,' said Arthur, who was on the lookout for the huge antennas that sat proudly on top of the building like candles on an enormous cake.

'There it is!' he declared a few minutes later, pointing. 'It must be a few miles up the coast and a mile inland, but we can see it as clear as day. Amazing!'

Millie negotiated the surrounding buildings, swooping up and around like a bird of prey, finally coming to rest eye to eye with the tallest tower. There were others, but this one, unlike the smaller towers that had helicopters dotted on top of them, was devoid of all aircraft. 'Let's park up between them,' said Millie, pointing to the two antennas that sprouted from the rooftop. 'Nobody is going to disturb us there.' She nestled the ship between the antennas before they clambered out onto the rooftop, next to a stairwell door.

'Wow!' was all they could both say – standing there surrounded by the most magnificent skyline.

Below them the streets were dotted with masses of bustling people.

From the roof they followed the stairwell down until they found a lift. 'Which floor?' asked Millie, leaning on the down button.

'Sixty-fifth, but when we get there I want you to wait outside while I go and chat with him. I want to play this one cool and not just rush in. The last thing we need in a packed building is for you to activate the curse. Providing, of course, he has the key piece here, or, indeed he still has it at all. Today I'll just check the guy out and see who we're dealing with. I know how I'm going to approach this, so leave it to me, OK?' Arthur looked and sounded in charge and Millie was more than happy to let him do some ground work.

'No problem. Come and get me if you need help,' she said, both hands raised in the air to signify surrender.

BING! went the lift as it arrived. Its doors slid gracefully open. 'Mmmm, nice music,' said Millie sarcastically and she again lent on the required button.

On the way down she greeted everyone who joined them in the lift with the same fixed grin, except one lady who she stuck out her tongue to, because she didn't return a smile.

Aidan Conor had the whole sixty-fifth floor to himself. His name was plastered everywhere, along with cosy couches, fancy teacups, and Cheshire cat receptionists. Millie curled up on a couch and Arthur saw to the cats.

'Yes sir, how may I help you today?' enquired the first receptionist, who looked as if she hadn't had time to put her makeup on before she came to work, so had just poured it all into a bucket and stuck her head in it.

'I would like to see Aidan Conor,' said Arthur coyly, while nervously running his finger back and forth under his buttoned shirt collar. Obviously a smiling cat with a make-up-laden face made him uneasy.

'Have you an appointment sir?'

'No, but I was hoping he would be able to fit me in.' His

expectant look must have worked in the past, but not with this lady.

'He is a very, very, busy man, sir, and he sees nobody without an appointment. I can fit you in next week if you like?' she said, consulting her screen.

'I'm sure if you tell him who I am he will see me.' Next week was no good, Arthur wanted to see him now.

'And who exactly are you?' The receptionist's tone had lowered just enough to say he still had no chance of getting in to see her boss.

'Lawrence Smiles.' It was the first name that popped into his mind.

The receptionist raised her hand and spoke into her mouthpiece. 'Sorry to disturb you, Mr. Conor, but I have a gentleman here who wants to see you,' she said, nodding to the voice on the other end and careful not to let her steely grin slide. 'Yes, I know sir, but he said if I told you who he was you—' she paused, cut-off mid-sentence, 'Lawrence Smiles.' More silence her end and then, 'I'll tell him that. Yes, I'll get his card.'

Arthur went to talk, but the pussy cat had now turned into a bulldog. Her grin had gone and been replaced by a wagging finger intended to stop Arthur speaking, but he did anyway. 'Tell him I've been sent over from the Gibraltar museum to discuss forged artefacts!' he blurted out. Not exactly the cool display he was hoping for, but needs must. She didn't need to tell him, as he heard for himself.

Arthur glanced back at Millie who had both thumbs raised and mouthed, 'Very cool Lawrence!'

'You can go in, Mr. Smiles,' said the receptionist, whose face was a picture of disbelief.

Arthur vanished through some towering double doors that were surrounded by fixed glass panels. Two tiny windows above the doors seemed to be open only for effect, because air-conditioning well and truly ruled the roost here. The receptionist switched her attention to Millie, who smiled sarcastically back at her and then buried her head in the magazine she'd previously plucked from the neat pile on the glass table in front of her. She wasn't really interested in its contents, but at least it shielded her from the receptionist's glare.

Aidan Conor's office was vast. You could fit Arthur's study into it fifty times over and still have room left for a marching band. If wealth in Chicago was defined by open space then this man was a very wealthy individual indeed.

'So tell me,' echoed a voice from across the room. The voice emanated from behind a thick leather high-backed chair partly obscured by an oversized desk that was home to nothing more than a monitor and a keyboard. Arthur edged over to the desk as the occupant of the chair swung round and dropped something into a drawer before closing it with great panache.

'I am Aidan Conor and you must be Lawrence Smiles,' said the man in the chair, which must have been tailor made for him, as he seemed to be moulded into it perfectly. He was dressed impeccably with a designer suit, matching shirt, and striking red tie. Above the neckline sat a head that was equally well tailored. Not a hair was out of place atop his immaculately sculptured face. Either he was born very lucky or his favourite surgeons were those of the plastic variety. 'Please take a seat,' said Aidan, casually dipping his head in the direction of the much smaller chair that sat on the other side of the table.

Arthur did as instructed and said, 'As I told your receptionist, I was sent by the museum in Gibraltar to discuss the artefact you gave them under protest about five years ago.'

'And?' said Aidan slyly.

'Well, it's fake.' *Might as well get to the point*, Arthur thought to himself.

'No.' said Aidan, slowly tapping his fingers on the table and fixing Arthur with an icy stare.

'It's a fake!' Arthur fired back. He didn't like to be called a liar. Well, at least in relation to the things he was telling the truth about anyway!

'No, Mr. Smiles,' said Aidan menacingly, 'I'm not talking about the artefact that I sent to Gibraltar. Of course *that's* fake. I'm saying no to the first part of your story.'

Arthur slowly shook his head in disbelief. He didn't expect him to just come out and admit to it being a fake straight away. This made him apprehensive about what might be next out of Aidan's mouth.

'I just got off the phone about half an hour ago with the curator of the Gibraltar museum who wanted to know if I had anything to do with a break-in that took place there. It appears that the artefact you're referring to was stolen – although strangely it was later returned – along with some paperwork with my name on it.' He looked into Arthur's eyes, who was forcing himself to remain straight faced, and then said, 'What interests me most is the *other* three pieces that were taken.'

Arthur didn't really have an answer.

'Well Mr. Smiles?' probed Aidan.

'I don't know about the other pieces.'

'I think you do, Mr. Smiles,' he said rising to his feet, 'and what's more I think you're the man behind the robbery, because the entire time I spent speaking to the curator he never once mentioned you would personally be paying me a visit. Don't you think that's rather strange, Mr. Smiles?'

Arthur sat silently, unable to think of a credible response.

'Now, I'm a reasonable man.'

Arthur doubted that, but he was glad to hear him keep talking because it meant he had more time to think of the answers to his searching questions.

'Like I say – I'm a reasonable man, so you keep your pieces and I'll keep mine,' said Aidan, now standing behind Arthur with his hands resting on the back of his chair.

Arthur's plan had well and truly fallen apart and he glanced back nervously towards the door.

'Oh, you can leave, Mr. Smiles, but I don't EVER want to see your face again. Is that understood?'

'Understood.'

Aidan span the chair around to face the door and Arthur got up and walked out, not once looking back. After what he'd just been through the receptionist's frosty look didn't seem quite so intimidating as before. The door closed silently behind him and he made his way over to Millie.

'Lawrence Smiles! Where did that come from?' whispered Millie, still amazed at hearing her grandad tell a lie.

'Old work colleague,' said Arthur forlornly.

'I can tell by your face that it didn't go as planned, Grandad?' His demeanour was a dead giveaway of how the meeting went, all downcast and sullen.

'Made a bit of a hash of that one, Millie.'

'Why, what happened?'

'He admitted the piece he sent to Gibraltar was a fake and that he still had the original, but I don't know how we're going to prise it out of him.'

'We'll come up with something, Grandad. We always have done before,' said Millie optimistically.

Arthur was still gazing down at the ground, scouring his

mind to come up with a solution. 'I'll tell you this, though. He is a nasty piece of work and we need to tread very carefully.'

The sight of Aidan coming out of his office and staring directly at Millie and Arthur was all Millie needed to understand her grandad's words of warning, because he certainly had a presence about him – one of a man not to be trifled with. All the same Millie held his stare until Arthur led her away. She might be a girl, but she could handle herself in a staring fight.

Several ideas were exchanged during the lift ride back to the top floor and again on the walk to the ship, but Arthur vetoed all of them. Aidan Conor had rattled him, big time.

'I think the key piece may actually be in his office, because he stuffed something in a drawer when I came in,' said Arthur, who was still deep in thought.

'The windows above the big doors to his office, Grandad, I can get in through those,' said Millie suddenly.

'I saw those too Millie, but I really don't want you anywhere near the man.'

Millie held Arthur's hand. 'I have no desire to get in there with him either, and I'm not going to. I'll just wait until he, and everyone else, has left and then slip in through the small windows and take on the curse. Apart from being attacked by a mean-looking photocopier I should be able to handle it.' Millie squeezed his hand a little tighter, and after a short pause Arthur reluctantly agreed.

'What if the piece isn't there, or he moves it tonight?'

'If that happens, Grandad, we'll have to follow him in this little baby until we do find it,' said Millie, tapping the ship's console.

The next eight hours until midnight dragged by. They occupied themselves by playing the countries of the world game between ten of them. Seven Millies against three Arthurs – was agreed after some debate – to be a fair spread.

At last the time arrived for Millie to go and check the coast was clear. 'Don't worry. Remember I can always fly myself out of trouble if needs be and I'll take the book as well,' said Millie, opening the door to leave.

'I'm coming out too, because if you're not back in thirty minutes I'll be down to get you, and as I can't open this door myself, I don't want to be trapped inside.'

Millie left her grandad on the roof and set off, armed to the teeth with the Holographic Replicator, Sense Enhancer, and the all-important book.

She decided to walk down the stairs in case taking the lift alerted any security guards that might be monitoring it. After four or five flights she gave up on the walking idea and flew down instead!

'Sixty-five,' she whispered to herself, as she landed beside a door with that number on it. There was a deafening silence broken only by the whirring of the air-conditioning fans from way above. Not a footstep could be heard, even with the Sense Enhancer on *Hearing*, either on the stairs or behind the door which Millie had her ear pressed against.

She slowly opened the door and peeked through into the dark hallway that led to Aidan's office. Millie decided against a torch and instead chose the moon to light her way. Not quite the same, but good enough when coupled with the visionary effects of the Sense Enhancer, and less likely to attract unwanted attention.

She was now a master of flying. Gliding up to the windows and down the other side wasn't a problem, but getting through them was more of a squeeze than she first thought. After wriggling her way through the frame of the window, she finally touched down on the office floor below.

Arthur had told her about the office, but all the same she needed a moment to take it in. The view from the expanse of windows was amazing. One more floor down and he would have had no view at all, because the adjoining tower, complete with its helicopter landing pad, came right up to the bottom of his window.

She walked slowly towards the desk, expecting with each tentative step to feel something. The pain that shot through her body when she neared a cursed key piece was *not* to be looked forward to, but Millie knew she had to experience it to get closer to completing the entire key. However, when she got to the desk without having felt the slightest twinge she knew the key piece wasn't in the room and sank despondently into Aidan's big chair, which engulfed her just like the one in her grandad's study.

She put her rucksack on the desk and, out of curiosity, tried the drawers to see what was in them, but they yielded nothing except neatly piled stationery and, inexplicably, the odd fizzy cola bottle. She was pretty downbeat by the time she slid the last drawer shut and span the chair round to face the city.

The windows must have been soundproofed because she didn't hear the helicopter landing directly outside Aidan's office. More worryingly, Aidan was the pilot and he'd just jumped out and was walking toward the side of the building.

Millie leapt out of the chair but it was too late. Aidan was already in the adjoining office and at the adjoining door. Millie couldn't get out in time so she ducked under the cavernous desk, slid into one corner, and held her breath.

The door opened and the lights flickered into life while Millie crouched silently, trying not to move a muscle.

'This office has a motion sensor alarm and *I* have a gun,' said Aidan from across the room. 'So whoever you are may

I suggest you come out of your hiding place right now?'

Millie stayed silent and Aidan remained standing in the doorway some fifty feet away.

'There are only two places to hide in this office,' he continued, 'behind the large plant in the corner and,' Millie closed her eyes, 'under my desk. I really don't want to have to put a hole in my nice desk and for that matter I've grown rather attached to the plant. I'm guessing you're still here because your bag is on my desk.'

Millie's heart sank. She'd put her rucksack on the desk when she tried the drawers and it was still there. She felt for the Holographic Replicator, thinking that she could overcome him that way and worry about the consequences later, but it wasn't on her belt. It must have dropped off when she squeezed through the small windows. The book was no help to her either, because it was in the rucksack.

'I'll count to three. One ...' What was she going to do? 'Two ...' She couldn't even fly because he had a gun and could shoot her. 'Thr—'

Before he finished he stepped into the room and Millie felt a shooting pain tear through her. If she thought things were already bad then they were about to get much worse. Aidan had the key piece on a chain around his neck and those few steps forward were enough to bring her in range of the curse. Now Aidan was no longer in control of his actions and Millie was struggling to fight the pain.

'STOP!' cried Millie, and came out from under the desk with her hands held aloft.

'YOU!' Aidan yelled; he was holding a gun in one hand and had eyes that were ablaze with hatred induced by the curse. He sprinted over, grabbed hold of Millie and pulled her back across the room and outside to his waiting helicopter – not even stopping to close the door. If she could see the key piece she might have been able to muster the strength to read the inscription once she touched it, but she had no idea where it was on his person.

'I'm not going to kill you here. I have a much better idea,' he said feverishly. 'I'm going to throw you out of the helicopter.'

As Millie could fly, this would have been a good thing, but the closer she got to a cursed key piece the more the pain level rose. She'd been too close for too long and passed out before they got inside. He dumped her on the passenger side where she fell back against the door, bashing her head on the glass, before taking the pilot's seat beside her and strapping himself in.

'You are going to die,' he said evilly, as he fired up the rotor blades and lifted off into the darkness.

No longer so close to the key piece, Millie regained consciousness, to see Aidan pulling the helicopter up high above the rooftops. The pain was still indescribable, but this was her moment. Perhaps her last moment?

She lunged out viciously with her feet as hard as she possibly could and smashed Aidan's head back against his door. She wanted to knock him out and she succeeded, but she hadn't thought any further than that. The helicopter was going down! She needed to get the key piece and get out.

As Aidan slumped forward onto the controls the key piece dangled down from his neck. Millie frantically grabbed it, ripping it from its chain and read, '*Where the sun's always smiling as it peers through the haze.*'

The pain went immediately, but her anxiety didn't. The helicopter was still falling fast and as much as she didn't like Aidan she knew his urge to kill her stemmed from the curse.

'WAKE UP. COME ON, WAKE UP,' she screamed, as

they plummeted lower, 'YOU HAVE TO WAKE UP!

Millie lent over and slapped him round the face. Suddenly he sprang into life, grabbed the controls, and miraculously managed to right the fall. Blood seeping from his head blocked the sight of a very relieved Millie flying out of her door and back to the Sears Tower. She knew that once he regained composure he would head back there himself, as that would be the last place he remembered being. She needed to get there first and she did.

She quickly scooped up her rucksack and the Holographic Replicator, which was lying by the tall doors, squeezed back out of the window and raced to the stairwell door.

'ARGGGG!' she shrieked at the face on the other side of the door.

'Shhh, Millie, it's me,' said her equally startled grandad. 'Are you OK?'

'Yes, Grandad, but we really have to get out of here.' Millie grabbed his hand and pulled him up the stairs to the top.

The only thing Arthur managed to say between huge gulps of breath was, 'Did you get it?'

'Yes!' Millie gulped back, 'but they don't get any easier.'

CHAPTER TWENTY ONE

AFRICA

To discover the final piece of the Key to Chintak use the Great Pyramid and your existing four pieces to unearth the sundown trail leading to the hidden city of Mu. The Eurasian Plate Line wind channel will provide your transport.

Seeing the clue appear in its full glory when Millie laid the fourth part of the key on the book was proof that this time the piece was not a fake. However, the clue caused Arthur to rethink his understanding of the Earth's crust!

'Why are you looking so puzzled, Grandad? Don't tell me you're stumped on something to do with geography!' Millie was stuck somewhere between glee that her grandad didn't know everything about the world, and worry that they might not be able to solve the clue.

All Arthur kept saying over and over was, 'Doesn't quite make sense.'

'What doesn't?' Millie's glee had now subsided and she wanted answers!

Arthur scratched his head. 'The Great Pyramid in Egypt was built for a pharaoh called Khufu, but I've not heard of a city called Mu in the same continent. There was talk that an underwater city discovered in the eighties might be part of the mythical civilisation known as Mu, but that was in Japan

– which is some way from Egypt!'

He paused to strum his fingers. 'I would say that what puzzles me more is the reference to the Eurasian Plate.'

'What's that?'

'The Eurasian Plate is one of a dozen or so plates that move independently of each other, but as a whole they form the Earth's crust. They're commonly known as tectonic plates and are always on the move – driven by the heat emanating from the Earth's core.' Arthur paused and stared blankly ahead.

Millie was tired and not really in the mood for a talk on crusty plates that squish each other around, but she had to ask. 'So what's the mystery?'

'The Eurasian Plate is hundreds of miles away from Egypt AND as for the wind channel … well wind certainly doesn't control the plates. At least I thought that was the case!'

'From what we've experienced since we set off I think we should keep an open mind on everything. I don't know anything about the plates, but I do know Zamorian and this Zamorian text in front of me says to use the Great Pyramid, so let's go to Egypt and see what turns up.'

*

They sat patiently in the ship until morning, when the Sears Tower would be teeming with people, and got ready to leave. They knew the ship didn't have enough power left in its Reflective Energy Cells so they thought hovering between the two antennas on top of the tower was as good a place as any to leave it. Probably one day they would return to use it again, but for now conventional flight won the contest over Zamorian travel.

'Autopilot on,' instructed Millie, who was standing by the door. 'Look after the ship until I return,' she said to the holographic image that appeared.

'This site is more than adequate because the antennas are providing extra energy,' said the autopilot.

Millie and Arthur waved in appreciation and stepped out onto the roof of the tower.

'Evade and protect measures enabled,' said Millie, and she watched as the door closed and the ship rose up to sit some way off the ground, but still snugly between the two antennas.

They got into the lift and journeyed down to the ground floor. The sight of one of Aidan Conor's secretaries stepping in on the sixty-fifth floor caused their hearts to flutter a little, but either she didn't recognise them or she pretended not to. Either way Arthur, at least, was happy not to renew her acquaintance.

*

O'Hare airport in Chicago was rather different to the one they caught sight of in Gibraltar, which had one runway that doubled as the main through road, and a terminal which serviced a handful of planes a day!

'Do you know there are fifty thousand people working here?' said Arthur, reading from an information board while standing in the check-in queue.

'I'm only interested in meeting the person who can upgrade us!' said Millie with a wry smile on her face. On every flight so far, excluding spaceship travel of course, she'd tried to squeeze an upgrade out when it came to seat allocation time, but had failed miserably. Today was no different. The sight of her hairline and eyes peering over the check-in desk next to her grandad and politely asking to be bumped up failed yet again.

'Oh well,' she said philosophically, 'at least I get to sit up front when I travel Zamorian.'

'I've never heard of Zamorian, do they give good flight rewards?' said a man standing behind her, thumbing through his vast collection of airline membership cards to see if he was already an affiliate member.

'Yes, but it depends on which planet you're travelling to,' said Millie with a straight face, before burying it inside a bag of sweets and wandering off to Passport Control. Arthur followed close behind.

'Kids!' he said to the man, as both of them blended into the masses.

*

Getting to Cairo, via a drawn-out connection in Frankfurt, proved to be an epic journey in itself as it took some fifteen hours to complete. It didn't help that they hadn't booked a hotel, and the only one they could find through airport information wasn't in the best part of the city. However, beds were beds, and not for the first time they were glad to fall into theirs. Even a death-defying taxi ride to the hotel in Giza did little to trouble their weary heads.

'It was far easier in the ship,' were the only words Millie uttered in the hotel room before getting some well-earned rest. Arthur didn't even hear her say that. He was out for the count before his head touched the pillow.

*

As always, Arthur was the first to rise, leaving Millie mumbling in her bed with her head buried under the pillows and her arms dangling over each side, while he went off to explore the local surroundings. Just in case of any unforeseen trouble he took the Holographic Replicator with him for strength in numbers!

Their hotel was located near the university on the west bank of the river Nile, about eight miles due east of the Great Pyramid. Arthur didn't have to travel far to discover this because the hotelier was a mine of information and even supplied him with tickets to the daily tour bus that picked up at the hotel. Not an organised tour of course, nothing in Egypt seemed to be organised – as Arthur knew from visiting the place several times in the past – but a sort of request stop tour. If you were in the right place at the right time and stuck out your hand then there was a fair probability the tour driver would stop – unless of course he didn't feel like it. Then you would just have to wait and chance your arm with the next one, in the hope that their mood was more forthcoming.

The temperature inside the hotel was bad enough because the air-conditioning was broken, but outside it was almost unbearable. The streets were still packed, although the people in them were mainly tourists. The locals were sensibly conspicuous by their absence, obviously smart enough to wait for the sun to lose its sting and the tourists to settle down to an evening's sunstroke before venturing out.

Arthur had never explored the Great Pyramid before. His previous visits always centred on the Valley of the Kings, which was located a few hundred miles further down the Nile near the city of Luxor. For him, the whole global trip was something of a busman's holiday, but without doubt this was the part he looked forward to most. The thought of discovering a hidden city in the land of the pharaohs was something he had dreamed of since he was Millie's age. His primary concern was of course her safety, but if they could finish their search unharmed AND find the city then Arthur would be the happiest man alive.

It was time to get started.

*

'Wakey-wakey!' announced Arthur, as he opened the hotel room door. Not unusually, owing to Millie's ability to sleep through most things, there was no response. 'Come on, get up! We've got a lost city to find!'

The curtains were still drawn so Arthur switched on the light and entered the room, to be faced with two empty beds. His was made up just as he had left it, but Millie's was not.

'Oh, where have you gone now?'

A few more steps into the room and Arthur was to find the answer. A note lay partially obscured on Millie's bed, which he picked up and read aloud.

You had me fooled for a while, but not any more. If you want to see her alive again, then bring me the missing piece. Meet me on the road to the pyramids at six. I will be standing beside my car. Don't be late.

Arthur slumped onto his bed, his mind suddenly awash with questions. Who could be behind the note? How was *he* supposed to find the other piece? The last clue said that the first four pieces were needed to find the fifth, so without them – they were gone, along with Millie – there was no way he could fulfil the note's ransom request, but that didn't mean he was short of a plan …

*

Arthur had a whole afternoon to kill, so he thought rather than sit around and worry himself stupid he would travel out to the pyramids to do some reconnaissance.

'Ticket good for day,' said the bus driver to Arthur, as he boarded and squeezed himself onto the end of a bench seat. When he first saw the seat it only seemed to be occupied by one woman who was covered in layer upon layer of robes which were taking up more room than she was. Only when he slid in next to her, balancing himself precariously on the edge with his feet sticking out in the aisle, did the robes start to come to life. First a small boy poked his head out, revealed a toothy grin and then disappeared, brushing against Arthur's legs as he went. Next out was another small boy. This one just appeared to be looking for the first and didn't stop to smile, but proceeded on his way. When the chicken appeared Arthur decided it was time to stop staring!

As more and more people herded themselves on, Arthur began to worry if he would actually be able to get off and had visions of being forced to wait until he got back to Giza before he could. *Perhaps that's why the ticket was valid for one day*, he thought to himself, *because someone might need several trips before they could leave the bus!*

The driver rambled away in English, clearly keen to further his language skills, although most of what he said was incomprehensible. Arthur did pick out something about an ancient pharaoh who had a vineyard next to an old oasis! He kept repeating this one so Arthur felt obliged to believe him, although he was rather unsure what a glass of wine from there would taste like. Dry no doubt.

Arthur needn't have worried, because when the driver shouted out, 'Nazlat as Samman,' most of the other passengers, including the woman sitting next to him, filed off. 'Next pyramid big,' said the driver as he closed the door and swung back onto the road. Arthur took this to mean the Great Pyramid.

The rest of the passengers, a gaggle of smiling Japanese tourists with cameras weighing them down, and a tiny woman with a huge backpack, left the bus when the driver slid up on the side of the road opposite the Great Pyramid.

Arthur, happy that he'd remembered his hat, felt as if he'd stepped from the bus into an oven. The sun was fierce, and he wondered how the little woman would cope as she staggered off into the distance with her rucksack pulling her down.

As he stood staring at the Great Pyramid, a shiver ran down his spine when he remembered why he was there. He was quickly pulled out of his bout of depression by the sound of people approaching.

'Managed to build one yet?' he said to the Japanese tourists who'd now joined him, cameras primed and ready for action. They just grinned at him, clearly not understanding his reference to their countryman's attempts to actually recreate the Great Pyramid, albeit on a much smaller scale. They'd failed, and so had everyone else who'd tried. It was an engineering feat, a true wonder of the world, which nobody had been able to replicate, even with modern technology. Arthur smiled back before continuing on his way.

He met another group of eager-eared tourists, who were listening intently to a young man with deeply tanned skin and a cherry red nose. His ragged blond hair and general appearance had a touch of the surfer look about it.

'This pyramid,' he said with great authority and theatrical hand gestures, 'is aligned with all four compass points, is one of the heaviest buildings on this planet, and is built on almost perfectly flat land. Can anyone explain to me how this was possible when it was erected thousands of years ago?'

Nobody said a word including, somewhat surprisingly, Arthur.

'Its design and location leave a lot of unanswered questions. If we can't replicate this structure using all that we know today then how did an ancient civilisation do it?' he said, finishing with a smile.

Arthur thought it best not to stick his hand up and suggest that maybe the Zamorians built it, but he did take the speaker to one side to quiz him.

'Hi, I'm Arthur Jarman. Can I ask you a question?'

'Dan Casey,' said the young man eagerly. 'Fire away.'

'Have you ever heard of a city in Egypt called Mu?'

'Nope! … Hang on, isn't there a Mu off Japan somewhere?' said Dan, now edging away into the crowd, 'but I guess that's a bit far away!' And then he was gone, swallowed up by the throng of tourists who themselves were keen to question him.

Arthur carried on alone to wander around the Great Pyramid, and the array of smaller pyramids that sat in its shadow.

Apart from looking at the pyramids for clues as to how the four key pieces could be used to locate the fifth and final piece, Arthur also explored the rest of the area that made up the complex of Khufu. He picked his way through an array of exposed temples, causeways, and tombs in search of an answer.

He knew he had the Holographic Replicator with him, but forgot that he'd tucked the Sense Enhancer into his pocket way back in Chicago. Switched to *Sight* it proved to be a useful tool and enabled him to get a close up view of all around.

With it he could see the top of the Great Pyramid was actually flat, never apparently finished off like most of the others with a cap stone.

Signs by the entrance told of a wonderful array of chambers and tunnels that burrowed their way up and down from the inside. Inexplicably, air vents also ran throughout the pyramid to the outside world. A picture of a mysterious door at the end of one of these vents, leading up from the Queen's Chamber, was detailed in such a way as to keep the viewer wondering exactly what lay behind it. The air shaft was two hundred feet long and far too small for a person to ascend. The image of the door, complete with its two handles, was actually taken by a robot camera that had been sent up to investigate what lay at the end of the shaft.

The more Arthur stood and read about the pyramids the more he began to wonder exactly who was behind their building. *Surely* the people who lived in Egypt when they were built were not advanced enough to complete such a feat of engineering?

Arthur's visit had turned up no definite clues to show how best the four key pieces could be used, so he decided to call it a day and head back to town. The time was fast approaching when he would find out who'd kidnapped his granddaughter.

Back at the hotel he still had enough time to peel off his dust and dirt-laden clothes and shower before going over his plan in his mind a few more times to get it right.

The plan was by no means foolproof, but one thing was for sure. Whoever had Millie had messed with the wrong man. Arthur had never been more determined than he was when he checked his watch and left the room with thirty minutes to spare.

CHAPTER TWENTY TWO

A SURPRISE VISITOR

'You see pyramid at night?' said the hotel receptionist to Arthur, as he descended the stairs. He would have used the lift, but there was a sign up saying it was out of order because the air-conditioning was not working. Quite how they were connected Arthur didn't ask.

'Er … yes,' he replied, before stepping out into the harsh afternoon heat.

The same driver who'd taken Arthur to and from the Great Pyramid earlier greeted him again when he pulled up outside the hotel.

'You go and see light at night?'

'Yes I do, but I'm meeting some friends half-way so—'

'It OK. I can stop,' he smiled, 'even with no tip I can stop.'

Arthur boarded the bus, and took the seat nearest the driver. Thankfully it seemed, before the evening rush.

'What your friend look like?'

Arthur didn't know. The only thing he knew about the person was that he'd kidnapped Millie and would be standing beside a car at the roadside expecting Arthur to bring something he hadn't got. 'I'll tell you when I see him.'

The bus bounced along the dusty highway for a few miles until a white car with a man leaning on it came into view by the roadside.

'That your friend?'

'Yes.' At least he hoped it was, because he didn't fancy walking the rest of the way on foot and being late for the rendezvous.

The bus slid up beside the man and Arthur peered apprehensively out of the window. He was reluctant to move at first because there was no sign of Millie, but then he spotted her rucksack on the back seat of the man's car. He quickly jumped to his feet and stepped off the bus. He'd made a mental note to tip the driver, but in his haste to confront Millie's kidnapper he forgot, which probably explained why the door was unceremoniously slammed behind him. The bus sped off into the distance kicking up a large dust cloud as it went.

When the dust cleared Arthur found himself a few feet away from someone who looked vaguely familiar. Arthur knew he'd seen him somewhere before, but just couldn't put his finger on where.

Before boarding the bus he'd tried to work out who might be waiting for him. He hoped it wasn't Aidan, because he really didn't like the man, and he really, really hoped it wasn't a Belendrian.

The man before him was well dressed, looked Indian, and was of stocky build. His handlebar moustache was the feature that made Arthur sure he'd seen this man somewhere before.

And then it came to him.

It was the official-looking man in uniform, who had turned up in India just after he and Millie had got hold of the first key piece. This was the man to whom Manik had passed an envelope, with instructions to help him 'be rid of the interfering pair'. Obviously Millie's plan to throw him off their scent at the airport hadn't worked out so well in the end. Somehow he'd managed to track them down to Egypt.

'My name is Anil,' said the man with an outstretched hand.

Arthur had no intention of taking it. 'Where's my

granddaughter?' he demanded.

'In due course, Mr. Jarman, in due course.' Arthur hadn't liked him when he saw him in India and he certainly didn't like him now. He was far too smooth to be trusted.

'Where is my granddaughter?'

'I have been trying to track you down from India. Let's say a mutual friend, who by the way is now serving life in prison, asked me to find you and get back what's rightfully his.'

In comparison to Arthur, who had sweat cascading down his face, Anil was dry-faced and appeared as calm as could be.

'What are you talking about?' Arthur knew full well what he was talking about – that Manik was the 'mutual friend' he was referring to.

'It doesn't take a genius to come to the conclusion that two people, fitting perfectly the description of you and your granddaughter, were sniffing around the tattoo parlour asking all sorts of questions about this.' Anil pulled the first piece of the key out of a trouser pocket and waved it in Arthur's face. 'Then a few days later it just vanishes from its secret hiding place and amazingly the police *and* the press turn up to find Ranjit's body in the exact same spot.'

Anil edged closer to Arthur. 'Stroke of genius, the press at the airport, by the way. I had to let you go then, but my job allows me to have certain privileges, shall we say – or at least it did when I still had it – and one of those is access to a details of airline passengers.'

A distant thumping could be heard from the back of the car and Arthur cocked his head to listen. 'IS THAT MILLIE?' His face was starting to redden with anger, but Anil remained calm. 'IF YOU HAVE HARMED HER I WILL ...'

'I'll tell you what you will do, Arthur. You will hear my story, then answer my questions, and give me what I want. *That* is what you will do.'

Arthur so wanted to take a swing at Anil, but he knew he'd no chance of beating him in a fair fight.

'It took a little time back in India to locate your hotel and then get your details from the manager, but once I did I was able to track you to Australia. Fortunately for you by the time I'd traced you to Ayres Rock you'd already left and so I carried on to South America, but then the trail went cold.'

'Why?' said Arthur.

'Why what?'

'Why, if the man who hired you is in prison, have you spent so much time trying to find us? Why didn't you just let it go?'

'Because he is my brother.' He paused for a second. His thoughts seemed to wander elsewhere before he recomposed himself and gazed deep into Arthur's eyes.

'All of the other family members and so-called friends have abandoned him, but not me. I swore to him that I would find you and now I have.' A single bead of sweat appeared on Anil's forehead, but it was soon patted off with the crisp white handkerchief that had previously been peeping out of his top pocket. 'I have nothing else to live for now, anyway. You see the authorities in India traced a lot of corruption back to my brother and most of it relates to me. If it weren't for a few forged passports, I wouldn't be here now. I still have a handful of friends in the right places who have helped me find you, but I'm under no illusions. If I'm caught, then they'll just disappear.'

Anil was a desperate man and Arthur knew it, but he suppressed his urge to panic. Instead he focused on his plan to get Millie back. He could still hear banging from the car boot and although this concerned him greatly – not least because of the temperature it must be in there – noise meant she was still alive and that was good enough for now.

'Travelling overland from South America to Chicago was a good way to cover your tracks, but after being so close on several occasions you could say I was exceedingly pleased to finally catch up with you in Egypt. Fortunately for me, this time you didn't book your hotel until you got to Cairo airport, and the people on the hotel reservation desk there were most helpful. Money makes everyone talk in the end. You just need to find the price.'

'What happens if they don't have a price?'

'Then they die.'

'You have it all worked out, don't you?'

'Well, I thought I did until I found these.' Anil plucked out the other three pieces and toyed with them in his hand. 'Now imagine my surprise when I find not *one* but *four* strange glowing artefacts in Millie's rucksack, and I'm reliably informed by your feisty little granddaughter, that you have a fifth.' Anil's cool persona was beginning to slip. He was now looking decidedly twitchy and was running his finger round the neck of his shirt to let some air in.

Arthur thought Anil was lying or that Millie had said what she did to buy some time. He also knew that Anil had no intention of letting either of them go. Probably the only reason they were still alive right now was because of his desire to find the last piece in the hope that he could get rich from it. Maybe he needed money to stay ahead of the police?

Arthur didn't really care what his reason was. All he cared about was rescuing Millie.

'I can give you the other one, but I want to make sure she is all right and then I want your word that you'll let us go,' said Arthur, biding his time. He wanted Anil to open the boot to make sure it wasn't booby-trapped before he put his plan into action.

'I'll show you your granddaughter, but first tell me what these are for.' Anil rolled the four pieces over and over between his fingers, like a card shark fondling his chips.

'I'll tell you, but first I want to see my granddaughter.'

'You are in no position to bargain, but I'll show you I can be a reasonable man.'

Now Arthur *really* didn't trust him.

Anil beckoned Arthur to follow him to the back of the car where he stuck a key into the boot and opened it.

'MILLIE!' yelled Arthur, showing his obvious delight to see her again but she couldn't respond because she had her back to him, was bound from head to foot, blindfolded and gagged.

'That's far enough. Where's the other piece?' He was nose to nose with Arthur and truly meant business.

WHACK! WHACK! It took two resounding blows from a fake Arthur to knock Anil out cold.

'I didn't really want to do that,' said fake Arthur, as he dropped a large rock to the ground.

'I know,' said the real Arthur, 'but I'm glad that you did.'

Arthur clicked the Holographic Replicator a few more times until he'd made enough copies of himself to pull Anil far enough away from the roadside and out of sight of any passing traffic. While they were doing that the real Arthur undid Millie's ropes and helped her out of the car.

She was hot and dehydrated and had a lump on her forehead, but still burst into speech the moment she was ungagged. 'I heard a knock on the hotel door, which woke me up. When I looked around the room I saw that you were gone and thought you'd forgotten your key or something, but as soon as I opened the door I was knocked to the ground. When I came round I was tied up in the back of this car.'

Arthur brushed the hair from her eyes and examined her bump. 'So you didn't tell him about another piece to the key then?'

'Nope, he never gave me a chance to say anything. I tried to use my power to move things, but because I was blindfolded and it was so dark I couldn't see anything to concentrate on.' Millie was shaking her head as if to say she'd failed in some way.

'Well, we're both safe and back together now.'

Millie smiled her first smile of the day and said, 'Yes, all nine of us,' and nodded towards the seven fake Arthurs waiting patiently behind him. Real Arthur turned round and they all chorused, 'HI!' before he switched them off.

Meanwhile Millie had pulled a large bottle of water out of her rucksack and gulped it down in one go, before taking the keys out of the boot and jumping into the passenger seat of the car. 'You'd better drive!' she said, dangling the keys in her hand.

Arthur slipped into the driver's seat, took the keys, and started the car.

'Great Pyramid please, driver,' said Millie, putting the four key pieces, which Arthur had picked up from the ground next to Anil's prostrate body, safely back into her rucksack.

The sun was beginning to set and Arthur said, 'The clue talks about the sundown trail. Any idea what that means?'

'Maybe if you look through the key pieces at the horizon just as it sets something will be revealed.' Her answer told its own story. She was obviously clutching at straws and hoping things would come together when they got to the pyramids.

'I went to see the Great Pyramid earlier and nothing really stood out. There are some smaller ones beside it, the smallest of which are known as satellite pyramids, but none of them gave me a burst of inspiration about how we might find the trail.'

They parked in the designated area and headed past the tour parties directly to the Great Pyramid. After spending over an hour traipsing around its base – and those of its smaller neighbours – they still had no idea what they were supposed to do with the key pieces. They spent most of that hour placing the pieces in various spots around each of the five biggest pyramids, but this proved to be a waste of time.

The sun was now falling fast. The last thing they wanted was to run out of light and be forced to stay another day.

The Holographic Replicator again proved handy when it came to getting around, although they had a close call with a couple of tourists when two Millies bumped into each other. 'Identical twins,' cooed the first tourist.

'Don't you just feel sorry for them when their mother dresses them exactly the same?' replied the second.

'I know what you mean,' said one of the Millies wryly, before they all went on their way.

Having turned up nothing and with the sun now sitting just above the horizon, Millie had another idea. 'Let's place them on top of the three medium pyramids and one small satellite pyramid and see what happens. If that doesn't work then we'll have to try the same with the Great Pyramid.'

Arthur agreed and three fake Millies were dispatched to the top of the medium-sized pyramids while Millie herself climbed to the summit of the smallest one. The distance between them, and the fast receding light, kept unsuspecting tourists from stumbling across their plan. Arthur remained at floor level, directing procedures with his hands. He, like Millie, who chose the smallest pyramid on purpose, had been drained by the sapping effects of the sun and by the day's events so far.

Real Millie had taken the Sense Enhancer with her to help her see if anything significant happened when all the pieces were in place. She reached her summit, along with one or two unwelcome tourists, a minute or so after the other Millies reached theirs – each of them raising their thumbs, as agreed. Well, the two nearest raised their thumbs, but the third one had vanished, obviously now outside Replicator range. Fortunately for the real Millie she could see the piece was in place and no tourists were anywhere near it.

Millie dropped her piece down, but much to her disappointment nothing happened. That was until she bent over to pick it up and a beam of light from the sun appeared, joined by one from the only star visible in the dusky sky – the North Star. The two lights were focused on the top of the Great Pyramid, which now seemed to have a gold cap stone shimmering on top, and then reflected off in two directions.

One led out to the middle of the desert about halfway between the Great Pyramid and the huge Sphinx, no more than half a mile away.

The other was aimed directly on her key piece, which was now standing on edge. She wasn't the only one to see the light, but everyone nearby clapped thinking it was part of the light show they'd been waiting for. As soon as Millie bent down and picked up her key piece the lights disappeared, much to the crowd's obvious displeasure, but the piece remained bolt upright in the palm of her hand and pointed, compass-like, towards the Sphinx.

The sun was almost set and the rapidly-fading light was having an effect on Millie's key piece. It was beginning to sag in her hand and she scrambled as fast as she could down the side of the pyramid. Finding the answer she was looking for, together with her desire to get to the point in the desert to which the key piece was leading her, had suddenly recharged Millie's batteries.

Once on the ground, and back in Replicator range, she sent another Millie racing to the top of the furthest pyramid to retrieve its key piece.

'Get the fakes to gather the key pieces, Grandad, and meet me out there,' gasped Millie, pointing off into the near darkness. 'Here, take the Sense Enhancer.' She thrust it into his hand. 'It will help you find me in the dark. I have to go – I'm running out of time.' Arthur couldn't argue because she was gone before he'd opened his mouth.

Millie charged across the desert following the line shown to her by her key piece. Even with a new burst of adrenaline she could feel her legs and her lungs screaming out for a break. Her body was being pushed to its limit, but the sun was barely peeking above the desert skyline and she was worried that maybe there was only one chance at this. Maybe if she were to try it tomorrow it wouldn't work again!

Suddenly the piece dropped flat in her hand and she looked up, to see the sun finally disappear from view.

Crowds cheered in the distance as huge searchlights burst into life beneath the great monuments.

Millie just stood there in the darkness, foraging with her feet in the sand for some clue, some reason, for her to be in this spot. What made this place so significant? Perhaps she wasn't in the right place at all. Perhaps she was a few paces too short when the sun went down?

She scanned the horizon for the familiar figure of her grandad. She also wanted to make sure no stray tourists were in the area, although it was hardly likely that any would happen upon her standing smack bang in the middle of nowhere! All the action was half a mile in either direction. To her left were the pyramids, and to the right the Sphinx, picked out clearly by the surrounding lights.

When Millie looked back towards the Great Pyramid she could see the outline of her grandad slowly making his way through the sand towards her with three Millies beside him. 'Hello, Grandad,' she said, switching off the fakes. He raised his hand to show the Sense Enhancer was doing its trick with his hearing. He was still a couple of hundred yards away so she started to hum, making it easier for him to home in on her.

Unable to find anything with her feet, she sank to her knees and plunged her hands deep into the sand, but not until she dug even deeper, and the sand was up to her chin, did she feel something solid. Her heart began to race as she clearly felt the outline of some words written on whatever it was that lay beneath the sand. There were too many words for her to make out with her fingertips and she began to panic a little.

Arthur's first words when he finally arrived did not help. 'Anil is here!' he said, in a hushed but alarmed voice.

'WHAT?' Millie wasn't so quiet. She pulled her hands out of the sand and took the Sense Enhancer from her grandad. True enough, standing in full view of the huge spotlights surrounding the Great Pyramid, was a rather dazed Indian man she recognised at once.

Arthur raised his finger to his mouth, 'Shhh, keep it down.'

'How did he get here?'

'No idea, Millie, but I do know we don't want to hang around to find out.'

They both stared back as he forcefully relieved a guide – who promptly ran off – of her torch and started flicking its beam across the dark desert floor. 'Oh great, that's all we need,' said Millie, who was now armpit deep in sand again.

'What have you found?' Arthur crouched down beside her and sunk his arms in to investigate. 'Some sort of stone maybe?' he ventured.

'Don't know for sure, but it has writing chiselled on it and I'm trying to feel what it says. It's Zamorian, but I can't make it all out,' said Millie, feverishly trying to piece the words together with her fingers.

'What?' she said when Arthur knocked her. She swivelled her head, taking a mouthful of sand in the process, to see Anil heading their way. He couldn't have known where they were. He must have been taking the shortest route to the Sphinx in the hope that he would find his prey there. One thing was for sure, if he carried on in the direction he was going he would be on top of them within minutes.

Then the worst thing possible happened. His torchlight flashed from side to side across the place where Arthur and Millie were kneeling. When it quickly came back to stop on Arthur, they knew they'd been rumbled.

They frantically started to burrow away like rabbits, but each time they cleared some sand away the surrounding sand just fell into its place. Even Millie's mind power produced the same results.

Millie's brain was now flooded with maybes. If they left now then maybe they wouldn't find it again, or maybe others would be attracted to investigate, or maybe even Anil would somehow work out how to decipher the writing. They had to work out what was written beneath the sand and they had to work it out now.

Millie shook the sand from her hands and picked up her

rucksack.

'What are you doing?' said Arthur, still vainly digging away.

Millie pulled the book out and said, 'Help me see what's hidden below.' She hoped upon hope that, unlike her request to be invisible, this request would be answered more favourably.

Suddenly the answer appeared before her eyes, for she could now read the inscription on the stone slab buried below her. Millie clutched her belongings and held onto her grandad as she read, 'Show me the way to the lost city of Mu.'

The ground beneath them suddenly started to swirl as if they were standing in the wake of a giant plughole with sand instead of water grabbing at their ankles. First their feet, then their legs, and finally their whole bodies were sucked into the sand and the darkness below. As quickly as it started, it stopped. The sand levelled out and displayed no trace of what had just happened.

Anil ran, huffing and puffing, straight over the spot where the secret entrance was and stopped a few feet from it. He had his hands on his knees – clearly he wasn't as fit as he looked – and sweat cascading from his face. The guide he'd snatched the torch from was close behind him, along with two other colleagues, and the sight of them all heading his way was enough to push him on towards the sphinx and further away from the spot where Millie and Arthur had vanished.

CHAPTER TWENTY THREE

MU

'Grandad, are you there?' wheezed Millie.

When she crashed down on the hard surface below the secret hatch, through which she and Arthur had just fallen, the air had been temporarily sucked from her lungs. If it wasn't for the sand that had dropped down and cushioned her fall then she may even have broken something. If *she* felt like that then how did her much older relative feel?

The blackness drew back when Arthur switched Millie's torch on with his only free hand. He was up to his neck in sand, with one arm protruding, and lay semi-horizontal a few feet ahead of Millie.

'I'm OK, Millie. Quite comfortable, really!'

Millie waded through her own pile of sand towards Arthur and helped pull him clear.

'Grandad, I have X-ray vision. I could see through the sand.'

Arthur turned sideways, and looked sheepishly at her. 'Can you see through everything, then?'

'It's strange. I can if I choose to, like I can see the contents of my rucksack because I just asked myself to, but normally I just see what you see.'

Millie was trying to act cool, but she was over the moon with her new skill. Just think – she could now play cards with the boys at school and show them who was boss. Not the first thought you would expect to pop into the mind of a twelve-year-old when she'd been granted such a thing as X-ray vision, but then Millie was no ordinary twelve-year-old.

After a good brushing down and a torch lit survey, Arthur

and Millie discovered they were at the end of a long tunnel which led off at a slight incline into darkness. A cool breeze channelled its way up the tunnel, brushing over their clothes, and even stirring the sand at their feet. Arthur was still shaking the stuff out of his hair when Millie noticed something on the wall beside him.

'Look!' Her voice shot off down the tunnel before echoing back in time with the breeze.

'Keep it down, Millie. We've no idea who or what is down here with us.'

'Sorry,' she said in a more hushed tone, 'shine your torch over there.'

Arthur pointed as instructed. 'Nothing there,' he said.

'Yes there is. Zamorian writing. Keep it still and I'll translate for you.'

Follow the tunnel to the end and then upwards until you reach a blocked doorway. To the right of that doorway a hole will appear when you place both hands on the wall. Slide into the hole and you will be carried down into the Arabian Plate Line wind tunnel, which in turn will take you to the much faster Eurasian Plate Line intersection and on to Mu. Do not wait too long after sundown otherwise you will be carried in the wrong direction.

'What do you make of that then, Grandad?'

Arthur stood shaking his head, sand billowing out of his hair as he did so, and said, 'What you just said blows the universally accepted theories of plate tectonics out of the water!'

Millie shrugged. 'Big words and little time. Short version, please!'

'The plates are supposed to be driven by hot molten rock that flows beneath them. So the short version is simple. If wind doesn't blow between the plate lines then *we* are going to be fried to death!'

It didn't sound too good, but they could hardly turn back now. Besides, they didn't know how to reopen the hatch above them, so they had little choice.

'Let's hope it's windy when we get into the hole, then,' said Millie, taking the torch off her grandad and making him walk a couple of paces behind, in case they came across the cursed key piece.

The tunnel was neatly carved out and more than tall enough for Millie to walk through. Arthur wasn't as lucky, and could often be heard behind her bumping his head and groaning.

They'd walked a good half mile before they reached the foot of some stone steps, but calling them steps was a massive understatement because they were about five feet high and eight feet across. Millie could touch the top of them but would never have been able to climb up without being able to fly. They seemed to stretch upwards for ever and ever. Arthur's face was one of sheer horror when he stood looking up at them.

'I can help you, Grandad.' Millie put her arm around his waist and pushed off from the ground. It took a few goes to get it right, because she needed a hefty jump to get airborne, but she managed to generate just enough power to leap from step to step.

Finally they reached the top and found themselves standing before a square stone block that barred their way forward. Arthur traced his finger around the outside of the block as if he were looking for something.

'This is the wall we want, Grandad.'

Arthur heard the sound of wind come alive beside him. Millie had opened the hole with her hands, but within a few seconds of taking them away it had closed up again. 'You'd better go first otherwise you could be left behind, Grandad.'

Arthur wasn't ready to go just yet because he still had a few unanswered questions. He looked up to see another hole above his head that measured roughly a foot square, but Millie hadn't created this one.

It seemed to be an air shaft of some sort, but his torch provided no answers.

'Well, I never,' he said to himself.

'What?' said Millie, eager to carry on.

Arthur pointed to the large stone block. 'Can you please tell me what's on the other side of that? Then we can go, I promise.'

Millie stood facing the block and said, 'Not far in front of it is another one that's similar. It's hard to see much beyond that. Both of them are very thick, but the closest one seems to have a couple of handles on it.'

'Do the handles have something hanging off them?'

Millie turned on her heels. 'How did you know that?'

'Millie, we're inside the Great Pyramid. The doors you're looking at have been a mystery to humans since they were discovered. Nobody knew what was beyond them because they're at the end of a very long, narrow air shaft leading up from the Queen's chamber, and the shaft is inaccessible for humans. I read about the doors when I came to the pyramids earlier today.'

This find had Arthur rocking on his heels. He was standing behind the secret doors in the Great Pyramid and he wanted to tell everyone!

Millie had to nudge him to bring him back to the real world. 'Grandad, we have to go. The message on the wall said we can't wait too long after sundown remember?'

'Yes, yes, sorry. Go ahead and open the hole again and

I'll go first.'

Once open Arthur took his hat off and stuffed it inside his shirt before sticking his head in the hole and exploring it with the torch. 'I can't see past the first bend.' He pulled his head out and blew a cobweb off his nose. 'If we're *really* going to fall into very fast wind tunnels then you need to secure everything to your person. Strap the rucksack to your front so you can grip it tightly as soon as you jump through, and keep your legs crossed.'

Arthur kissed Millie on her forehead. She responded with her trademark thumbs up. 'Good luck,' he said, disappearing down the tunnel clutching the torch. Millie took a deep breath and jumped in straight after him. She heard the hole close up behind her and held on tight to her rucksack.

They slid down and down, countless times banging themselves on the side of the dark, dank tunnel as they fell. The initial drop reminded Millie of the Black Run water slide, minus the water, at her local swimming baths. It twisted its way down and round and down again towards the ever-growing roar of wind from the Arabian Plate Line wind tunnel below. She might even have enjoyed it if she hadn't been so scared and apprehensive about where she was actually going to end up.

Suddenly the bends evened out into a steep slide designed for one thing only – speed. As she skimmed down the slide like a stone being flicked across water, she picked up more and more velocity, and with each passing moment the roar of the wind grew louder and louder. She clutched her rucksack as tight as possible and squeezed her eyes shut and then … WHOOOOOOSHHHHH!

Nothing could have prepared her for this. She thought she was belting along before, but it was a snail's pace compared to the speed at which she was now travelling.

Millie was zooming along in the centre of a stream of wind, held perfectly in the middle of a tunnel by its force. A good thing, because travelling at the speed she was she would've been ripped to shreds if she'd hit the sides.

Even if she had wanted to ask the book for help, she couldn't. It was a struggle to hang on to her rucksack let alone reach inside it. No, she was in this one for the ride. After a few minutes the tunnel swerved slightly to the left and a minute or so later all hell broke loose.

'AAAAAAAAAAAAARRRRRRGGGGGGGGHHHHHHH!' she screamed when the tunnel she was in joined another one. The vicious change in direction to the right was extreme enough, but the sudden increase in speed felt like she'd just been blasted from a cannon.

Millie was now trying desperately to keep her legs crossed, they having clearly made up their minds they wanted to go back in the opposite direction. She could feel her cheeks wobbling frantically as her whole body fought against the force of the wind.

And then it stopped.

She was plonked down and slid into the back of her grandad, who dropped the torch on the ground.

'I managed to keep hold of it until now,' said an extremely windswept Arthur. His hair was veering off at all angles and his clothes seemed to have worked their way around his body.

They must have slowed gradually, but it sure didn't feel like it.

'Sorry, Grandad,' said Millie, who was still straightening herself out and checking for any damage. Apart from a few scratches neither of them looked the worse for wear. Arthur collected the torch, but they didn't need it as the place where they were standing was filled with light.

Only once they had fully composed themselves did they take in their surroundings. They were in a magnificent cathedral-like room. Its ceiling was vaulted – almost out of sight – and laden with stalactites hanging like chandeliers from above.

As quickly as the wind had died it started to pick up again.

'MOVE FROM THERE NOW!' shouted a distant voice.

They clambered up and out of the deep gully. The wind was fast picking up – only this time in the opposite direction – and they needed to move quickly. Millie grabbed hold of Arthur, who was struggling to get a foothold, and with one big push they both floated up and out, onto flat land.

'We have been expecting you,' said the voice.

Millie and Arthur stood rooted, both waiting to see who the voice belonged to. They didn't wait long before they caught sight of a tall, thin man, dressed in dark flowing robes. His feet were bare but it didn't seem to hinder him as he picked his route across the uneven floor. Eventually he came to a stop just before them, turned to Millie and said, 'My name is Tewani, the ruler of Mu. Welcome to my kingdom.' He swept his hand gracefully before them and bowed politely, first to Millie and then to Arthur.

Millie was a little taken aback by the gesture and replied with a rather lame dip of her head. 'My name is Millie and this is my grandad, Arthur.'

'You are the Chosen One.' Millie wasn't sure if Tewani said this as a statement or a question, but a nod seemed to do the trick because he greeted it with a broad smile.

'We mean you no harm,' said Millie.

'And we mean you no harm either. It's not our way. I know you seek the key piece and we have it safe for you.'

'Nobody can be around when I'm near it otherwise they'll

be taken over by its curse.' Millie wanted to make sure they weren't just about to rush out and present it to her!

Tewani slowly lowered and raised his head to express agreement. 'Aurora told my forefathers all about the curse. We will make sure no person or thing is near you when the time comes for you to collect it. Now please come with me as I expect you need rest and water and have plenty of questions to ask.'

Millie couldn't think of too many, except where is the key piece, but as for Arthur – well – his mind was positively overflowing with them!

Tewani led the way and the others followed. They passed through more cathedral-like chambers, which had grand entrances of ornate stone carved pillars and dozens of passageways running off them in all directions.

Everything in the chambers was carved out of stone with the most exquisite detail. Some of the rooms had stone tables topped with stone candlesticks, although they were providing no light, and perfectly proportioned stone chairs slid neatly beneath them. Others had beautifully carved statues. Some statues, like those depicting people and animals, Millie recognised, and some she did not.

The deeper they went the more people appeared, all wearing similar clothes to Tewani. They all displayed the same expression of fascination and bowed politely if Millie or Arthur made eye contact with them.

'What is this place?' Millie whispered to Arthur, who didn't respond because he was too transfixed and goggle-eyed to hear her.

They came at last to a smaller chamber. Unlike the others, this one had a domed ceiling that was devoid of stalactites and had a definite air of formality about it.

'Please take a seat,' said Tewani. 'I'll go and get the

others.'

They sat down as everyone else in the room stood up and bowed. There were maybe a dozen people scattered around, some reading from stone tablets and others inscribing them. Further inspection of the room revealed it to be stacked high with even more book-shaped tablets.

'It's a library,' said Arthur, now nodding in turn to everyone in response to their greeting.

'We're under water, Grandad.' Millie didn't hear what Arthur said, because she was far too busy looking through the walls to see what was beyond. Directly above them was water. Lots and lots of water. 'There's something carved on the outside rock. It looks like an animal,' said Millie. Even with X-ray vision she was struggling to make out its exact shape.

'Millie, I find this almost impossible to comprehend, but I think we're in the fabled underwater city of Mu, just off the coast of Japan. The exterior to this building was only recently discovered by local divers, but the geological community has been divided on whether it's man made or natural.' Arthur was struggling to believe his ears, and *he* was saying the words!

'Technically speaking you are both right, although we did have Zamorian help with the structure. However the large exterior carving you refer to, Millie, which is a turtle, was all our own work – before the land was flooded of course!' Tewani had returned with two others. The first, who'd just delivered that speech, was much shorter and broader than Tewani, of oriental appearance, and walked with a slight stoop.

Millie and Arthur both stood up when they entered, but were quickly ushered to sit down again by a wave of Tewani's hand. 'Please sit,' he said, as he and the other two pulled stone stools across the floor and sat themselves down. 'Please, everyone, go about your business.' The others scattered around the room tried their hardest to comply, but were clearly fascinated by the new arrivals.

'This is Golden Valley,' Tewani said, pointing to the plump Chinese man, 'and this is Le.' Both of them nodded politely and Arthur and Millie did the same. Millie thankfully managed to suppress her urge to laugh out loud because she'd just been introduced to someone with the same name as her local Chinese restaurant. The mere thought of that gave her hunger pains and an overwhelming desire for chicken chop suey!

Le was female and much younger than the other two. Her hair flowed endlessly down her back, and she looked to be of Mexican or Spanish descent.

'Water?' A young man arrived and handed out two stone goblets full of water, one each to Millie and Arthur, then promptly left again, bowing politely as he went.

'I expect you have questions,' said Tewani.

Arthur didn't know where to start so he went for an easy one. 'Is this really Mu?' he asked, his voice shrouded in disbelief.

'Yes, it is,' said Golden Valley.

Not wanting to be left out, Millie joined in with a question of her own. 'How did you get your name?'

Arthur shook his head ever so slightly. Just enough to tell Millie what he thought of her question to Golden Valley.

'It's a question with meaning and therefore relevant,' he replied. Millie patted her grandad's back and lent forward to hear the answer. 'This city is full of many people from many different parts of the world. The Zamorians who originally visited our planet were a friendly and helpful race. They warned our ancestors of two natural disasters that threatened our very existence.'

'Which were?' said Arthur eagerly.

'By far the most important thing the Zamorians told us was that the molten mass that drove Earth had almost burnt out and this planet could explode at any time. So they placed an alternative power source in the Earth's core to stop that happening.'

'How does it work?' Arthur was struggling to contain his excitement at hearing how the world *really* functioned.

'The Zamorian power source needs to vent its waste as lava. It uses the fractures in the Earth's crust, like volcanoes, to do this. As well as expelling waste, volcanoes also suck in huge amounts of air, which is used to cool the power source. The warm air generated by the cooling cycle is then dispersed evenly, using the plate lines. How it all functions and where the waste is expelled depends entirely on the pull of the moon. All of this meant that Earth carried on evolving exactly as it would have done before.'

'I wondered why the air in the wind tunnels felt so warm,' mused Millie, who could feel herself start to glaze over and had to make a concerted effort to stay focused as Golden Valley continued.

Golden Valley paused and Arthur waved him to continue 'Please carry on. You said there were *two* very important things.'

'Yes, the second warning was of a forthcoming ice period that would be like no other we had experienced. Ice would freeze this planet and not thaw for many generations and when it did a lot of the Earth's surface would be under water. During the time when they helped us prepare for this, many cultures came together.'

'But the last ice age was twenty thousand years ago! Common historical thinking is that, at that time people weren't advanced enough to travel vast distances and build such places as this.' History was Arthur's subject and hobby and he wasn't about to pass up questioning someone who might be able to fill in the gaps of the last two hundred centuries!

Le spoke for the first time. Her voice was melodic and subtle and her tone not the least bit condescending. 'Common or modern historical thinking is wrong. At the time of the ice age, as you call it, we were far more advanced than you have been led to believe. With the help of the Zamorians we were able to build shelters like these, both over and under ground, and gain a better understanding of how the plate lines worked. Generally we were very self-sufficient.'

'What happened after the ice age?' asked Arthur.

'After the ice age, all the shelters – or underground cities as we now call them – were covered with water. We stayed below the surface for many centuries until the ecosystem above settled down.'

'So you used the plate line wind tunnels to travel between the underground cities?' Arthur chipped in.

'Exactly,' said Golden Valley.

'Fascinating. Just fascinating,' said Arthur, who was trying to take as many mental notes as his brain could cope with. Just whom he was going to relay these notes to was anybody's guess. Anyone he did choose to tell, especially in the scientific or historical community, would have him sent to a madhouse for sure!

Millie raised her hand, 'Er … you still haven't answered my question about how you got your name.'

'So sorry. I must apologise, we haven't spoken to any outsiders for three hundred years so you must stop us if we go on. Every male in my family was called Golden Valley so I am just following on a tradition. The son of the original Golden Valley designed this city. Of course back then it was in a valley above water and when the sun came up it would light the buildings and they shimmered like gold.' Golden Valley bowed his head apologetically for taking so long to explain.

'Hence the name Golden Valley,' said Millie.

'Yes.'

'You were telling us what happened after the ice age. Why did you stay down here all this time?' said Arthur.

It was now Tewani's turn to give a brief history lesson. 'After the ecosystem on the planet's surface settled down many of our ancestors went out to explore, but we'd grown so used to our life below ground that the people of Mu chose to stay. All of the underground cities around the world did the same, and we carried on like that until the Belendrians arrived.'

'What happened then?' Millie sat up. This was what she wanted to know about. Sure, Mu history was interesting, for her grandad at least, but Belendrians, now *that* was a different matter.

'The balance in the underground cities changed when the Earth's core was filled with Zamorian children. Their being there drained our power and made sustaining multiple underground cities impossible. As we were the largest one, a decision was made to move everybody here. That is why today you see so many different races of people in Mu,' said Tewani.

'Why didn't you go above ground?'

'It was too late for us then, Arthur. We couldn't integrate into the society that had developed up there. We have never had a war amongst ourselves, and on the occasions when people were sent above to investigate life on the surface they always seemed to return with stories of fighting and hardship. The closest we came to feelings of such anger was when the other cities had to be abandoned, but those feelings were born out of not knowing what was going on in the core.'

'And then Aurora turned up,' Le said, taking over from Tewani.

'*And?*' said Millie eagerly.

'He just appeared one day in the wind tunnel chamber and asked to see our leader. When he told our ancestors who he was they were in no mood to entertain him any longer, but once he explained his motives and the plight of the Zamorian children they began to trust him more,' said Tewani.

'Not all of our ancestors trusted him,' said Le.

'Yes, but the majority did,' said Tewani, slightly agitated by Le's comment. 'That is when he left part of the key for the Chosen One to collect.'

'Did you fear the arrival of other Belendrians?' asked Millie.

'No. They never knew we existed. Only Aurora did, because his work back on Zamora allowed him access to such information. It was never really clear why he kept this information to himself, but in the end it all worked out because we provided him with a perfect hiding place for a key piece and he provided us with some hope for the future,' said Golden Valley.

'Any more questions?' asked Le.

'Where's the key piece?' said Millie, eager to get down to business.

'Actually, I have one more.'

'Yes, Arthur?' said Tewani.

Millie just wanted to get on, so her grandad's interruption

didn't go down too well.

'Why did we have to enter the Arabian Plate Line wind tunnel to come here and how do we get out?'

That was two questions, but once Millie heard them the annoyance she felt towards her grandad subsided. They were good questions, because if something went wrong it would be a good idea to know exactly how to get out!

'Since the Zamorian children arrived the Plate Line wind tunnels run much too fast to jump into without first picking up speed. The only time you can get into them is when the wind changes direction, but you need to know exactly where to be standing when this happens. Only decades of experience can tell you where the right place to stand is, because it's different each time. Aurora couldn't tell you for sure where that place would be, because he didn't know when you would find the book. That is why you were eased into the ride via a pyramid tunnel made by Aurora himself. You will not have the same problem when you come to leave because we can help you then,' said Tewani.

'I would like to add that apart from knowing where to stand, there are certain times of the day when you can't enter *any* tunnel because they are all out of sync,' said Golden Valley.

'What would happen if you *did* enter at one of those times?' Millie's morbid curiosity was getting the better of her.

'You would get ripped apart in the underground network,' replied Golden Valley.

'Or worse,' said Le knowingly.

Golden Valley nodded. 'Oh, yes, I forgot.'

Millie looked on pensively. 'What's worse than that?'

'You could be shot straight out of a volcano … but that almost never happens!' said Le.

Millie pursed her lips and winced. 'Ouch!'

Tewani and the others all rose to their feet in unison and Millie and Arthur followed suit. 'Let's take you to the key piece, so you can be on your way.'

CHAPTER TWENTY FOUR

THE FINAL PIECE

Their journey from the library to the key piece took them past crowds of curious-looking and politely bowing people of all colours, shapes, and sizes, who'd spilled out of the adjoining corridors. Millie wasn't sure what to do so she just smiled, while Arthur delivered his best impression of a nodding dog.

The group went through the wind chamber and came to a halt when Tewani pointed into a side room and said, 'You wait in there Millie, and I'll clear your path to the key piece. I'll make sure nobody is within a few hundred paces. Arthur, you'd better come with me.'

'Just a second,' he said, and went with Millie into the side room. 'Do you think we can trust them?' he whispered.

'Yes I do. Think about it. They want the children out of the core as much as we do because it will restore power to the underground cities and make their lives much easier. Here, take this just in case.' Arthur took the Holographic Replicator from her outstretched hand. 'I have my powers to help me and now you have *you* to help you!'

Arthur nodded in agreement – slowly at first but then with great vigour – before leaving in pursuit of Tewani.

The room Millie found herself in was full of the most amazing array of artwork and she spent the next few minutes just gazing at it.

'Are you really the Chosen One?' said a small voice in the doorway behind her.

Standing in the dimly-lit opening was the same young man who'd served her and Arthur water back in the library.

He was a wispy little fellow with tufty hair and a frightened grin. He looked Asian, but it was difficult to tell, as he was partly obscured by shadow. In one hand was a stone tablet and in the other a small hammer and chisel.

'Can I have your autograph?' he enquired almost apologetically, bowing his head.

'Er,' said Millie, somewhat taken aback by the question. She'd never been asked for such a thing before and the request made her blush with embarrassment.

She started to walk towards her admirer but the sound of some footsteps approaching scared him off. By the time she'd poked her head out of the room he was nowhere to be seen.

'We have cleared your path,' said Tewani, approaching alone from the other direction. 'The others are all back in the library and this whole section to the wind chamber is empty.'

'Somebody was just here asking for my autograph.' said Millie, as if it didn't really mean anything.

'Yes, I saw Kier running off. He was so excited when he found out you were here, but I thought letting him serve the water would be enough! Never mind, I'm going back down that way and I'll make sure he's gone. You need to go to the end of this corridor,' said Tewani, who was pointing in the direction he'd just come from, 'and what you seek is in the last room on the left. There's nothing else in there so you only have the piece itself to contend with. We will wait for you to come and find us.'

'Thank you.' Millie stood and watched Tewani hurry away and disappear into the maze of side chambers.

When she could no longer hear him she tentatively set off down the corridor until the effects of the curse started to kick in. This time she was determined, more than ever, to fight through the pain barrier and counter the curse as quickly as possible. The thickness of the stone walls seemed to be helping because, although it was biting at her body from all directions, the pain was still bearable.

At last she approached the room. The key piece was only a few feet inside, but a sudden surge of pain rocked her backwards.

'Right,' she said, building herself up, 'this is it. This is the last time I'm going to feel such pain.' She filled her lungs with air and jumped through the doorway.

CRACK!

'I wouldn't count on that, if I were you,' said Kier, who was standing over Millie's motionless body with blood dripping from the stone tablet in his hand. He'd doubled back in an innocent attempt to snag the signature of the legendary Chosen One. Unfortunately for Millie he picked the wrong room to hide in and he was now, like many others before him, not in control of his actions.

Kier picked up the key piece and twiddled it in his hand. 'So this is what you seek,' he said, standing over her, staring down intently. 'If you take this then you will leave, but I want you to stay for ever. I must get rid of this thing.' He knelt down and stroked Millie's bloodstained hair. 'Don't worry, I will be back.'

Millie awoke, feeling as if she'd just been hit by an express train. 'It's gone,' she muttered, looking up from her prone position. She could feel a faint trickle of blood running down her neck as she rose unsteadily to her feet.

She staggered to the doorway and looked up and down the corridor, just in time to see Kier, key piece in hand, shuffling off towards the wind chamber.

'STOP!' she shouted desperately after him.

Kier ground to a halt and glanced back over his shoulder.

'I SAID I WOULD BE BACK FOR YOU!' he bawled, before continuing on his way.

Millie started after him as quickly as her legs would carry her, and wasn't too far behind when Kier entered the wind chamber.

He hurried over to the edge of the wind channel – where Millie and Arthur had first arrived in Mu – and held the key piece out above it.

'NO!' Millie screamed as she came running into the chamber.

'STOP!' Arthur shouted from way over on the other side where he'd been patiently waiting for his granddaughter's all-clear signal.

'I have to,' said Kier and before another word was uttered he dropped the key piece into the howling wind below.

Millie's run broke into flight, and she dived down after it with both arms outstretched. It was almost in her grasp when first the key piece and then Millie were sucked into the raging torrent.

'What is going on?' said Tewani, who'd just arrived at the scene. 'I heard shouting and—'

Arthur motioned towards Kier. 'He threw the key piece into the wind channel that leads to the tunnel and Millie went in after it. I have to help her.'

'You can't, Arthur it's not safe. If Millie jumped in then she'll already be dead. She needed to build up some speed because the wind is at its strongest right now.'

'She did have speed. She *flew* into the wind,' said Arthur, hoping against all hope she really was going fast enough.

Tewani didn't respond to Arthur. Instead he turned his attention to a rather dazed and confused looking Kier. 'YOU!' he shouted.

Arthur put his hand on Tewani's shoulder. 'There's no

point in shouting at him. He would have been under the control of the curse. It's not his fault. Believe me, it's not his fault.'

Arthur walked across the chamber to the young man, who was standing forlornly beside the wind channel.

'What happened?' said Kier, eyeing his blood-stained tablet.

'Nothing. Go now and everything will be OK.' What else could Arthur say? The poor lad was confused enough as it was.

Tewani said nothing when he crossed paths with Kier to stand alongside Arthur, who himself was looking rather dazed as he stood staring hypnotically at the raging wind below.

'If she gained enough speed she may still be alive in there, but at this time of the day the wind stream will terminate back at the pyramids at the base of another secret passageway.'

'Why do you say "but"? Surely that's good news.'

'Arthur, the secret passageway is sealed and can only be opened if she places both hands on the wall as she must have done in the Great Pyramid.'

'So?'

'So she will be arriving at the wall at breakneck speed and will not have enough time to react. This was your route out, but she has entered the channel too early.'

They both stood motionless, gripped by the sound of the wind as it rocketed by.

'Millie will find a way,' said Arthur, who was forcing himself not to think of the consequences if she didn't.

Tewani bowed his head. 'It will not be long before the wind slows enough for you to enter, Arthur. I'll come with you to help in whatever way I can.'

Arthur felt Tewani's hand on his shoulder. Although grateful for the gesture of support, he could think of nothing else but Millie.

*

The Eurasian Plate Line wind tunnel was pulling Millie along at an immense speed. Her hair was streaming down the back of her perfectly flat body, with her arms outstretched and her feet dangling behind.

Left, right, left, right she was pulled ever onwards, changing direction at a moment's notice. Her rucksack was strapped firmly to her back, but its bulk provided almost too much drag for her to catch the key piece still hanging tantalising in front of her hands.

Her determination to get it was all-encompassing, even going so far as to mask the pain she normally felt when so close to a cursed key piece.

Millie managed to find just enough extra power from somewhere to increase her speed. Finally she grabbed hold of it. The burning pain she always felt when this happened was again evident, but she was determined to read the inscription.

The wind was so intense that she couldn't focus and so used her flying skills to slow herself down. She couldn't stop, but she slowed enough to see the words at last.

'*Where*—'

WHACK!

She'd hit the wall leading to the secret passageway at the base of a pyramid. Her pace was slowed by her attempt to read the inscription and her outstretched hands had triggered the wall to open, but she was still going a great speed when she flew through the hole and bounced to a stop on the floor. The key piece shot out of her hand and rolled off into an adjoining room.

For a moment, Millie lay where she fell, catching her breath and regaining her senses.

Wind was no longer lashing at her face and whistling past her ears, although it could still be heard raging in the tunnel behind her until the secret passageway closed up and her world fell silent.

Pain started to work its way through her body. Not from the curse, although she could still feel that in the background, but from her wrists and her head wound. Her head was pounding as before, but her wrists felt as if they were both broken. She could still feel her fingers and they had a little movement, but the pain was immense when she used them to take her torch out of her rucksack and turn it on.

Opposite to where she lay was a room with a sandy floor, and in one corner was a huge sarcophagus, its lid balanced upright on the edge of the open stone coffin.

Millie slowly got to her feet in preparation for her final assault. She looked an awful mess as she stood there with a bloodied head, limp arms, and sand encrusted clothes. The pain from holding the torch with a broken wrist was too much and she dropped it on the floor, watching it finally bounce to a halt facing half in and half out of the room.

With her head down and heart thumping she stumbled forward towards the key piece, but with each step her legs felt heavier and heavier until she realised that the sand on the floor was clawing at them and trying to pull her down. Her knees started to buckle under the pressure and then the desert carpet engulfed her.

She reached out and took hold of the key piece, but the sand plumed up from beneath, lifting Millie right off her feet and slamming her into the empty sarcophagus. The key piece flew into the air and came back down to land on the lid, span a little, and then fell flat.

If the lid hadn't crashed down as Millie was thrown inside the sarcophagus then the piece would have landed straight in her lap, but now it was a couple of feet away lying flat on top of her burial chamber.

At first the lid sealing her in sent Millie into a deep state of shock. She could no longer feel the pain of her broken wrists or even the curse. Those feelings were replaced by ones of horror, worry, and fear. Her chest felt tight and her skin as cold as ice, and she became acutely aware that she may not be alone in the coffin.

And then it started.

Millie couldn't make out what it was at first. All she could hear was a faint scratching noise from above. The cursed key piece had sprung upright, much as the one in Millie's hand on top of the satellite pyramid in the Egyptian desert had done. Only this one was not leading the way. This one was inscribing three letters on the blank stone lid.

R.I.P.

Millie heard it settle flat once more and suddenly it came to her what to do. '*Where the clouds are sleeping in a far away land,*' she gasped.

It had taken her some time to think straight, but when she did she remembered her latest power, X-ray vision. Once the key piece had settled she could clearly read the inscription that was written on it.

However, even without broken wrists – they healed themselves once the curse had been lifted – and all her powers fully functioning, Millie still couldn't shift the lid, however much she huffed and puffed. She tried a combination of flying and telepathic energy to move it, but only succeeded in bumping her head and grazing her hands. The sweat ran off her as she rapped on the walls of the sarcophagus, all the time screaming at the top of her voice to be released.

If only she had the Holographic Replicator to generate lots of Millies to help her!

The stale air was growing thinner and she could feel herself getting light-headed from the lack of oxygen. The absolute darkness allowed her imagination to run wild. She didn't see anything else in the tomb when she was thrown in, but she couldn't help feeling she wasn't its sole occupant. Was her mind playing tricks or had she just heard a scratching sound?

Suddenly a shaft of light appeared, causing her to shield her eyes. This was swiftly followed by the welcome sound of two familiar voices.

'MILLIE! Are you OK?' shouted Arthur.

'You did it, Millie,' said Tewani, who was struggling with Arthur to pull the lid far enough over for Millie to get out.

'That's enough,' said Millie, poking her head out and filling her lungs with a welcome dose of air. It may have been stale, musty air, but she didn't care one bit.

Arthur helped pull her free before dispensing one of his characteristic bear hugs, while Millie let out a huge sigh of relief.

'Here you are.' Tewani held out the final piece of the Key to Chintak for Millie to take.

'Thanks!' she said, pausing briefly to admire it before stuffing it safely inside her battered rucksack.

'Follow me,' said Tewani, and he led the way back out into the passageway and onwards towards a dead end. 'This is where we exit.' He placed his hands against the wall and a hole appeared. 'The Zamorians also taught us how to do this,' he said with a grin. 'Now go through.'

Arthur and Millie ducked through the hole, Tewani

followed and it swiftly closed up behind them. They were once again standing at the top of the giant stairs leading down to the secret passageway between the Great Pyramid and the Sphinx.

'To reopen the hatch you came in through from the desert, you need to stand directly below it and repeat the words you said before.'

'Thank you, Tewani. If we succeed, and the Children of Zamora get to return to their home planet, then the balance will be restored in the underworld and your people can once again inhabit the other cities.'

Millie couldn't have said it better herself if she'd tried.

'My people will be indebted to you for ever if that happens. Good luck. Now I must go. My journey back is going to be a long one because the wind has changed direction, so the sooner I get started the sooner I can tell them the great news.' Tewani placed both hands on the opposite wall and disappeared into the hole that materialised.

They watched the wall magically repair itself before Millie helped Arthur down to the base of the pyramid. It was far easier for both of them going down than when they came up. They still used Millie's flying power to help them, but this time gravity was on their side and they managed to clear three or four stone steps with each leap.

'I wonder who'll be at the gateway to greet us when we open it with the key?' said Millie, as she and Arthur made their way purposefully towards the overhead hatch at the end of the tunnel.

'Show me the way to the lost city of Mu,' she said, stepping back away from the hatch to avoid taking any more sand on board. She was already a walking desert, with her hair and clothes full of the stuff.

Sand started to sift down from above and then – PLONK! – a huge amount was deposited at their feet when the hatch swung down, narrowly missing Arthur's head.

'Hold on to me, Grandad.' Arthur grabbed hold of Millie and they flew upwards before coming to rest on the desert floor above. The secret hatch resealed itself and quickly disappeared from sight when the surrounding sand tumbled in on it.

'Let's get out of here,' whispered Arthur, and he led the way as they both trudged back to the car park where there was only one car left, waiting for its owner to return. The light show had finished, and as quickly as they'd arrived to ogle at a great wonder of the world the tourists had left.

The solitary car belonged to Anil, but he was nowhere to be seen and Arthur had the keys.

'I can't see any movement,' said Millie in a hushed tone. 'Let's take it and go. I really don't fancy the walk!'

Arthur had reservations about the idea, but he too had no desire to walk to the site where they needed to assemble the key. In fact he'd no desire to walk any more at all!

They crept across the car park to the waiting car and Millie shuffled excitedly as Arthur unlocked her side before racing round to his.

'I have been waiting for you.'

Arthur slid to a halt as he rounded the bonnet. There, crouched on the floor in front of him with blood-matted hair and two huge lumps on his head, was Anil. In one hand he had a gun, and he trained it on Arthur as he climbed unsteadily to his feet. Millie had her door open, but the sound of Anil's chilling voice and the sight of the gun was enough to keep her from getting into the car.

Thoughts of using her telepathic powers to open the door on him were quickly dispelled in case the gun went off as he fell. A cursed key piece was no longer involved, so this time if Arthur was shot dead then he would stay dead.

'Throw me the bag,' he demanded of Millie. 'NOW!' he roared impatiently. The click of the gun being cocked was enough to make Millie do as instructed and slide her rucksack across the roof to Anil who unbuckled it with his free hand – never once taking his eyes off Arthur – and shook out the contents.

Anil flicked his eyes back and forth between Arthur and the contents of Millie's rucksack, and it didn't take him long to find five key pieces instead of the four he'd previously stolen from the pair.

'I don't know how you managed to knock me out before, but all is now forgiven as you have so kindly brought me all five,' said Anil with a slimy smile.

He fiddled with the pieces, assembling them like a jigsaw, until only one was left and then he did something he was to regret for the rest of his life – he slotted the final piece in place.

'NO ... HELP ... SOMEONE ... PLEASE ...' he shrilled. The assembled key was creating some sort of vortex around itself, and Anil was struggling vainly not to be pulled into it.

Millie and Arthur could feel its magnetic strength too. Arthur was trying his hardest to hold onto the car, and not be dragged off by the swirling wind that had now whipped up the desert sand and was in the process of consuming Anil.

Anil finally lost his battle and was sucked in. His flailing feet were the last part of his body to disappear from view. Arthur looked set to be the next in line when Millie, who was making full use of her flying power to fight against the whirlpool of wind and sand, slammed her door shut. This displaced the key pieces, causing the vortex to disappear instantly.

Nothing much could surprise the pair by now and this event was no different. They both grimaced in tandem – seemingly too tired to say more than one word to each other about Anil's timely demise.

'OOPS!' said Arthur.

'PHEW!' Millie exclaimed, retrieving her rucksack and the five separate key pieces. Arthur was using the car to hold himself up, but still had enough strength to thank Millie with a nod and a smile.

They both clambered into the car, neither speaking again about Anil's fate. In fact they sat in silence all the way to the excavation site where the book was originally discovered, fully aware that their momentous journey was coming to an end. What they weren't aware of was how their lives would change when *they* assembled the key.

CHAPTER TWENTY FIVE

CHINTAK

'This is it,' said Arthur, switching off the engine and applying the handbrake.

Who would have thought that three words could provoke so much feeling?

Arthur sat tapping the steering wheel and staring out of the window towards an excavation site that had long been abandoned. Unlike the Great Pyramid this was not a place visited by many. Only a half-submerged stone boulder with an identification plaque crudely bolted to it gave any indication of the significance of the place. He couldn't help wondering what might be in store for them when they eventually got out of the car. Were they really doing this deed for the good of a race that had seen millions of their kind persecuted by a few, or were they playing right into the hands of that very same few? Could they really be sure who wrote the book and what the outcome would be?

Now the searching had finished and they'd arrived at their goal there still seemed to be just as many questions as answers.

Millie was pondering something she'd read in the book about the Key to Chintak. That it should only be assembled in one piece when they reach this spot in case a Belendrian detected the power in it and came to investigate. Because Anil had already pieced the key together, albeit briefly, were a group of murderous villains about to make an untimely appearance?

Arthur was the first to speak. 'Not too impressive.'

'Nope.'

'Still, this is where they found the book.'

*

The ancient black book was discovered in the Egyptian desert in 1952 by a group of French archaeologists who were excavating an underground tomb.

While carefully clearing sand from around the tomb one of the crew noticed a small black object poking out.

It turned out to be a corner of the black book, which, once pulled out and cleaned off, was greeted with confusion when it was discovered to have no writing in it. Its only real feature was the embossed cover, which in a certain light appeared to look a little like the outline of a door. Once the assembled crew had all inspected the find it was stowed away for later examination and the dig continued.

Next to the book the archaeologists also found a strange rock that didn't appear to any of them to have come from the area. Their curiosity as to what lay in the tomb drew them to decide that the rock must have been part of a meteorite. Being of no real interest to them, it was quickly discarded.

The tomb was eventually opened and its contents examined. Much to the disappointment of the team, it yielded nothing of great interest.

The only other significant entry in the archaeologists' journal of events at that time was that one of the crew reported seeing a shimmering light appear briefly as he was marking out the far end of the tomb. But as he was the only one to see it and the sun was particularly strong on that day, his colleagues put it down to a combination of sunstroke and a vivid imagination.

The book found its way back to a museum in Paris where it stayed for many years, and then over the ensuing half century it was passed from country to country in order to try to solve its mystery.

In 1983 the British Museum dated it to around AD 900, but due to its remarkable condition several other museums disputed this even though their own dating methods corroborated the findings.

And so it came to pass that at the turn of the twenty-first century the book arrived at the museum where Arthur Jarman worked and took pride of place in their Egyptian showcase. It was due to stay there for three months until it was handed back to its rightful owners in France.

Half way through the loan period, however, the museum had to shut down for a week to undergo some renovation work. It was during this time that Arthur decided to take the book home for what he described as 'a little light reading'. Little did he know what lay beyond this tongue-in-cheek comment that he made for the benefit of his workmates.

Arthur's colleagues couldn't understand why the book fascinated him so much. They'd long since reached the conclusion that the book must have been made for an Egyptian nobleman who died before he had a chance to write in it. Another of many theories offered, was that it must have been buried with someone who believed that whatever awaited them on the other side could be written down.

*

Millie opened her door to get out, but Arthur pulled her back. 'It'll be OK, Grandad. I know it will,' she said calmly. He let go and they both climbed out and walked over to the stone to read the simple inscription engraved on the plaque.

Entrance to tomb discovered in 1952.

Arthur took a compass out and got his bearings before pacing off in one direction with Millie tagging along behind. Her heart rate seemed to go up a notch as she watched him walking in front of her. She could feel the hairs on the back of her neck and even hear herself breathing by the time he stopped and said, 'Are you sure you still want to do this?'

He knew the answer, of course.

Millie nodded.

She knelt in the sand and spread a small area flat with her hand and took out the five key pieces. One by one she neatly assembled the first four. The wind that was blowing when they first arrived was now conspicuous by its absence. Perhaps even Mother Nature was curious as to what might happen next.

Millie held the final piece tight in her hand and looked at her grandad for his approval for what she was about to do.

'Go on,' he said.

She lowered it into place, at the same time saying 'CHINTAK' in her loudest, clearest voice.

What happened next was surreal, to say the least. The sand started to swirl, vortex-like as before, but this time it wasn't sucking in – it was spitting out.

'NOOOOOOOO! GET AWAY FROM ME!' squealed Anil, as he thumped onto the ground. He leapt up in front of the equally startled pair and ran as fast as his legs would carry him back to his car, yelling incomprehensibly as he went. Moments later he was bouncing the car across the sandy desert and out of sight.

Whatever had happened when the key consumed him certainly had a profound effect!

'I doubt if we'll see him again,' said Millie.

The vortex, which was briefly subdued in freeing itself of Anil, rose up again from the key, swirling around faster and faster as it gained height. Millie and Arthur had to shield their faces from being sand-blasted by the mini storm, but it quickly died down and the desert became calm again.

'WOW!' said Millie, absolutely astounded by what she saw.

'Ditto.'

After all this time, after all the pain and anguish, there they were standing side by side in front of a ten foot square gateway which led to a hidden continent. The gateway had no discernible markings, but it was there all right, almost like a blank canvas ringed by the desert skyline.

'LOOK, GRANDAD, LOOK! SOMEBODY IS COMING!' Millie couldn't contain her excitement when she saw some figures appear in the gateway. At first they were just specks, but they quickly became larger, seemingly floating towards her and Arthur.

'I see them, Millie. I see them.' Arthur was a mixture of excitement and apprehension, as the figures got closer and closer until they became recognisable to the human eye.

They were Zamorians and one of them was coming a lot closer than the others. The images of the Astronaut carved out in the Nazca Plains and in the hidden cavern in Australia were spot on. They were short, about Millie's height, and had human features with the obvious exception of a nose.

'And hello to you,' said Millie. She just couldn't believe she was standing face to face with a distant relative. This was her goal. She had wondered if it would ever be achieved, and at times if the Zamorians ever really existed; but they did because one of them had just said hello to her telepathically.

'Translate what they're saying out loud for me, please, Millie.' There was no way Arthur wanted to miss a word of what went on from here. He'd done his fair share to get to this point and he wanted to know what happened next.

The figure on the other side of the gateway drifted towards Arthur. 'There's no need for her to translate. I will speak out loud in your language.'

'Thank you,' said a very awestruck Arthur.

'My name is Fitar and I am very pleased to meet you,' he said to Arthur, before turning to Millie. 'Both of you.'

'Introduce yourself, then,' prompted Arthur to Millie, who was standing with her mouth ajar and her manners askew.

'Sorry. I'm Millie and this is my grandad, Arthur.'

'No need to be sorry. I expect you have had an arduous journey to get here and have questioned your sanity many times,' said Fitar.

Fitar had a voice that could put the most nervous person at ease in his company. His whole appearance was one of calm. Millie felt her worries start to melt away just from being in his presence.

One thing was for sure – all Zamorians seemed to look alike. Those gathered excitedly behind Fitar all looked the spitting image of him, with big eyes and small mouths that were upturned at the corners. Maybe the arrival of Millie and Arthur was the reason for their fixed smiles or maybe they were just born happy!

'You can say that again. My presence set off the curse on the key pieces and caused havoc whenever we came near one …' Millie's words tailed off. She felt guilty even thinking that her problems compared to those of a people who had been imprisoned on a foreign planet for centuries, knowing all their adult relatives had been slain.

'You do not need to feel guilt for telling of your journey. Each of us experiences and deals with problems in our own way and yours are no better or no worse than anyone else's,' said Fitar, displaying an uncanny knack of reading emotions as well as minds. 'I only wish Aurora were here to see this day.'

'Do you know how he died?' quizzed Millie.

'I last saw Aurora six years before I passed this book back through the gateway. He was anxious to tell us something almost as soon as he appeared. The words "a young" had just passed his lips when someone stepped up beside him. The mere sight of the mysterious stranger seemed to relieve Aurora of his ability to speak. It was only when the stranger reverted to his natural state did we all realise who it was – Kiptiziz.

We all recognised immediately the leaves of the deadly Joxgovia plant when Kiptiziz pulled them out and shoved them forcefully into Aurora's mouth. A drop of blood from another Zamorian on the skin of someone suffering from Joxgovia poisoning was the only cure. We could see from the way Kiptiziz stood sneering over his fellow Belendrian that he felt no guilt for his actions.

Aurora's own curse was all that stood between his living or dying. On one side of the gateway stood millions of children willing to offer their blood as a cure, but unable to do so, and on the other stood the most hated Zamorian alive, who was in no mood to make such an offer.

Aurora had one last act of defiance left in him, though. Something had distracted Kiptiziz and as he turned away to investigate Aurora threw his key through the gateway. As soon as he did so the gateway closed and that was the last we saw of the Belendrians.

He knew that we could not pass his key back through as the Belendrians would most probably detect its power and come to retrieve it, but we could pass the book through in the hope that it would eventually find its way into the right hands.'

'What happened after you sent the book through?' said Millie, thankful that she and Arthur had managed to avoid

Kiptiziz along the way.

'We threw a large rock out at first to test the gateway and then followed this with the book. A group of us sat for a while staring out at the sand as it rolled its way across the skyline and then reluctantly we closed the gateway to avoid detection, leaving our hopes resting in the desert. In the ensuing days we reopened the gateway to see if the book was gone, but all we ever saw was it slowly being consumed by the sand. Once we lost sight of it completely we decided only to reopen the gateway every few years or so. Each time we did we were always met by the same landscape, until one day we opened the gate to see someone digging in the sand very close by. We closed it immediately hoping that they'd not seen us.'

Arthur nodded. 'They did see something. At the time the book was discovered it was recorded that one of the workers saw a shimmering light, but when he and others went to investigate they couldn't find anything and put it down to a desert mirage.'

'You bonded with humans before the last ice age. Did you mean that to happen?' Millie enquired.

'Not at first, but we were forced to communicate with your race,' he motioned towards Arthur, 'when one of our probes, spaceships I believe you call them, malfunctioned and the pilots had to abandon ship. They were spotted, but both races quickly came to trust each other and shared information. At the time, interaction between races was actually prohibited and so it was hushed up by our leaders.'

'If it was hushed up then how did *you* find out about it?' Obviously this was a subject that interested Millie.

'Aurora told us. He used to work with the historical archives and one day he discovered a reference to it when he was accessing a restricted section. That was also the time when he found out about the underground cities. He never told the other Belendrians, not because he wanted to protect anyone, but because he wanted to rule them himself. It was only when he started to feel guilty about what he'd done to our race that he let us in on his secret. His guilt was further compounded when we told him that we were probably depriving the underground cities of power because there were so many of us in Chintak,' said Fitar, who was bobbing gently about in the air.

'Whose idea was it to put a key piece in Mu?' asked Millie.

'Aurora's. He wanted to explain the reason why they were suffering, because they wouldn't have known, and to tell them he had a possible solution.'

Millie had often stood back when her grandad was firing off questions, but now *she* had them all lined up. 'How did the book give me powers?'

'It didn't. All the book did was allow you to bring out the powers that were buried deep inside you. The ones you would never have tried to channel because you would have grown up in a human world.'

'So it brought to life powers I already had?'

'Yes. It could not give you any new ones. We just hoped you possessed enough powers to get you through.'

Millie scratched her head. 'That's why I didn't go invisible when I asked,' she whispered to herself.

'That is right,' said Fitar, reminding Millie that he could read her mind!

Everyone stood – or floated in the Zamorians' case – each of them contemplating what they'd just been asked and told, each of them dealing with it in their own little way.

Arthur played with the sand with his feet, thinking about the implications of truly discovering another race – not to mention an underground city and a hidden continent – and what it all meant to science. He couldn't help wondering what else was out there waiting to be found.

Millie was mesmerised by the gateway and the people beyond. A people that she felt part of – indeed *was* part of. She no longer thought about the past but only the future, and what she could do for the Children of Zamora to help them get home.

Fitar just smiled. He didn't know if his future plans involving Millie would be a success, but he was happy that his last plan had worked, because it gave his people hope for the future.

The silence was broken when Arthur said, 'So where do we go from here?'

'We need you to find the crystals to drive the Molto device we have in Chintak so we can, providing the climate is stable enough, return to Zamora and start again. The Belendrians can't retake anything you bring into Chintak because, thanks to the curse, they will die if they pass through a gateway to our continent.'

'But they can get us on the outside?' said Arthur slowly.

'Yes they can, and once they know what you are up to they will try with all their might to bring you down.'

'How many crystals?' asked Millie, choosing for now to ignore the danger ahead.

'Six. Each Belendrian has one, except Kiptiziz who has two because he took Auroras', and we need all of them. If they have not detected the opening of this gateway, you will have an advantage over the first Belendrian you take on.'

'Which is?' said Millie.

'Surprise.'

'But after that they'll know about us?' Arthur's tone was one of great concern.

'It depends if they notice the crystals have gone or not,' said Millie positively.

'Optimism, Millie. A true Zamorian trait,' said Fitar.

'Hmm,' said Arthur, not entirely sure it was a trait to be admired when it blocked out such obvious dangers.

'Where are the crystals?' said Millie.

'We don't know.'

'How are we going to find them if you don't know where they are?'

'Arthur, we have no way of tracking the Belendrians, but we do know that wherever they are it will not be far from a gateway. The problem is that all the gateways on Earth, except this one have been moved many times over the centuries. They never bothered moving this one since it was cursed and is unique because it was the first built and only leads to Chintak.'

'So we don't know where the other gateways are, either!'

'No we don't, Millie, but we know how to find out.'

'How?'

'We need you to come into Chintak. This gateway only leads IN to Chintak, but the one on our side leads OUT to all of the others. Once inside you can go back out through any gateway you choose. All the others lead to and from each other. This is the sole reason we got you to find the key. So you could use it to come into Chintak and then travel on from here.'

Arthur's immediate excitement about taking a look inside the hidden continent was swiftly knocked back by a healthy dose of reality. 'You mean Millie, don't you?'

'Yes. If you, a human, were to step through then the *flaming curse* – another of Aurora's legacies – would burn you to death.'

'But Zamorians can't come through into Chintak either?'

quizzed Millie. She wanted to help them, but not to die at the first hurdle.

'That is true. Zamorians will lose their heads before being obliterated to dust if they attempt it, but we believe that as you are part-Zamorian and part-human you are the *only* person who could come through.'

'I don't want to sound negative, but you said I would escape the curses of the key pieces – but I didn't.'

'Millie, you *did* escape the full force of the curses, otherwise you would not be here right now.'

The mood had certainly turned darker. Up until then Millie had successfully managed to mask her fear and reservations. Now it was easy to tell from her expression that she was unsure what to do next.

'Can I ask a question?'

'Go ahead, Arthur.'

'Why didn't Aurora just curse all the Belendrians to death and steal the crystals himself?' Millie had asked him this question on their journey to Gibraltar. His reply then was about to be proved right.

'Simply put, he was too scared to go against all five of them. They are powerful individuals, but as a group they are much stronger.'

This was a good distraction for Millie and she waded in with her own Aurora question. 'Was Aurora the only one to know about the ship?'

'Yes. He had planned to use it just for himself. It was something else he discovered in the Archives and …'

The theory about Zamorians being born with a permanent smile wasn't true, because Fitar's sentence had just tailed off with a distinctive grimace.

'What is it?' asked Arthur.

'Yes what's wrong? Millie too could see his instant

change of mood.

Fitar said nothing. He just raised his hand and pointed back over Millie's head. What Millie saw when she turned round stunned her to silence.

'What? What is it?' said Arthur hurriedly. He'd also turned round, but couldn't see anything.

'A SPACESHIP, GRANDAD! IT'S A SPACESHIP!'

'Millie, you have to come through now – right now. I don't know who is inside, but I am fearful of who it could be,' said Fitar. The urgency in his voice clearly indicating his unease at the sudden change of events.

Millie shook her head and turned back to face Fitar. 'I can't leave my grandad.'

'Millie, if you don't come through now then all your good work will be undone.'

'Millie, go. They'll probably not harm me. I'm of no threat to them. Go now – I'll make it.' Maybe he would be allowed to live or maybe not, but Arthur felt that if Millie stayed she would be given no such choice. Her safety and life meant much more to him than his own. Going through the gateway now seemed a better option than sticking around in the Egyptian desert.

'I'll come back for you, Grandad.'

'STOP!' said Fitar, who was now holding both hands out in front of him. 'Don't move.'

Millie had started to walk towards the gateway, but immediately ground to a halt. 'What now?' She didn't know if she was coming or going, and Arthur felt the same way.

'I don't believe it,' said Fitar, with the smile returning to his face.

'What?' Now it was Arthur's turn to try to get a straight answer.

Fitar didn't respond to either of them, apparently

transfixed by the spaceship which had now settled on the ground.

Millie watched as the ship's door opened and a Zamorian stepped out. Arthur took up a protective position in front of her, but she moved him aside. 'There's no need to be afraid, Grandad. This is Aurora. He has brought the ship over from Chicago. The Reflective Energy Cells were recharged by the antennas we left it between.'

'How do you know that?' said Arthur.

'He just told me.'

Arthur wasn't entirely sure how much more of this his heart could take. 'You're dead!' he blurted out to Aurora.

'How is this possible?' asked Fitar. He might also have connected with him telepathically before the ship landed, but how had Aurora survived? He was as much in the dark as anyone.

'You thought you saw me die, but as you can see I am still very much alive. Kiptiziz left me for dead in the desert, happy that when the Joxgovia plant had finished with me the wildlife would clean up afterwards. What he didn't account for was that I didn't come to the gate alone. I came with another Belendrian.'

'Who?' Between Fitar, Arthur, and Millie, only she could come up with the most basic of questions. The other two just stood in shocked silence.

'Me.' Another Zamorian suddenly appeared out of thin air, right beside Aurora.

All of the Zamorian children floating behind Fitar vanished in an instant at the shock of seeing someone just appear.

'This is Phix. His mother's name is Phxzandria,' said Aurora.

'And his father's name is Kiptiziz,' said Fitar.

'Will somebody please tell me what's going on?' Arthur desperately needed to make sense of it all!

'I will explain,' said Aurora, 'Phxzandria was Kiptiziz's girlfriend when he abandoned the planet, leaving all adults to die. But Kiptiziz didn't know she was pregnant with Phix at the time and that anyone who was pregnant survived when the Belendrians took all the children to Earth. Every other adult Zamorian died. We now know that an unborn child maintains the Juju balance of the mother carrying it. On Zamora, at that moment, thousands of women were pregnant. All of them survived to keep the population going – albeit on a minute scale compared to before.'

'I guess that made you unpopular when you grew up and they feared you would become like your father?' Millie directed her question at Phix, who apart from one word had stood silent until now. What she asked and what she meant were two different things. What she meant was, how do we know that *we* can trust you?

'I was not popular on Zamora. That is why I left to seek revenge for what my father and the others did. To prove to all Zamorians that I am not like HIM.' Phix said the last word with such vitriol in his voice that the others felt compelled to believe him. 'I am a Belendrian, but that is where the similarity ends between my father and me. Besides, not all Belendrians are bad. Are they, Millie?'

It was true. She *was* part Belendrian and although she hated doing the washing up and had been known to eat as many strawberries as she could at the 'pick your own' farm she felt that didn't put her in the same bracket as Kiptiziz and the others!

'Of course! It was you who saved Aurora in the desert.' Fitar's puzzled expression of the last few minutes now began to clear.

'Yes. It took me centuries to track Aurora down on Earth. Shortly after I did, we came to this gateway together to tell you the news. I was invisible and acting as Aurora's lookout when I saw Fi – another of the Belendrian six – standing at the top of that sandbank.' He pointed to a distant dune to the left of the gateway, 'I went after him. I didn't see Kiptiziz come up behind Aurora until I was almost on top of Fi. When I did see him I raced back down, but before I got anywhere near them he'd already made Aurora eat the Joxgovia plant and stolen his crystal. There was no way I could take on two Belendrians on my own so I made a noise to distract Fi. He panicked, thinking that some humans were around, and waved for Kiptiziz to leave. Once they'd gone I had just enough time to administer the cure.'

'Your blood.'

'Yes, Millie, my blood.' He walked forward and headed directly for Millie. '*I* was crucial then, but *you* are crucial now Millie. You always have been. We have waited almost three hundred years for you. Neither Aurora nor I could do what you have done in order to open this gateway. Our plan was to wait for the key pieces to go missing and then track you down. In fact we were on your trail even before that happened, because we both lived in India and knew where the key was hidden. Every day we used to go between Manik and his family in the hope that something was about to happen. It was on one of those visits to Ranjit's tattoo parlour that we struck gold. We knew he had a grudge against his father and was letting slip his knowledge of his father's secret, but it was beyond our wildest dreams when you turned up while I was waiting in the alley outside the parlour.'

'We didn't see you,' said Arthur, before realising what he'd said.

'I was invisible. I used to sit there most days stroking Suna and just waiting.'

'How did you know we would come there?' said Millie.

'I befriended Ranjit, when I took my human form, and got him to tattoo the missing Taj Mahal door handle – which looked similar to the key piece you were looking for – onto a tourist and I put a curse on him once it was done.'

'A curse on who?' said Millie, with a frown.

'The tourist. The curse worked a bit like a homing device for Zamorians. If one was near then he or she would be attracted to it, but only you would know why. I kept encouraging Ranjit to tattoo the design on more people in the hope that one day you would come along. The man you saw it on was in fact the third person to have it done.'

'Hang on. If you can curse then why didn't you just undo all of Aurora's curses?'

'Good question, Arthur, but only the Zamorian who cast the curse can undo it.' said Aurora.

'So you see, Millie, we were watching you from afar all the time. In fact I was helping you long before you were born because I put a similar homing curse on the book when it was passed back through the gateway, but it never worked because you, or your ancestors were obviously too far away to detect it.'

'That's why I felt drawn to the book when it was in the study,' Millie said to herself.

'So you've been around in every continent, then Phix?' said Arthur.

'Yes, although sometimes we have been too far behind you to help.'

'Like when?' Arthur wanted to know why they didn't help more when they were needed most.

'You have to realise that we had to be very careful. It

would have been fatal for us to get too close to the key pieces, but it was I who knocked your leg in the alleyway outside the tattoo parlour to warn you that Ranjit was slipping past unnoticed.'

'And it was I who reopened the secret door twice in the rock in Australia once I realised you were trapped inside because your escape route had been flooded,' said Aurora.

'Thanks,' said Millie, waving her hand to attract everyone's attention, but Arthur wasn't quite finished yet.

'You must have got Molto to work again on Zamora because you're here. So why can't you just transfer the children straight back to your planet?'

'Not possible, Arthur, unless the crystals are in place in Chintak. It's also not now possible for me to go back to Zamora, because after I left the Zamorians set *their* Molto device so nobody could be transported from the Earth's surface – they were afraid of who I might bring back with me. They doubted my motives and not one of them would come with me to help. The only way now for us to get back is for the Molto in Chintak to be brought to life so that all the children can return home and restore the link to the Earth's surface.'

'And the only way for all that to happen is for me to get the crystals,' said Millie.

Nobody answered her. They didn't need to. Everybody, including Millie, knew she was the only one that could restore order to the Zamorian people.

Millie's mind was crammed to bursting point by now as she tried her hardest to take everything in, but as it all whirled around inside her head she managed to pluck one thought out. It was something she couldn't believe she'd forgotten about until now, the guiding voice she'd heard in the tunnels in Gibraltar. However, she had no time to pose the question, because the time for talking and asking questions was brought to an abrupt end when the assembled key started to shake and distort the gateway.

'Millie, you have to go now. The key is not holding up. YOU HAVE TO GO,' said Aurora firmly.

'Go, Millie. We will look after your grandad and will help you when you come through a gateway.'

The ground was now shaking and the key started to smoulder.

'Go, Millie,' said Arthur, with tears in his eyes.

'But—'

'No buts, Millie. Contact me when you come back through. We'll all be there to help you.'

Millie gave Arthur a quick hug and jumped into the gateway just as it disappeared and the key turned to dust.

THE END

Watch out for the next instalment …

Thanks for reading this far. I hope you enjoyed it. If you did then please feel free to drop me a mail via the book's website: **www.Zamorian.com** (Contact page). Your comment might even appear on the website itself! You can also use this page to register your interest in the next book in the series.

Please, please, please tell your friends about
The Key to Chintak.
I <u>need</u> you to spread the word!

If you didn't enjoy it … well I guess I will have to try harder next time!

Oh yes, I almost forgot – I guess you are wondering why **you** could see the pieces of the key? Well, I'll let Millie explain below …